BECOMING
LIZ TAYLOR

Elizabeth Delo trained as a teacher and has worked in schools in London, Birmingham, Paris and Somerset. After writing fiction in her spare time for many years, Elizabeth took a break from teaching to do a Masters degree in Creative Writing at Bath Spa University, graduating with Distinction. She runs creative writing classes and has worked as a freelance editor.

Elizabeth has a degree in French from Goldsmiths in London. She has travelled in Europe, Asia and the United States, but always returns to her beloved France. She loves cities, cinema and dance.

She lives in Somerset with her husband and has three children.

BECOMING LIZ TAYLOR

Elizabeth Delo

ALLEN&UNWIN

Published in hardback and trade paperback in Great Britain
in 2023 by Allen & Unwin, an imprint of Atlantic Books Ltd.

10 9 8 7 6 5 4 3 2

A CIP catalogue record for this book is available
from the British Library.

Hardback ISBN: 978 1 83895 805 3
Trade paperback ISBN: 978 1 83895 806 0
E-book ISBN: 978 1 83895 807 7

Typeset in Sabon by Avon DataSet Ltd, Alcester, Warwickshire

Printed by TJ Books Limited

Allen & Unwin
An imprint of Atlantic Books Ltd
Ormond House
26–27 Boswell Street
London
WC1N 3JZ

www.atlantic-books.co.uk

MIX
Paper from
responsible sources
FSC® C013056

In loving memory of
Patricia Palmer

ONE

I t was probably safe to dress up now. No one came to the house at this time of night. No one really came at all. Val went upstairs, took off her day clothes and stood at the wardrobe in her slip. She ran her fingers across all her purple dresses, selected one and laid it on the bed. She changed her underwear, put on her conical bra. It was hard to find them now, those bras. They were all the thing in the fifties, and they gave women a lovely silhouette. That pointed bosom, that nipped-in waist like an inverted triangle. Val's waist was far from that after two babies and now the spread of her seventy-two years, but the bra still lifted and separated, which she found pleasing. She pulled the dress over her head and zipped it up at the side, then sat on her bedspread and rolled the nylon stockings up her legs. She always put gloves on to do this – it saved snagging, especially with the 10 denier she insisted on buying. They were so fine they could ladder easily if they weren't treated with care. She did this part slowly, easing the stockings over her toes and then using the flat of her palms to unroll them up her leg. It felt as though she was being slowly coated in silk. She squeezed her feet into a pair of stilettos which she kept in a shoebox in the wardrobe. There. She admired herself in the full-length mirror. She put her hands on her hips and stood with one knee slightly bent, just how Elizabeth Taylor posed in that white bathing suit in *Suddenly, Last Summer*. She slid her fur coat from its hanger and eased it on, then pulled it around her and twisted this way and that. The coat caught the light and moved like molten bronze.

She sat at her dressing table and smeared coral on her thin lips. They weren't as full as Elizabeth's – Miss Taylor had a real sultry pout. Val's lips were thin now. They looked more like a crack in the wall. She was sure they had been plumper when she was young. Age seemed to thin a person's lips, made it look as though they were grimacing even when they wanted to look chirpy. Val followed the arches of her brows with the kohl pencil until they were thick and dark and perfectly symmetrical. Then she twisted the beauty spot onto her cheek. The photograph leaning against the mirror had been taken in Elizabeth's heyday in 1962. Her face was in profile; she was looking at something off to her left. Val liked to think Richard had appeared in the doorway just as the picture was being taken. But it might just as easily have been a photo shoot, the photographer saying, 'This way, Miss Taylor!' 'Ooh yes, move your head the other way!' 'That's it – turn your body towards the camera!' How exciting it all must have been. Anyway, the picture helped Val get the position of her spot just right: mid-low on the right cheek. Mind, she'd drawn it on so many times she probably didn't need it anymore. But she liked it there on the dressing table. She liked the glamour of it.

She held onto the banister rail as she went downstairs, side-stepping in her heels. Sometimes when she did this, she would imagine she was at the Oscars, making her way to the podium to accept Best Actress Award for *BUtterfield 8*.

In the kitchen she made a coddled egg and ate it sitting at the table next to the wall. She lit a cigarette. She didn't smoke, but liked the elegance of the Bakelite holder resting in the V of her gloved fingers. The smoke hung in the room in layers of blue.

From the front room she heard the ticking intro of *Countdown*, that hypnotic metronome, calling Britain's elderly to pick up their pens. Val sat in her armchair in front of the television, crossed her ankles and angled her knees to one side. She liked to sit like a lady. She scribbled capital letters onto her little pad, mouthed the beginnings of words, explored consonants on her tongue. Sometimes she got the conundrums even when the contestants didn't. You just had to keep staring at the letters along the bottom of the screen.

When the programme had finished, she turned off the television. She sat in the quiet room looking at the ornaments on the mantelpiece. The Portmeirion bud vase she'd brought

3

back from her honeymoon in Wales; the copper box where she kept the matches for the gas fire; the perpetual desk calendar. Every day she turned the tiny wheel on the calendar so that the metal plates flipped over to show the right day, date and month. At either end of the fireplace stood her Staffordshire china dogs, a wedding present from Len's parents. She still remembered the excitement of when she'd taken them out of the box the day Len carried her over the threshold. Such a grown-up thing to receive. She still dusted them every day and put them back on the same spot, positioning their haughty faces to look proudly over her front room. For a while she watched the torsion pendulum under the glass dome of the anniversary clock on the mantelpiece. Len had bought them the clock to mark their fifth anniversary. The four gold balls on the pendulum rotated left, rotated right, and then back again, smooth and precise, as if dancing a polite minuet. A single oscillation took exactly eight seconds. Sometimes Val found herself spending full minutes contemplating the mechanism spinning gently back and forth, back and forth.

Elizabeth evenings usually made Val feel better. The silk lining of the fur coat gliding up her bare arms, a dainty puff of face powder, a sparkling fake rock on her finger; it calmed her. In the quiet of her terraced house and hidden away from the world, the burden of being Val was lifted, and for a time she could pretend she lived a more glamorous life, one that brimmed with diamonds and adventure in Bel Air,

Los Angeles. The loss she still dragged around from day to day fell away, and for a few short hours she was able to forget. Dressed as Elizabeth, she could almost be happy.

When Val woke in the morning, she found she'd been crying again. She took a tissue from the quilted box on the bedside table and wiped her eyes. Five decades since she lost Duncan and Len, yet still she dreamed about them. The dreams were a brief, blissful return to those happy days with her husband and son, until she was confronted on waking by the terrible reality yet again. Strange how she still felt the shock of it. How could it be possible still to be in the grip of grief all these years later? They say sorrow eases with time, but Val felt it got harder. Every year that passed pulled her further away from the two people she'd loved more than all the world.

She was due at the hairdresser at ten. Although she kept her more elaborate clothes and make-up for the evenings, she still enjoyed putting on a bit of glamour. Having her hair done was an occasion, and she clipped some sparklies onto her earlobes and put on her favourite dress. It was dusky mauve with fabric buttons down the front and a matching belt which threaded through a loop on either side of the waist. The petticoats underneath gave the skirt a fullness which made it float as she walked. Val pulled her raincoat over the dress, closed her front door, and stepped out onto the pavement.

The sky was charcoal grey, and a light rain was falling steadily. Val tilted her umbrella in the direction of the wind as she walked towards the main road. She and Len had bought the house on Palmer Street just before they were married. It was halfway along a Victorian terrace, three streets back from the seafront. Two symmetrical rows of houses on either side of the street converged at a point at the end, like the orthogonal lines on a perspective drawing. There were no bay windows or front gardens – the windows ran flush against the front wall and the doors gave straight out onto the pavement. Val always thought this made the street look tidy. She'd been proud to live in Palmer Street when they'd first moved in, but the area had changed since those early days. Now, it was rather down at heel. The butcher, haberdasher and department stores on Meadow Street had been replaced by charity shops and stores where everything cost a pound. The grocer on the corner was now a tattoo parlour. Regent Street had become a dirty artery of amusement arcades and takeaways, the shop windows permanently grubby from the crawling traffic.

Val crossed Alexandra Parade and walked along Walliscote Road. This street was grander, lined with imposing Victorian villas. Grey-stoned, with cream stucco surrounds to both bay windows, top and bottom. Most of the buildings were still whole houses, their front gardens tidy with slate chippings and bay trees behind the low walls, smart front doors and expensive drapes at the windows. Roof gables were finished with intricate carvings and ornate finials. The dark morning meant that lights were on in some of the sitting rooms, and crystal chandeliers sprinkled glittery light across pale walls. Further along the street some of the buildings had been converted into flats, but even these were large and well-heeled. Val glanced down into basements where spotlights lit up kitchens like cruise ships. They had shiny marble-topped islands and fridges like wardrobes. Everything seemed bigger than it needed to be. Even the wine glasses on the draining boards were as big as soup bowls. Val had always hoped she and Len would eventually live somewhere like this. When the children were born, she used to walk past the semi-detached villas on the grand streets that curved away from the seafront, wondering if they'd ever be able to afford one, thinking they'd soon need an extra bedroom, a bigger garden. One or two of the roads had French names: 'Montpelier', 'Boulevard'. Now, there would have been an address to be proud of. Of course, she hadn't needed to move in the end. They didn't need the extra room after all.

She crossed the road at Clifton Street and walked beside the crenelated stone wall along the edge of Clarence Park. Leaves scratched along the tarmac paths in the park. The bite in the breeze was a reminder of the end of summer.

From under the hairdresser's hood dryer, Val looked at her reflection in the mirror. She smoothed her index fingers across her cheeks, pulling the skin taut. For those few seconds she could almost be a young woman again, all the creases gone. But when she let go, the skin puckered back into place and the bags under her eyes reappeared. Her resemblance was closer to Elizabeth Taylor's later years now, she thought, when she'd become a garish presence on the chat show circuit, rather than the glamorous star of her early movies. Even Liz became grotesque in the end. Val once read about a speech she'd given at a charity fundraising event in Santa Monica, where she'd apologised to her fans for ageing. Under the dryer, Val repeated Miss Taylor's words quietly in a faux-American accent: 'I'm sorry I've gotten old,' she said.

Outside, on the pavement, people were walking past the salon, busy coming and going. What had everyone got to do all the time? No one's got time to think anymore. A tall man with a ginger beard carried a little girl of three or four on his shoulders, clasping her ankles in his big hands. He bent his knees to exaggerate each footstep, making the child bounce up in the air and giggle with glee that was all of her. Be glad of what you've got, thought Val. Treasure these times. Treasure the times when you can tuck them up all cosy and safe.

She was pleased with her hair. The firm set meant the rolls would keep their volume, and the colour was just what she'd asked for. She'd gone a bit darker. 'Cleopatra Black', she'd described it to the hairdresser. As she left the salon, she took another glance in the mirror. When she stepped out onto the pavement, she imagined a line of flashbulbs and she smiled, held her head to one side and then the other, her neck extended. With its mille-feuille layers of lace petticoat, she loved how her dress moved forward and back as she walked off towards the seafront, like a bride walking up the aisle.

It was colder along the front. The wind came in sudden gusts from the Bristol Channel, the cries of seagulls hysterical or mournful depending which way the wind caught them. Val watched a gull flap across the sand and settle on the low wall between the pavement and the beach. Up close, she'd always found the size of them astonishing. Len used to joke that gulls were the gangsters of the bird world. 'If they were human, they'd carry flick knives, and would use them too if you looked at them in the wrong way,' he'd say. As she passed, Val eyed the bird's malevolent stare. The tide was out – the sea somewhere out there across the flats, so far away it was hard to imagine it was there at all. The sand was the colour of rain. Lights on the Grand Pier flashed dismally, but there wouldn't have been many pleasure seekers today. The bright red of the helter-skelter at the end of the pier stood out against the grey sky. The roller coaster was still. Those carriages would sit up there on the rails until next summer. A tourist train trundled along the promenade, carrying a few local people to save the long walk from town.

Up ahead on Beach Lawns, next to the ugly sprawl of Pirate Adventureland, the Weston Eye, an observation wheel carrying

9

thirty caged viewing pods, revolved slowly. It was a recent addition to the seafront, promising spectacular views over the whole sweep of the bay. Val had promised herself a ride one of these days. Having lived in Weston all her life, she would love to see the view from up there, the pattern of the streets from above. She'd like to try and spot her own house among the rooftops. Perhaps on a warmer day she'd come down to the front and do it. Although, it wouldn't be much fun on her own. It was the sort of thing you did with somebody else. On the pavement underneath the wheel, she felt its heavy rotation and heard its mechanical whine, its clicks and creaks.

A pram was parked next to the ticket kiosk at the foot of the wheel. It was angled so that Val was able to look in as she approached. The baby was asleep, its head to the side, its tiny mittened fists up by its ears. The yellow waffle blanket with its wide satin hem was identical to the one she'd had for Duncan. It took her right back. Val looked around. The baby appeared to be all on its own. There was a man in the ticket kiosk talking on his phone, his back to the window. There was no sign of a mother. No sign of anyone. If Val had looked up, she might have noticed that one of the wheel's pods was occupied. If she'd listened, she might have heard the giggles of a child above her head, and the sing-song 'wheeee' of a woman.

Val didn't think about it. She didn't even break her stride. She kicked the brake off the pram and pushed it as if she did it every day. Her palms wrapped around the contours of the handle, fitted into the grooves in the blue plastic as if it were made for her hands. She picked up her pace. Walked faster than she had for thirty years. Her heart thudded. Left right left right, the swift rhythm of her steps like an organist's pedals. She passed the amusement arcade, all its electronic noise hanging in the doorway. Left right. Faster. A man in a leather bomber jacket hurried past with his head down, a tabloid rag under his arm. The baby slept. Val's fingers gripped tighter. She looked through the handle of the pram and saw her feet walking and walking. She felt her heartbeat. She felt her pulse in her arms. She glanced behind her. The big wheel was far away now. The pavement was empty, save for an old couple in bobble hats sitting on a bench staring out to sea.

TWO

In Brighton, Rafe unlocked the door of the charity shop and carried in the bin bags that had been left outside. No matter how many signs you put in the window, people still dumped their unwanted possessions in the doorway when the shop was shut. He piled the bags up out the back to sort through later. For now, he wanted to finish the window.

The look he was aiming for was 'Autumn Celebration'. In the last few days, he'd been through the rails, picking out clothes in autumnal hues – oranges and reds and russets and browns. He didn't like Hallowe'en – it was way too American for his tastes – and so his display would simply be a celebration of autumn, full of brown leaves and apples and ears of wheat. He'd drawn a template, cut horse chestnut leaves from sugar paper, and stuck them around the edges of the window. He passed the steam iron over the long orange 70s dress he'd chosen for the mannequin. Holding the darts on the bodice between his fingers, he ironed each one into a sharp pleat. He pulled the dress over the mannequin's head and arranged it, gathering the fabric at the waist, and fixing it at the back with safety pins. Then he draped a length of gold organza over its shoulder, twisting it gently so that it fell to the floor in soft folds. He covered the silk in little paper leaves, fixing each one in place with double-sided tape. He liked how the pleats in the fabric looked like the autumn wind making the leaves scurry and dance. From a hanger on the wall Rafe chose a scarf with a blackberry and bramble design and tied it around the mannequin's head. He hung a green leather bag from its shoulder and slipped a pair of flat red pumps onto its stiff feet. On a small wooden step ladder he'd found out the back, he placed bowls of conkers and sheaves of wheat and grasses from the florist, tied with green velvet ribbon. He scattered more conkers and leaves around the mannequin's feet. Rafe stood out on the pavement and studied the finished display and smiled. He'd always had a flair for window design. Jim had always got Rafe to do their windows in the gallery. 'You've got such an eye for it,' he used to say. Rafe wondered whether Jim would still appreciate the artistic skill of his windows if he saw this one. Alright, it was a charity shop not a gallery, but there was still a professionalism to it, a finesse.

In their art gallery, it was Jim who had been the salesman, Jim whose charisma had bounced off the walls. Jim was one of those larger-than-life men: plump, six foot three with a rich, deep voice that meant everyone listened. One of the 'characters' of Kemp Town, he knew the whole street and it knew him. Jim was interested in everyone and everything. He was the life and soul; he was a force of nature. He was also the love of Rafe's life.

They were together for over twenty years. They had set up the Kemp Town Gallery, along with a shop on Portobello Road and a stall at Spitalfields market, sharing their time between all three. After their break-up though, Rafe found the fast pace of London overwhelming. Crowds frightened him. More than once he'd had a panic attack on the Tube. Soon after that disastrous party, Jim had taken over the London shop and Rafe hadn't set foot in the capital since.

The door rattled open, and a teenage girl came in. She scouted around the shop.

'Can I help you?' Rafe said.

'I'm looking for some gloves. Like, posh ones, you know?'

Rafe took her over to the formal wear and pulled out a tub of accessories from under the rail. The girl rummaged through it, pulling out various gloves and matching them up. She found a pair of black opera gloves and tried them on, pushing her fingers into each of the tight spaces, then rolling them up the length of her slender arms. She brought them over to the counter to pay.

'What's the occasion?' Rafe asked.

'They're for my prom,' the girl said.

Rafe smiled. School proms seemed to be all the thing these

days. They certainly hadn't had proms in Weston-super-Mare in the 1980s.

He carried the bin bags from the back of the shop to the counter and started to sort through the donations. The condition of some items people left had shocked him at first. Split seams, grubby bras, shirts stained yellow at the armpits, soiled underwear. He had once found a used sanitary towel still stuck into a pair of pants. Nothing fazed him nowadays. Anything unwashed he just put in a pile to run through the machine out the back. He seemed to be able to keep the shop in far better order than he could his own flat.

Most of what came in was decent however, and some of it was exceptional. Sometimes the quality that came out of those sacks made him gasp. He often knew it was good even before he pulled it out. The feel of the fabric, the weight of it, the stitching on the seams and hem. A particularly well-tailored jacket, or an expensive shirt. A ball gown. Sometimes he'd discover the most exquisite finishing – a beaded bodice, a diamanté neckline, some particularly rich embroidery. Formal wear he always found thrilling. He would hold up each piece of clothing, inspect it in the light from the shop window and wonder about its history. Every garment told a story. Where had a tuxedo suit and cummerbund been bought? By whom and for what occasion? A wedding, perhaps, or an exciting date. Maybe it had been a reluctant purchase for a function the wearer would rather not attend. Every garment had history, bought by someone somewhere, loved, then put at the back of a wardrobe until eventually given away.

He lifted another bin bag onto the counter. It was heavy, and from the way the weight was distributed, it felt like a single garment. He untied the knot and reached inside. The black plastic bag fell to the floor as he pulled out the coat. It was knee-length, had three-quarter sleeves and a Peter Pan collar. Mid-brown fur with faint horizontal dark-chocolate stripes. It must be mink. Rafe ran his palm over the front of the coat; held the seal-sleek pelt to his face, inhaling old musk and a thousand cigarettes. It smelled of parties. It reminded him of his mother.

THREE

Val turned away from the seafront onto Alexandra Parade. Her heart still thumped; her feet continued to propel her forward. She couldn't have explained what she had just done, or why. There was something about the way the baby was lying, with its head to the side, its little fists up next to its ears. Something about the satin hem on its waffle blanket. Whatever it was, when she turned the corner into Palmer Street with her pram, fifty years suddenly dropped away.

For a time, it was as if she was floating above the pavement, watching from outside of herself. The revving of an engine at the garage on the corner, teenagers scootering down the middle of the street, the caw of the seagulls – they were distant sounds, outside the cocoon that encased her and the baby. There was only the rhythm of her feet on the pavement; her hands clenching the plastic mouldings of the handle. There was only the child lying asleep, like a cherub. She looked at each front door as she passed, anticipating a neighbour stepping out. Someone who knew she wouldn't normally be pushing a baby. Before she reached her house, she saw the Polish taxi driver from the end of the street pulling his front door shut and turning to walk along the pavement towards her. Would he recognise her as the woman from Number 76? The woman he'd never seen before with a pram? He glanced up as he passed, gave her a nod, then carried on walking with his hands stuffed in the pockets of his anorak.

Val stopped outside her house and rummaged in her handbag for the key. Now that the pram was here, outside her front door, the sight of it shocked her. She looked back in the direction of the seafront and began to panic. You've got time, she said to herself. You could turn around and take it back and claim something about a misunderstanding. What would you say, though? What would you say? She couldn't think of anything she could say. Then she considered for a moment and felt calmer. Don't forget, she said to herself. Don't forget the baby had been left on its own. There was no one else in sight. Clearly, it'd been left for someone to find.

'Who's this scrumptious bundle, then?' Caroline stepped out from the house next door, making Val jar in horror. She wore fuchsia lipstick and turquoise tassel earrings that were clipped on so tightly her lobes were red. Her perfume smelled like boiled sweets.

'I didn't know you had a grandchild, Val,' she said, wrapping her hand around the side of the handle and bending in so that she filled the entire space under the hood. Val looked down at Caroline's dyed-blond hair, swept into a side ponytail. They weren't close as neighbours; they only knew bits about each other. Caroline had recently turned forty (the party had thumped through Val's wall for most of the night); she had two children but they both lived away. She had half a dozen cleaning jobs. She was a nice enough girl, but it wasn't the same as back when Suki lived next door, when all the children were little, all in and out of each other's houses. When Val first moved to Palmer Street, she'd known all the neighbours. So much more of life was lived outside. People walked everywhere rather than scuttling out of their houses straight into their cars. Val couldn't even remember cars lining the street like they did now. The garden gates at the back of the houses were all left open and the children barrelled up and down the passageway. Lines of washing, paddling pools, Lego on the paving slabs, cap guns and roller skates. Tonka toys in sandpits made from wooden pallets. You knew everyone then; you lived each other's ups and downs. Rafe was always in next door with Suki's kids, especially after Duncan and Len. Val didn't know what she would have done without Suki and the way she'd helped her through the hell of losing one and then the other. She'd been a good friend all those years. Last Val heard, when she bumped into Suki's daughter Becky at the doctor's surgery, was that Suki had met a man on the internet and was living in Shrewsbury. Becky had even given her the address, which Val had written into the little embroidered book she kept in her handbag. She'd meant to get in touch but hadn't found the nerve. She wouldn't have been able to think of anything interesting to say. It sounded as though Suki had an exciting new life now.

'Boy or a girl?' Caroline straightened up and looked Val in the eye, waiting for an answer.

Val hesitated. It hadn't occurred to her what it might be.

'Oh, um . . . it's a boy.' How nice that would be, she thought to herself.

'Your son's little one, is it?' Caroline looked back into the pram, smiling at the baby. Val tried to remember what she'd told Caroline about Rafe. Was it conceivable she would have a grandchild? Perhaps it was better to say she was childminding for someone. Who? Who?

'Yes, my son's,' Val said, unable to think of something plausible.

'I can't wait to be a grandma,' Caroline said. 'All the fun, but you get to hand them back, don't you?'

'Exactly!' said Val, still trying to find her door key.

'It won't be long for me,' Caroline went on. 'My Leanne's pregnant with her first. She sent me the photo of her scan yesterday. Here, let me show you.' She zipped open her shoulder bag, pulled out her phone and held it out to Val. On the screen was a constellation of the baby inside the womb. 'Zoom in on it, Val, and tell me if you can see what I can see.

20

I'm sure that's a little winkie there,' she said, pointing. 'I said that to Leanne, but she won't have it.' Caroline thrust the phone into Val's hand. 'Zoom in on it,' she said again. Val didn't know what 'zoom' meant. She stared at it, wishing Caroline would take the thing off her.

'Like this, look,' Caroline said, moving her finger and thumb on the screen and making the picture larger.

'Oh, I don't know how to do that,' Val said. 'I don't have one of these.'

'What, you don't have a mobile?' Caroline said. She turned from the phone and looked at Val, stunned.

Val shook her head. 'I've just got the phone in the hall,' she said.

Caroline was enlarging the photo again. 'What d'you reckon, Val? Is that a willy or what?'

Val peered at the screen. She wished Caroline would leave her alone. 'It's hard to say,' she said. 'It could just as easily be his finger, couldn't it?'

'Ah! You said "his!" You've called it, Val,' Caroline said, zipping the phone back into her bag. 'That's one of those slips of the tongue, isn't it? I'm gonna tell Leanne.'

Val smiled along, although she ached to get inside her house.

'Oh. Just to say,' Caroline said, getting in her car. 'It's Sylvia's birthday tomorrow. Ninety! Some of us are going to pop round in the afternoon. About three. Just for an hour or so. Cut her cake with her, you know.' Sylvia lived on the other side of Caroline. 'You're welcome to come. Bring the baby!'

Val smiled and watched Caroline drive off towards the dog leg kink at the end of the street. She pushed open her front door and lifted the wheels of the pram carefully over the threshold, then pressed the brake down with her foot. The baby was still asleep. Val stared at the pram in the quiet hallway. For a moment it seemed monstrous, taking up all the space like that. The thick plastic handle, the lime-green checked pattern, the hi-tech system of buttons and levers, it was incongruous next to Val's wall plates and collection of ballerina figurines on the windowsill. But then she looked at the child, its head turned to the side, the soft contours of its face, and it felt right. Suddenly, unexpectedly, there was a baby again in the house, half a century since the last one.

Val hurried upstairs. It was hard to pack, not knowing how long she'd be away. A week? A month? Far longer than that? She puffed out a sigh, looked around the bedroom. Think. She knelt next to the ottoman where she kept all her baby things and lifted the lid. Under the photos and Rafe's school reports she found Duncan's old rattle and his stuffed giraffe. She opened a wooden box which contained all of Rafe's milk teeth; the plastic clamps from her babies' umbilical cords; the wrist bands they had worn in the hospital. In a small envelope she'd kept the curls from Rafe's first haircut. Of course, there were no lockets of hair or kiss curls of Duncan's, but she'd kept the sleepsuit she'd found him in that morning. She'd folded it in tissue paper, double-wrapped in plastic bags, hoping it would preserve his smell. She looked towards the doorway. She didn't have much time, but she couldn't resist opening the bags, unfastening the ribbon around the tissue paper and holding the suit to her nose. She breathed in. Was it still there, the scent of her baby? Was it there? It was so faint it was barely there at all. Maybe she only imagined the smell of him now. It had been fifty years after all. She parcelled it up again and laid it carefully back in the ottoman. She found what she was looking for: nappy pins. She'd even kept some terry towelling nappies, all neatly folded. Proper nappies they were, in those days.

She pulled her suitcase down from the top of the wardrobe. It was a heavy, cumbersome thing with a hand-stitched trim and metal clasps. Val lay it open on the bed. She put the baby items inside, along with her polyester trousers, a couple of jumpers, four of her purple dresses and a nightie. Then she rummaged in the chest of drawers for her conical bra. She folded a lace negligée into the case along with her silk dressing gown and her satin peep-toe mules. They had kitten heels, and plastic straps decorated with pale-pink feathers. Her 'fluffies', she called them. She pulled her fur coat from the wardrobe and held it up in front of her, wondering, then slid it from its hanger and folded it on top of the rest of the clothes. Wherever she ended up, she might still be able to watch the television of an evening in a bit of fifties glamour. Even with a baby to look after, she had standards.

Into her vanity bag she put her powder puff, a bottle of L'Air du Temps, the kohl pencil for the arches of her brows and the beauty spot on her cheek. Next to the portrait of Elizabeth Taylor on her dressing table there was another photograph. It showed Val on the promenade near the pier, her hand on Duncan's pram and Rafe behind her on the sea wall in shorts, socks and sandals. He had his arms out wide, holding his bucket and spade aloft, a smile as wide as Marine Lake. He would have been four years and three months old. Val could probably say the exact number of days, too, if pushed. It was the only photograph ever taken of her with both her boys. She picked it up and peered into her own eyes. If only you'd known, she thought. Keep him safe, that little mite in the pram. She clutched the photo to her chest, just for a moment, then tucked it into the elasticated pocket of the case, along with the one of Elizabeth. She pressed the clasps on the suitcase, fastening it with a clunk.

Her savings were under the sateen lining of a hat box in the cupboard in Rafe's old room. Most of the notes were new fifties and twenties but some were old currency – obsolete ten-pound notes from the seventies and eighties. Even a couple of postal orders she'd never cashed. She should have paid them in years ago, but it was probably too late now. Still, when she counted the money, it amounted to nearly three and a half thousand pounds. Enough, surely, to get themselves established somewhere if that's what was needed.

Down in the hall, the baby began to splutter. The first choked coughs of a cry. Val stood for a moment looking over the banister, trying to think. The sight of the pram was startling. She felt her stomach turn over. What had she done? The baby was beginning to wail as she bumped the case downstairs.

'Keep calm, Val,' she said to herself.

The baby's cries echoed round the walls.

'Shhhh, the whole street will hear you,' she said to the child. She tried to make her voice sing-song, but she heard its crack of alarm.

She pulled back the yellow blanket and lifted the baby out. 'Shhhh, dearie,' she said, and she held its little body to hers and pressed it close. Such a natural fit, as if the years had fallen away. For a moment, there was only the physical. The weight of the child, the position of Val's hands – one under its bottom, one on the back of its head. She closed her eyes at the ache of it. Her body found its own sway. She turned her face and put her nose against its cardigan and breathed it in. As she exhaled, she let out a sound. 'Oh.' She did it again. Breathed in slowly. Held it. Let it out. 'Oh.'

The baby was becoming distressed now, its cries long and loud.

'Come now, little one,' Val said. 'Hungry? Let's see what we've got.'

Holding the child with one hand, she unzipped the tartan bag that was hanging from the handle of the pram. Linen squares, disposable nappies, a teething ring – she rummaged around until she found what she was hoping for. She unscrewed the lid of the bottle and breathed in the sweet, malted smell of formula milk. She put it in the microwave and soothed the baby while the bottle rotated behind the glass, and then she shook some drops onto her hand to check the temperature. She wondered whether she should delay the feed until after they'd left Weston. Who knows how long they had? Her shoulders tensed at the thought of a knock at the door. But you can't ignore cries of hunger. She sat the baby on her lap, its head against her breast. The crying stopped immediately, replaced by huge thirsty sucks. As the baby settled into the feed it made tiny, contented sounds. Its eyes stared up at her, big as two brown conkers. All Val's stress from taking the pram, the fear that had spread up through her back as she'd pushed it home, all now fell away, and there was just her and this little human in her kitchen, already connected. 'You'd been deserted, little one,' she said, lost in the baby's gaze. 'It's OK though. You're safe now. Mama will look after you.'

The baby's eyes were tipsy with milk. It would be due a nappy change soon, but she didn't want to unsettle it now. The nappy didn't feel too full. Anyway, it was probably best to get on the road. She laid the baby on the couch while she attempted to dismantle the pram. It seemed such a complicated contraption with all those levers and clips. She pressed buttons, pulled at catches on the frame, but she couldn't get anything to budge. She felt herself begin to panic.

'Just stay calm,' she said aloud. 'There must be a way.'

She looked underneath the body of the pram, her heart racing, and tried another lever. Somehow this time she managed to release the carrycot from the chassis. Once it was off, it was easy to collapse the frame. Val opened the front door a little and peered out. The couple across the road were coming out of their house. They looked up at Val standing there on her doorstep. She smiled quickly, then closed the door again and peered through the net curtain until they got into their car and drove away.

Her own car was parked on the road outside the house. She rarely drove. Most of the time she walked, or if she was going up to Worle she normally took the bus. Up until four years ago she still had Len's old Morris Marina. It had broken her heart to get rid of that car. All the fun family times they'd had in it – trips to Bristol Zoo, picnics on the Quantock Hills. Len had picked her up from the hospital in that Marina; she'd brought both her babies home in it. The engine had begun to splutter however, and there was rust in the wheel arches, and the man in the garage said it was beyond repair. Eighty quid he'd given her for it. She watched the scrap metal lorry tow it away, knowing that the memories of that car were far more valuable than the cash in the pocket of her pinny. She'd wanted to replace it with a new Marina, but apparently they didn't make them anymore. She wished Len had been around to help her choose a new model. She didn't know the first thing about cars. In the end the man in the garage found her a little red Peugeot which he said was a 'good little runabout'. In four years, she'd barely driven two hundred miles in it. The thought of the journey ahead – wherever she was going – filled her with fear. But she couldn't think about that now. She had to press on.

It was a bit of a fiddle to get the pram chassis into the boot, but she managed. The bag and suitcase had to go on the back seat. It was only a small car, but if Val slid the front passenger seat right back the carrycot part of the pram just fitted, wedged between the seat and the dashboard. In her day they just used to put the carrycot on the back seat, but she wasn't sure that was allowed now. The seatbelt stretched around the carrycot just far enough to be able to clip it in. It looked safe and couldn't slide forward wedged up like that against the dashboard. When she had more time, Val would work out how to fasten it properly. Before setting off, she rooted through the big books at the bottom of the display cabinet in the front room until she found Len's *AA Road Atlas of the British Isles*. The cover said it was from 1974. Hopefully, wherever she was going, most of the roads would be the same as they were then. She threw the map on the back seat of the car, lay the baby in the carrycot, and pulled away from Palmer Street.

FOUR

At five o'clock Rafe locked the shop and set off through Kemp Town. The sky was darkening, and a breeze blew up through the streets from the sea, but it was mild for October. The businesses along St James' Street were packing up for the day. In the window of the butcher's shop, Rafe watched a man with fat red fingers gather up piles of sausages to take back to the fridge. Pools of pale-red blood puddled on metal trays. In Kemp Town garage, an engine was being over-revved, and the tang of exhaust fumes hung in the open gateway. A blue neon light in the shape of a mouth beamed a fluorescent smile from the wall of the orthodontist surgery. Two large white poodles stepped from the door of the dog grooming parlour, curls piled on top of their heads like little judges' wigs, tails preened like topiary. They were followed onto the pavement by a woman in her twenties in a scarlet puffer jacket and crimson nails an inch long. She clipped along the pavement in high-heeled ankle boots, holding the dogs, one in each hand, on leopard-print leads. Gay anthems shrieked from a pub doorway. Christ, thought Rafe. The in-your-face kitsch of Brighton's gay scene irritated him. Did it all have to be so fucking tasteless? He paused briefly to study the window of Kemp Town Bookshop, felt suddenly starving and decided to call into the Doorstep on the way home to pick up one of their fat baguettes. He tried not to buy food out as a rule, but he could eat half now and save the other half for his dinner tonight.

He pushed open the door. The cafe was full of the clatter of coffee beans being blitzed in the grinder; the violent bash of an espresso filter against the waste box; the bright babble of conversation; nutty tones of Americanos and flat whites; the sweet tang of caramel syrups. The leftover baguettes had been placed at the front of the display cabinet under the counter. Rafe walked towards it, peering to see whether there was still a Prawn Marie Rose on granary.

Then he froze. Jim was sitting to his right, on an orange velvet sofa along the window. He was squashed up against a man in a grey houndstooth suit and shouty designer glasses. Rafe's heart hit his throat. They were looking at something on Jim's phone, thighs touching. Rafe saw the big mug on the table in front of Jim; knew he would have ordered 'a latte but in a mug not a glass, thanks'. The man in the suit was leaning into Jim, and they were both laughing at something on the phone. Jim flicked his thumb across the screen, then said something that caused them both to explode. That great big barrelling laugh. Rafe was suddenly back at Florence Road. Saturday breakfasts in bed with papers and cats; Sunday lunches in Sussex pubs. Walks at Cuckmere Haven, at Portslade, at Beachy Head. Even on the night of the party, Rafe remembered that laugh coming from the sitting room, being the host with the most. Trying to impress Lucas.

'What would David Niven do?' he'd heard him bellow. It was one of Jim's favourite sayings back in the Florence Road days. 'Pour a stiff Martini and slip one to the lady!' he roared, reaching for the decanter like he was Jay bloody Gatsby himself.

Those lavish, extravagant parties. The exotic people that came. Models, actors, photographers Jim knew from fashion shoots. Champagne cocktails, the odd line of cocaine chopped out on the mirrored coffee table they'd bought in Fitzrovia for obscene money. It all stopped after that stupid argument.

Rafe stood halfway between the door and the counter. The grind of the coffee machine, the quiet chatter of people sitting at tables, the scrape of chair legs on the wooden floor, all of it faded into the background. Rafe felt hot panic prickle up his back. If he turned to go, it would look obvious. If he bought a sandwich . . . How could he possibly buy a sandwich? All he could do was stand still, aware of the presence of his former lover; a presence that was always as big as the room, aware of that rich voice, that gargantuan laugh. Aware of him with another man. All over another man.

Rafe glanced across at them, tried to assess whether he could sneak back out onto the road unseen. He didn't care how it looked to the baristas behind the counter, the dozens of people sitting at the bistro tables and on the sofas. He just didn't want Jim to see him. He was unprepared; caught completely off guard. And suddenly aware of his appearance. His Diesel jeans were a decade old, and his corduroy jacket was grubby and stained. His hair had got longer and greyer; it kept falling in his face, making him look wild and unkempt. He needed a bloody shave.

Rafe seemed to be unable to move. He stood rooted to the spot, his panic like paralysis. Then Jim looked up. They saw each other. Just for a moment, it was as if it were just the two of them, sheathed within an invisible bubble. And all their history, everything that had ever mattered to them, everything they had been to each other, was encased in there with them. But then the moment was gone and there was just awkwardness. There was so much to say to each other and yet there was nothing. It was over. He'd always known this would happen – it had been inevitable. This was the moment. This was the moment when you meet your ex in public and you just accept it and realise he has another life. He has another life while you haven't. Extraordinary, actually, that it hadn't happened before now, given that they'd broken up five years ago and both lived in the same town. He'd heard that Jim had moved over to Hove, but it was still Brighton, more or less.

The man he was with had noticed that Jim's focus had moved from the phone. He looked up at Jim, and Rafe heard him say, 'You OK?'

'Yeh!' Jim said. Was that panic in his voice? Could Rafe hear Jim's heart hammering with nerves, same as his own? Did part of him feel as sick as Rafe did?

A look of uncertainty crossed Jim's face, as if the confidence he wore like a second skin had momentarily failed him. But then he gathered himself. Of course he did. He put his hand up to Rafe.

'Hi!' he called, getting up from the sofa, sidling round the low table. He had put on a bit of weight – he'd always struggled – and his hair was cut in a shorter style; his curls waxed down. He was wearing a burgundy shirt splashed with a daisy motif, beige trousers in a delicate check, tan Loake brogues. Yellow socks. He only ever wore yellow socks.

Suddenly Rafe's hand was in Jim's. That huge hand, the hand he used to know as well as his own, the hand that used to smooth his face, touch him in bed. How ridiculous that they should shake hands. But what else was there? They couldn't stand dumbstruck in front of each other, in front of the whole cafe and Jim's companion. So they went through this jolly facade. They were just two friendly guys who happened to know one another in some way. Acquaintances. Of course it came easier to Jim.

'Rafe, how are you?' Jim said, smiling. There was that warmth. That ability to make you feel interesting and important to him. He did it with everyone, and now he was doing it with Rafe.

'I'm good. Good. Yeah.' Rafe found himself grinning like an idiot, overcompensating. 'You?'

'Yeah. Yeah, I'm good,' Jim said, smiling. Rafe couldn't help noticing that he was doing that thing with his hands – running his fingertips round each of his knuckles – that he always did when he was nervous. Rafe didn't hear any of the words they were speaking. They were all just sounds, stupid pleasantries. Blurred meaningless fluff. Don't look at the man he's with, Rafe thought. Don't look across.

'How's the shop?' Jim said.

'Oh, you know. It's quiet.' Rafe wished he could say that business was booming, or that he had the wit, at least, to spin Jim a lie. How could he tell him his life had sunk so low he'd had to give up the gallery and was volunteering in a charity shop?

'No one's got any taste anymore,' said Jim. 'Everyone wants Tuscan landscapes, Brighton sunsets from behind the West Pier. Prints of fucking Banksy!' Typical Jim. Even under pressure he could manage to come out with something relevant and witty.

'We were just saying,' he continued, looking over at the man he was with. 'Kemp Town's lost its edge, don't you think? Everyone's in the North Laine now, in those appalling pop-up galleries.'

When Jim looked towards the man on the sofa, Rafe too glanced over.

'Oh, so sorry, let me introduce you.' He gestured Rafe over to the sofa. 'Clem, this is Rafe. Rafe, this is my husband Clem.'

Husband. Rafe's blood ran cold. The room suddenly felt airless.

'Nice to meet you,' Rafe smiled. Clem's suit was expensive, his mustard tie skewed slightly below the open top button of his shirt. His hand was small, but his handshake was all confidence. Rafe tried to match Clem's warmth, covering for the horror in the pit of his stomach by holding Clem's hand harder and longer than was necessary. 'I didn't know you got married,' he said, looking at Jim.

'Oh, we just went and did it one day,' Jim said, his voice booming into the space in the middle of the cafe. 'Decided in the morning, phoned the registry office. Turned out they had a bloody space that afternoon at five. Can you imagine? It was mental. We grabbed my brother as a witness, then went and got rat-arsed in The Geese. Came out of nowhere! Great day though.'

'Congratulations,' said Rafe. 'I'm really pleased for you,'

he said, looking at Jim, then smiling fleetingly at Clem. There was a pause.

'Oh, why don't you join us?' Jim said. 'They've got a licence. We could order a bottle of wine.'

Rafe held his hands up as if in front of a firing squad. 'Oh, no, no,' he said, looking towards the door. 'I've got to be going.' He felt his throat constricting. 'I only popped in for a sandwich, and I can see from here the Prawn Marie Rose have all been snaffled.'

'You'd be lucky, this time of day,' laughed Jim. Rafe noticed him twisting his wedding band round his finger. Rafe was picturing the moment he could walk out of the door.

'Anyway, good to see you,' he said to Jim benignly. 'Nice to meet you, Clem.' He tried to make his smile appear genuinely friendly. He couldn't bear having to shake both their hands again. 'And congratulations once again,' he said, putting his hand up to them in a wave, before turning and barrelling out of the door.

He marched off along the pavement at a pace, his face contorted, his heart hammering. As he walked, he made sounds in his mouth. '*Fuuuuuccckkkk*,' he said. '*Fuuuuuu-cccckkkkkkk. How fucking awful fucking embarrassing fucking awful was that?*' He spoke like a ventriloquist, not letting his lips move in case people in the street thought he was talking to himself. *Married. What the fucking hell fuck was that. Fucking married.*

FIVE

The traffic stop-started along Locking Road. Val watched people traipse up and down the pavements. How strange that they were all going about their normal business while she'd taken a baby. Shuffling mindlessly around the shops or strolling back to work after lunch, while her blood hammered. She couldn't understand why nobody was pointing at her. When she stopped at a red light, she dipped her head and looked down into her lap. Her little Peugeot felt huge and obvious. Her shoulders tensed, anticipating flashing blue lights in the traffic, but there were none. Time and again, the traffic light changed to red then green, and Val slowed and stopped with the other cars, then pulled away without incident. Nobody stopped her. Nobody noticed her. But then why would they? The baby had clearly been abandoned, the mother wanting someone to take care of it. Why else would she have left it on its own like that? It must have been a cry for help. It was just so fortunate that Val had come along when she did. She was a perfect fit. All those years ago she'd lost a baby. And now she'd found one.

A thin drizzle had started, and Val flicked the windscreen wipers onto intermittent. Once they reached the main road out of Weston, the traffic moved more freely. The baby stared at the sky through the window. Val offered her index finger into its small curled-up fist. When it opened its hand a little, Val wriggled into its grasp until it was clutching the length of her finger. She glanced across at the infant. She wondered if it was a girl or a boy. The yellow leggings, the cream cardigan over a Toy Story vest, didn't give a clue either way. And how old? Three, four months maybe. Years ago, Val would have been able to tell. She knew what age the milky dots of teeth pushed through the gums; what age babies started to babble. It's easy to forget all that when you're out of practice.

At a roundabout a few miles out of Weston, a police motorcycle stopped alongside the car. The police officer pulled up the visor of his helmet and gestured for Val to wind down the window. He shouted something and pointed to the baby, but she couldn't hear what he was saying over the thrum of his bike.

'Pardon?' said Val. Her heart was in her throat.

The light turned green, and the policeman pointed at the road beyond the roundabout and shouted something about a lay-by. He pushed his visor back down but didn't move until Val had pulled away. Then he followed her. For one surreal moment it flashed through her mind to tear off. Just put her foot down and race away from him. Even if he pursued her, she wouldn't have to stop. She could just keep driving. He'd probably get fed up in the end. But then, that would be ridiculous. She was a nervous driver, already daunted by whatever journey lay ahead. She rarely drove at the speed limit, let alone above it. Anyway, why should she run, she reminded herself. She had done nothing wrong. She'd rescued an unwanted baby, that was all.

In the rear-view mirror, she saw the policeman behind her, gesturing for her to pull into the lay-by ahead. She indicated to pull in, but flicked the wrong arm on the steering wheel, setting the wipers onto high speed and making them judder and squeak across the glass. Panicking, she pushed the arm back down and found the indicator. Oh, now he'll think I'm a fool, Val thought, as she pulled into the lay-by and watched him climb off his bike. She sat small in her seat, watching him in the wing mirror as he walked slowly and deliberately up to the car.

'Afternoon, madam,' he said. He removed his white helmet. His movements were unhurried, which made them more unsettling. Val looked up at him and tried to give him her best smile. He had a fat moustache and thick black hair in his nostrils.

'Good afternoon, sir,' she said. Had he heard the crack in her voice?

'Can you turn your engine off for me please, madam?'

Val did as she was asked.

'Off anywhere special?'

'Um, no, not really,' said Val.

The police officer kept his eyes fixed on hers, then looked along the length of the car, and across at the carrycot sandwiched between the front seat and the dashboard.

'That child should be in a car seat,' he said.

'I did try my best,' Val said, putting her hand on the seat belt that she'd fed around the hood of the carrycot.

'That's not safe, nor legal,' he said. 'It needs to be strapped into a proper baby seat.'

'Well, that's typical of my daughter!' Val said suddenly, giving a theatrical roll of her eyes. 'She asked me to look after this little chipmunk while she and her husband have a break. It was only once they'd driven off that I realised they still had the seat. I'm not surprised she forgot about it – they were so excited to be going away!'

Val heard her words and couldn't believe the ease with which they were tumbling from her mouth. Daughter? She didn't have a daughter. Val had barely told a fib in her life, and here she was lying through her teeth to an officer of the law. It was necessary though. She had a duty now, to protect this baby. Poor little mite had been left high and dry, with no one looking after it. It had been such lucky timing that Val had found it when she did; it was in the safest hands now.

'You can't drive with it like that,' the police officer continued. 'You need a car seat.'

'It's funny you should stop me now, then,' Val said. 'I was actually just on my way to Halfords to buy one. Fancy that!' Val even heard herself laugh, as if they could both enjoy the irony of his timing. 'My daughter called me earlier. She said that if I buy it then she'll pay me back when they get back from the Cotswolds.' The story was just spilling out of her. It was like a natural defence reflex. They always say a woman will go to any lengths to protect her child.

The police officer didn't speak for a while. He appeared to be thinking. Traffic droned past behind him. Fuzzy, broken voices and faraway police sirens crackled from the radio fixed to his jacket. A woman was saying 'Charlie two zero six', through static and white noise. Eventually the man said to Val: 'Well, OK, please make sure you do,' and he gave a slight nod of his head as if to enforce what he'd said.

'You're very kind,' said Val. 'And forgive me. I'm a bit all at sea. I'm not used to having sole charge of this little Bonny-boo!'

The police officer said nothing, but she thought he gave her a strange look. His radio hissed and squelched. He replaced his helmet and walked back to the motorcycle. Val's heart thudded. She watched in her mirror as he pushed his visor down, kicked the bike into gear and pulled away. He turned his head to look at her as he passed.

Val sat in the lay-by and tried to gather her thoughts. Had she seemed suspicious? He must have believed her, or why would he have ridden off? He must be right about the seat, though. If anyone knew the law, he did. She would try and buy one somewhere on the journey. It dawned on her that she had no idea where she was going. She hadn't thought that far ahead. It would have to be somewhere remote, she supposed, somewhere far away. The wipers scraped the windscreen. Val flicked them off. The baby began to stir again. Quick, thought Val. Think. She couldn't think. Her mind was beginning to race. She tried to put the car into first, but it wouldn't go. Several times she tried to force the gearstick into position, but it seemed stuck in neutral. She began to panic. She turned off the ignition; took a deep breath. Waited a moment, then turned the key again. This time the gearstick clunked into place. Damn these new cars, she thought; everything felt so tight. What she'd give for the Marina now, with its easy gears and great big boot. Oh well. She'd have to make do. She indicated to move back onto the road, and pulled away towards the M5.

SIX

It was at Weston lido during the hot summer of 1968 that Val first met Len. A Saturday, one of those unending days of a high yellow sun; the sky was a dome of whole blue. Val queued on the pavement along the high sandstone wall with her best friend Marion. They'd left school two years before and had both found clerical jobs at rival banks in town. Stuck all week in dark offices, when the weather was warm, they spent every evening and weekend at the pool. While the queue moved forward, Marion rested her elbows on Val's shoulders.

'Which side gets the sun for the longest?' Marion said, looking up at the high wall, shielding her eyes from the sun. They wore the matching sunglasses they'd bought the week before in Walker and Ling on the high street.

'That side, I think,' said Val, pointing to the side nearest the pier. 'Halfway along, near the lifeguard's chair.'

The girls shuffled forward, then clunked through the turnstiles. The concrete was hot under the soles of their feet.

Marion picked across the sun terrace, pulling up her knees, exaggerating her steps.

'Oh my god! My feet are burning!'

She stopped on the terrace, hopping up and down, pulled the flower flip-flops out of her bag and wiggled them on.

'Here,' she signalled to Val, and they lay down their towels. Val saw her glance across at two boys who were sitting a little way along the terrace. Marion undid her zip slowly, wriggling herself out of her skirt. She crossed both arms across her front and peeled up her shirt, pulling it slowly over her head and stretching her arms. When she saw the boys looking over, she dug Val sharply in the ribs and laughed. Val looked down, embarrassed. Why did Marion have to be so obvious, she thought. Secretly though, she admired her confidence; she would give anything for an ounce of that. At least she felt she looked quite good in her gingham bikini and matching headscarf. The girls sat on their towels and reclined on their elbows and looked up at the sky from behind their matching sunglasses.

'Look at that one,' Marion said, nudging Val and nodding over at the boys. 'He's like a Greek God. I'll take him and you can have his mate with the badges on his trunks.'

'Marion!'

Marion sat back up. She pulled a book out of her bag, opened it to the first page and shut it again. She squinted into her compact mirror and reapplied her lipstick.

'I'm going over,' she said, getting up.

'Marion!' Val said. She was horrified and excited all at the same time. 'You can't just go over and talk to them, just like that.'

'Watch me,' Marion said.

Marion walked over to where the boys lay on their towels, and the way she moved was all swing. Val watched her talking and laughing with the boys, her knee bent, her slim hips thrown forward. With her wand-curled hair and brown frilled bikini, she looked like Raquel Welch in *One Million Years BC*. She pulled the boy she liked up by the hand. They went over to the side of the pool and pantomimed trying to push each other into the water, before falling in together. When they surfaced, they smacked the water with their hands, making it splash in each other's faces, laughing. As Val watched them, she became aware of the other boy. She could feel his eyes on her. She glanced along the terrace, then looked quickly away. Without Marion she was exposed and felt shy and awkward.

He stood up and walked over to the deep end. He had the body of a swimmer: muscular, with a broad V-shaped back. He must have been nineteen or twenty, but he had a man's physique. It looked as if his torso had been chiselled out of marble by one of those Renaissance sculptors. Val tried to remember the name of that famous one from her school History lessons. Michelangelo, yes that was it. Or maybe

Leonardo da Vinci. He dived in off the side and Val watched his strong arms propel him through the water with tight, neat power. There was a fluidity about him. No splash or wasted energy, he cut through the water like a dart. After he'd swum a few lengths, he pulled himself out of the pool and walked over to the diving platform. He climbed the steps at the back of the board and appeared at the first level. Val watched him walk out across the water and curl his toes round the end of the board. From behind her sunglasses, she saw him look over at her. He raised his arms straight up above his head, his fingers stretched up to the sky, bounced slightly, then launched himself from the board. He entered the water as straight as a pencil. When he pulled himself out of the pool onto the side it was effortless, graceful. He went back to the diving platforms and climbed the steps again, higher this time – to the second tier. This time he somersaulted from the board, tucked up like a tennis ball, before straightening out and slicing the water with barely a splash. Val watched as he walked back to his towel on the sun terrace. She wished she could call over and say something clever, compliment his dives, but she was too shy. She wasn't like Marion. What would she possibly say? But then he stopped in front of her. She could see the trickles of water running under the blond hairs on his shins. His thighs were thick, his chest defined. He had swimming badges sewn onto his navy-blue trunks.

'Mind if I sit down?' he said.

'No. No, that's alright . . .' She gestured to Marion's empty towel. Her heart hammered.

He was still out of breath from the diving and his taut stomach moved in and out. She was aware of her own body, of the unbearable intimacy of their swimwear.

'I think we've lost those two,' he said, nodding at Marion and his friend climbing the steps at the back of the diving platform, his hands already cupping her waist. 'Where are they going to come out, d'you think?' he said. 'First or second tier?'

'First, without a doubt,' said Val. 'Marion's got some nerve, but she's actually scared of heights. There's no way she'll jump off anything higher than the lowest board, it'll terrify her.'

Something about the boy's manner made Val feel bolder, suddenly. 'Not for you, though' she said, turning to him. 'You're clearly not scared of heights.'

He smiled at her. 'I've been diving for years though.'

'You're really good.'

'Thank you.'

'Is that what the badges are for?' Val said, then felt suddenly embarrassed that she'd drawn their attention to that region of his body.

'Yeah, they're for diving and lifesaving,' he said. 'I know it's what kids do, have their badges sewn on their trunks, but I don't care. I want to show them off. These are pretty recent. I got most of them in competitions last year.'

Val liked that he was proud of his swimming badges. There was something endearing about him wanting to display them like that.

'Can you dive from the top, then?' she said, pointing up to the highest board.

'No, I'd never dive from up there,' he said. 'You shouldn't. Not without being properly trained. Nobody except the professional divers is allowed up there. Only experts know how to jump from that height. If you hit the water the wrong way, you can break your neck.'

'That's awful,' said Val.

'I know. You'd need a death wish to jump from up there,' he said. 'Or be a kamikaze or something.' He was sitting with his elbows on his knees, face cupped in his hands.

'How frightening,' Val said.

'The professionals do it, though,' he said. 'But they've had the proper training. They're incredible. Have you ever been here on competition days?'

Val shook her head.

'Oh, you should. Tell you what, there's one here next weekend. It's an international. They're the best.' He looked across at her. 'Will you come with me?'

Val felt a prickle of excitement run up her back. 'Alright,' she said.

He turned towards her. 'What's your name?' he said.

'Val.'

He put his wet hand out to her. 'Pleased to meet you, Val. I'm Len.'

She shook his hand. There was something unusual, something intimate about shaking hands with him when they were both wearing so little. He wasn't that much older than her, but there was a formality about him that Val liked. She risked a shy smile, felt her skin tighten.

'You've got lovely eyes, Val,' he said. 'They're unusual. What colour are they?' He leaned towards her and peered into them. 'They're purple. Violet. Like Liz Taylor's.'

Nobody had ever paid her a compliment like that before. She'd seen Elizabeth Taylor in magazines, knew her astonishing beauty. She smiled. She couldn't stop smiling. One ordinary afternoon, and life had suddenly become exciting.

They sat in silence for a few moments, the sun clutching their skin.

'Come on,' he said, jumping up and holding his hand out to her. Her heart beat wildly. He led her over to the fountain. Water spilled from the upper tier onto the ground. In the sunlight it was a curtain of glitter. Children ran in and out, their bodies glinting. Val and Len plunged their hands through the water, trying to interrupt the flow, but the weight of it forced them down. They ducked inside, leaving the heat haze of the lido, and entered the secret watery grotto underneath. It was a 360-degree circle of noise. Len shouted something to Val, but she couldn't hear him. She shrugged and laughed and put her hands up to her ears. They sat on the low seat that hugged the fountain's central column and were cocooned behind a solid wall of water. There was only the water thundering around them, their wet bodies side by side, their bare legs nearly touching, but not quite.

SEVEN

To the west the sky was lavender. A formation of geese wheeled across the sky towards the coast. Val was on the M5, heading north. Suddenly there were cars on every side. Lines and lines of traffic, zooming up behind her, pulling out around her, overtaking this side and then that. Slowing slightly, before accelerating again. The little Peugeot felt hemmed in. Val tried to pull over to the left, but had to swerve back. There was a car there too. It was bewildering. She barely knew where to look, her eyes flicking from the road in front of her to the rear-view mirror and back to the road. Should she be using the side mirrors too? She didn't know. Her back was tensed. Still they came, looming up behind, then pulling round her and flying up the outside lane. And so fast! She'd never seen cars driving at these speeds. It was alarming. She should probably keep to the slow lane, but it was hard to move over to it when everything was whipping past her left and right. For a time she found herself caught between two huge lorries. They towered above her, high as houses, both travelling at the same speed. She began to panic and hung back so that they would pass. *Bwwwaaaaat!* One of them blasted its air horn right next to her, making her leap out of her skin. She eased her foot off the accelerator, willing the trucks to move past her. Her hands were wrapped tightly around the steering wheel and her fingernails were digging into her palms. She sat rigid, hardly daring to look around her. Was it always like this on the motorways? She'd certainly never driven on one. It dawned on her that she may not have been on one before. If she had, it could only have been with Len – she hadn't really been anywhere since. Although she wasn't even sure if the motorway existed when he was alive.

A sleek saloon pulled alongside her. The driver, a middle-aged man with a shaved head and a goatee, stared across at her. She looked straight ahead, trying to pretend he wasn't there. A hot flush spread up her neck and into her ears like she hadn't felt since the menopause. The traffic dispersed again, and the driver took off up the outside lane. Val moved over to the left and stayed there. A steady fifty-five miles an hour meant she could let everything else go past. If they were all in such a rush, then that was up to them. She wasn't in a hurry; she didn't need to drive like the world was about to end. Anyway, she had to be extra careful, given her precious cargo.

The child had closed its eyes and the gaps in the barrier of the Avonmouth bridge meant that the sunlight flickered across its face. Val stole glances at the perfect half-circles of lashes on its pale skin, its cheeks round and smooth as a bisque doll. The tiny movements of its mouth in sleep. It looked more peaceful than Rafe ever had. God, he was hard work, that child, always trapped full of colicky air. Val thought of the photograph of him on the picnic rug in the back yard at Palmer Street. Squirming like a grub on a leaf, his great wailing mouth nearly as big as his head, fists tiny balls of temper. Face pickled in that spotty rash for all those months. Val used to walk on whenever someone stopped to look in her pram. Her baby looked diseased. He scarcely smiled until he was nearly three. It might be easier with this one. Maybe this one would be more like Duncan.

After the bridge the motorway split. Val looked at the signs: M5 Midlands; M4 London; M49 South Wales. She scanned the place names. She had no idea where she was going. She took a deep breath, tried to calm herself down. She wished she could stop again and just think, but there was nowhere on the motorway – she was caught in the forward momentum of the traffic. She grimaced suddenly, imagining the implications of what she'd done. Why on earth had she taken a baby? What was she thinking? This was absurd. For a few miles, she raged at herself, overcome by what she'd done, tormented by the possible consequences. Then she calmed down, convinced herself she was worrying over nothing. She'd been thinking of the baby; that was all. She'd done the kindest thing. She'd been thinking about the welfare of the baby.

'You'd been deserted,' she said, looking across at the child. 'Nobody wanted you. But don't worry – you'll be alright. You've got a new mama now.'

The slip road for the M49 ran parallel with the M5 for a stretch. Val studied the intersection, considered the signs. London. Midlands. South Wales. She weighed up her options. Which route would get her away from the motorways? Where could she have some time alone with her baby? She thought of the remoteness of North Wales, the narrow roads, the beautiful green of the mountains. She thought of her honeymoon with Len when they'd stayed at Aberdovey. Flicking her indicator down to the left and moving onto the M49, suddenly she felt more relaxed. She pushed her index finger into the baby's little fist again and felt its fingers clamp around it. She felt its dependence.

To the west, the sun had found a hole in the dark clouds and as Val drove between the pylons of the Prince of Wales Bridge, it cast a thick silver wedge on the water and lit up the green girders of the stay cables. The car felt small in the six lanes of traffic. Just after the bridge she passed a road sign showing a red dragon and the words *Croeso i Gymru*. The sign brought on another surge of nerves. Suddenly she was in a different country. She felt sticky inside her clothes. There was a strangeness to everything. The duality of the languages on the motorway signs was confusing. She didn't know whether to turn off or keep going. Where was *Casnewydd*? Was that the same as Cardiff? Did it matter anyway since she didn't know where she was heading? She tried to give it some thought now, to picture where some of the Welsh towns were. She drove past motorway junctions, not knowing what anything meant, not knowing her destination. In the end, when she could no longer stand the stress of driving aimlessly along a motorway, she chose one at random. Head to the countryside – that was the best thing to do. The slip road led up to a huge roundabout. She stopped at the traffic lights and frantically scanned the signs above the various lanes. When the lights turned green the car behind her beeped. Her stomach lurched. She looked in the rear-view mirror at the man in the car behind. She pulled away and the man overtook her on the roundabout, giving her a hostile glare. She circled the roundabout twice, reading the signs aloud, trying to visualise the map of Wales. She recognised the name Abergavenny and remembered passing through there with Len on their honeymoon. She turned off the roundabout. If only Len were here, Val thought. He'd know what to do.

Val had ragged her hair to go to the diving competition, so that the curls fell to her shoulders and bounced when she walked. She'd pulled it back off her face with a cotton scarf and tied it at the back, like the model she'd seen on the cover of *Vogue* at the newsagent's. It was another day of searing sun, and she was worried she might be too hot in her lemon-coloured dress with its tight cap sleeves and full skirt. She'd never been out with a boy before.

She headed along the seafront towards the pier where she'd arranged to meet Len. As she walked, she opened and closed the metal clasp on her handbag. Her nerves were so tight they could snap. Somewhere in the distance she could hear the drone of the traffic along Marine Drive, the shouts of holidaymakers down on the beach. She wished she was down there with them, eating a 99, making sandcastles or playing cricket, instead of being dressed up to the nines going to meet someone she barely knew. It was incomprehensible, suddenly, the thought of spending all afternoon with a boy. How was she supposed to behave? What on earth would she think of to say? She tried to think of topics of conversation, but couldn't come up with a single thing. She wished it was a double date so that she could at least hide behind Marion. Part of her hoped Len wouldn't be there. It would be better to be stood up than to have to go through with this ordeal. Before she got to the pier, she darted into the public toilets to check her hair and make-up. As she stared at herself however, she thought of the elegant way he'd dived from the board, his broad smile, how they'd sat under the fountain, their bodies so close together, and she felt a shiver of excitement. She took a step closer to the mirror, remembered what he'd said about her eyes. A rush of excitement shot through her, and she hurried back out onto the promenade. Oh, please be there!

As soon as she saw him sitting there on the railing, waving and grinning, holding the tickets above his head as if he'd won the Football Pools, she was glad he hadn't stood her up. There was nothing to be nervous about. He jumped down and kissed her hand, then stood back and looked at her. 'Hang on,' he said, screwing up his face and holding his fingers against his forehead like he was trying to remember something. 'I've got it! *Suddenly, Last Summer.*'

'Pardon?' laughed Val.

'Liz Taylor in that iconic dress and scarf tied round her head. Alright, the dress was green not yellow, but you're a dead ringer for her. I told you last time, didn't I?'

Val's stomach did a flip. Did he really think she looked like a film star?

'One of her greatest roles, I would say,' Len went on. 'Katharine Hepburn and Elizabeth Taylor – they don't make flicks like that anymore.'

They set off along the promenade towards the lido and Len draped his arm around Val's shoulder. Already, she felt like his girl.

It was a big day in Weston. All week the diving competition had been advertised on billboards in the town. On the beach the 'Gold Rush' treasure hunt was in full swing, with people crawling across the sand, sifting for gold. Donkey rides, sticks of rock, swing boats, foil windmills on sticks spinning in the wind.

They pushed through the turnstiles and took their seats on the blue-and-white-striped deckchairs on the terrace. The poolside was packed. A man's voice blasted over the Tannoy. 'Today, ladies and gentlemen,' he said. 'You are in for a jaw-dropping spectacle! We have divers from across Europe: from France, from West Germany, from Switzerland, Belgium, and Austria. We have world champions here. We have three Olympians! And they will all be performing here, at this wonderful pool in Weston-super-Mare. The setting, over the decades, for the most exciting dive shows and swimming competitions. Not only that, but our world-famous beauty pageants, judged by stars of stage and screen. Over the years we have welcomed Stan Stennett, Tommy Cooper, Chico Marx. Even Laurel and Hardy.' The crowd burst into applause. 'The centrepiece of the lido, of course,' the commentator went on, 'indeed of Weston itself, is this spectacular diving platform. Ladies and gentlemen, this is a breath-taking example of 1930s architecture. The tallest diving stage in Europe, the top board protrudes an eye-watering ten metres over the surface of the pool.'

Val and Len got the giggles at the way the man was putting emphasis on the first syllable of his words. 'He sounds like a bingo caller,' Val said. Len roared at that. She was pleased she could make him laugh.

The speaker continued: 'Daring in its vision, audacious in its design, sublime in its execution. You will notice the central tower reaches in a sleek arc over the water, with four cantilevered platforms springing from its huge semi-circular arch. I'm sure you all agree it is a structural fanfare, a paean of art deco design. It is if you will, ladies and gentlemen . . .' He paused. 'A symphony of geometry.'

Len nudged Val and grinned. 'He certainly knows how to build this up, doesn't he?' he said.

'Anyone would think he was reading from a script,' she quipped, and Len laughed.

All around them, people were hastening to their seats, licking ice creams, smoking cigarettes. People who didn't have tickets had climbed up onto the perimeter wall and sat along the top with their legs dangling down.

Val watched the show, mesmerised. The divers twisted and somersaulted in mid-air. They left the board forwards, backwards, from a handstand start. Their dives mirrored the graceful arcs and sweeping curves of the board itself. At the end of the show there were comedy routines with acrobats fooling about, appearing to fall accidentally, their bodies changing in mid-air from clumsy to balletic. One man held another by his ankles from the top board and they leaped off as one, separating just before they hit the water. Even a small trampoline was set up at the top, the divers bouncing off it to give them more velocity. A man in a clown suit stood on the edge, his arms windmilling, pretending he was going to fall. He stood on one leg, then the other, leaning out over the water. The crowd laughed and roared. Then he set up a step ladder, jumped from it onto the trampoline, flung himself into the air and landed with a neat splash.

After each burst of applause, Val and Len rested their hands between them on the wooden frames of the deckchairs, nearer and nearer, until their fingers brushed together. On the way home they held hands and detoured up around Anchor Head, not saying as much but both knowing they were looking to get away from the crowds. In an iron shelter above Birnbeck Pier he kissed her, his tongue suddenly enormous in her mouth. Her coyness all gone, Val's desire for him was physical, urgent. When he pressed his body against hers, she pressed back. He made a low moan through his kiss.

Six months later, Len proposed at the end of Clevedon Pier. Val was eighteen.

'I'm sorry I can't give you a Krupp diamond like Richard Burton gave Liz Taylor,' he said. 'I'm only a humble railwayman, I'm afraid, living in Weston not Beverly Hills.'

'She can keep her fancy cars and diamonds,' Val said. 'I've got something much more precious.' And she kissed him, leaning back against the railing of the pier while the water moved and swelled around the columns underneath them.

*

The wind had got up, tugging at the poplars on the hills off to the east, and the rain was beginning again. Val flicked on the wipers, and they dragged across the glass. Just outside Raglan, she pulled into a garage. She filled the car with fuel, then unfastened the seatbelt and lifted the carrycot out of the car. It wouldn't be fair to wake the baby, but she wasn't going to leave it on its own, not like its mother had. Inside the shop there was a small selection of baby essentials. Val studied the tins of formula milk and the range of ages. She'd never used formula with her little boys. Rafe had switched to cow's milk early on, greedy little tyke that he was, sucking her dry. After she lost Duncan, they gave her tablets to dry up her milk. It took a long time to stop lactating, and once or twice she found to her horror that her breasts were still leaking several weeks later. She picked up a tin labelled 3–6 months and read the information on the back. How much to give, how often to feed. There was a chart with an upward curve showing a baby's expected growth. Suddenly Val felt the weight of responsibility. How could she be sure she was choosing the right milk when she didn't know the baby's age? She'd guessed four months, but now it really mattered. Uselessly, she looked down at the child. Yes, it must be about four months. She put the 3–6-month tin in a basket, along with a couple of bottles. She studied the other items. Picked up a twin pack of dummies, then hung them back on the hook. She'd never used dummies with hers – it felt wrong trying to silence a baby by shoving something in its mouth. She would far rather give it a cuddle. She looked at the packs of disposable nappies. She'd never used them before, but they would save all the palaver of buckets and liners, she supposed. Especially being on the move and all. Convenience was everything. She put some nappies in her basket, along with cotton wool and wet wipes. On her way over to the counter she picked up a sandwich from the fridge, and a bar of chocolate.

'Any fuel?' the man behind the till said.

'Uh,' she looked out to the pumps. 'Number six.'

The man scanned the items. Suddenly Val noticed the monitor on the wall behind him: nine rectangles showing nine different views of the forecourt. The shock of it hit her in the throat. She watched the man's face as he scanned the baby things; imagined him as a witness, describing her to police, telling them what she'd bought. A phrase popped into her head: 'On the run' . . . 'on the run' . . . Was that what she was? She caught sight of herself in the two-way mirror by the coffee machine. Her hair had held its set from this morning, the stiff black curls as high as a hat. She imagined how she must look to the man in the garage – the full net petticoats under her dress, the diamanté earrings she'd worn to have her hair done. She'd been in such a hurry to leave with the baby she hadn't thought to change. She looked conspicuous. She would be memorable, dressed like this.

'Going anywhere nice?' the man said, glancing at the baby.

'Just. No, not really,' she said, handing him some bank-notes. 'No.'

She couldn't think of a single thing to say that would sound convincing. As she took the receipt from him, she imagined how curious she must seem with her curt replies, her black bouffant, her handfuls of cash.

Outside on the forecourt she opened the car door and threw the things onto the back seat and strapped the carrycot into the passenger seat. She had to get away. CCTV cameras were everywhere she looked now. They all seemed to be pointing at her, burning into her skin like lasers. But she couldn't find the car key. She patted her pockets. She looked on the floor, felt down the side of the seat, under the pedals. It wasn't there. The baby flinched suddenly, thrust its hands out with a jerk. The first hiccoughs of a cry. Val felt between the seats, around the handbrake. Her hands were cold and clammy, and they weren't doing what she was telling them. Part of her just wanted to put her forehead against the steering wheel and let someone come to her. Let someone come and take her away and turn her in. It was preposterous what she had done; she could feel it now. So enormous it didn't even feel real. But here she was with this baby and the nappies and the milk powder and the man in the garage and the CCTV. She tried to think. She couldn't just put her head on the steering wheel. She couldn't let things unravel now. No, somehow she'd have to keep going. She opened the back door again and rummaged through the shopping. There was the key, under the nappies.

She thought again of the pram on the pavement. Come on, Val, she said to herself. Don't give up now. Anyhow, had she done wrong after all? Wouldn't any mother have done the same, finding a baby all alone? No one would be looking for her, Val decided. The baby wouldn't even have been reported missing because the mother had wanted it to be found. Why would anyone go to the police? If anyone was the criminal, it was the mother for leaving it abandoned. Val had done her a favour, whisking it off to safety in the way that she did. Even so, she still felt the cameras on her, imagined them swivelling, following the car, as she pulled out onto the road.

EIGHT

Even though it was beginning to get dark, and the air had turned cold, Rafe needed to walk. He wanted to lose himself down by the sea.

'Spare any change, please?' A man sat blocking the pavement outside Tesco Metro, his hood up, the metal sticks that were his lower legs exposed below the hem of his trousers. Normally Rafe would have given him some change, gone back to the Doorstep even to buy him a cup of tea and a flapjack. Instead, he stepped around him into the road, buttoned his old corduroy jacket, stuffed his hands into his pockets and marched down Portland Place towards the seafront.

He crossed the main road at the bottom and went down the steps onto the walkway above the beach. The sky was the colour of steel. Beyond the rusting turquoise railings, beyond the banks of pebbles, the grey waves tumbled and heaved. Seagulls screeched mournfully, their bodies buffeted on the thermals this way and that. A dirty bassline thudded from a bar under the arches. The breeze was jerk chicken and sticky rice, battered fish, seaweed and brine.

Rafe played the scene in the cafe over and over in his head. How must he have looked, fixed to the floor like that between the door and the counter, his jeans dirty and his hair in need of a cut? Since the party he'd gone awfully grey. What must Jim and Clem have thought? Clem. Poncey bloody name.

For some reason, it was knowing that Simon had been a witness at their wedding that seemed like the bigger betrayal. It was ridiculous to feel like that, Rafe knew, not having seen Jim's brother for five years. But he'd always got on so well with Simon. Still thought of him as family, somehow.

Down on the beach Rafe scrambled across the pebbles and down the shingle banks. They gave way under his weight so that he sank with each footstep, making the going hard, escalating his frustration. He skidded down the last of the banks, stood on the shore and shouted into the roar of the waves. He stayed there for a long time, hollering his despair at the sea. He wasn't even sure how he felt. Embarrassed? Angry? Jealous, certainly. Over on the concrete breaker, a seagull pecked at cold chips from a discarded cardboard cone.

Rafe moved back from the shore and sat down on the beach. He raked through the shingle with his fingertips, picked out a few larger pebbles and flung them towards the waves, but they fell with a clack at the shoreline. He couldn't even get them as far as the water. He drove his heels forward and back in the shingle, scoring deep gullies, watching the stones skitter down the bank.

Clem. He supposed he'd always known that Jim would end up with someone like Clem. Some younger media type. As he thought about the scene in the cafe, he began to feel a little ashamed that he hadn't asked Clem more about himself. He could have been friendlier. Should have been. He worried now that he'd come across like some pathetic, angry cuckold. It was just such a shock, seeing them in there together. Seeing Jim. The unbearableness of loving someone.

In his rational mind, he was happy for them. Jim was a good man, that was the trouble. He deserved happiness. He was one of those people who carried an aura of generosity and fun and what the bloody hell is life for if it ain't for laughing. Let's not take it all so seriously. Rafe did. Rafe took everything seriously. So bloody seriously that his obsessiveness had driven Jim away. He'd ruined everything. All he had left of those wonderful years with Jim was a maddening string of 'if-only's' buzzing around his head. Stupid bastard. He deserved to feel like this. Jim didn't. Jim deserved a big new life with a husband called Clem who wore trendy glasses and worked in Media.

He cupped his face in his hands and watched the grey swell of the sea, sensing the energy of the waves. He watched each one gather and grow, then smash onto the shore, its wash and the next wave merging in foamy confusion. Near the breaker, a single line of wooden posts ran down the beach to the sea. Themselves sinking into the shingle, they leaned at odd angles, mutinous. A row of drunken sailors. Over by the pier, the lights reflected in the water, rides illuminated against the navy-blue sky. The long arm of the Booster ride held its terrified thrill-seekers upside down over the water and Rafe could hear their muffled screams. Jim often used to drag him onto the pier. Rafe would indulge him by agreeing to go on the ghost train. Jim could never get enough of it – they had to do it every time. Clattering through the darkness in their metal carriage, Jim would cower and shriek in his exaggerated way, while Rafe sat next to him po-faced. Rafe was acting up, too, pretending not to be scared. It was just a thing they always did on that ride, mucking about – one over-reacting, the other stoic and straight, their role-playing all the more enjoyable because of its predictability. They both loved the Dolphin Derby however, and were fiercely competitive. Two pairs of quickfire hands fired balls into holes, making the dolphins buck across the course. Afterwards, they would stop at the seafood kiosk and sit on the beach eating vinegary cockles with wooden forks out of polystyrene pots, then position the empty pots on the shingle and aim pebbles into them.

The wind was colder now, and the last light had drained from the sky. Rafe was glad of his jumper now and pulled the polo neck up to his chin. Shaking himself out of his daydream, he made himself get up and start back up the beach. What's done was done. It wouldn't do to get maudlin. There'd been enough of that.

Even as he approached Duke's Mound, he knew that whatever was about to happen would be trashy. What a fucking cliché to go there now, when he was already feeling worthless. Oh, but who cares? He climbed the steps from the beach and headed up towards the dark shapes of the bushes.

NINE

A dark band of cloud hung low in the sky, but it was no longer raining. The baby's choky coughs had stopped now, and as they drove along it was making happy, gurgling sounds. Val thought again about Rafe, and how he used to fret in the car, making every journey a trial. Always contrary, even at that age. This one was a good baby, Val decided. You could just tell these things.

A few miles after the garage, she stopped the car again, pulling into a lay-by on the side of a dual carriageway. She opened the road atlas and found Wales. As her eyes flicked across the pages, she tried to think of a plan. With her index finger she traced roads, possible routes. Lingered over the bigger towns. She pictured the days ahead – what the baby would need, where might be the best place to hide, if indeed hiding was what she needed to do. She couldn't imagine anyone would be looking for her. Who would miss her anyway, given that she barely saw a soul from one day to the next?

Her finger stopped on Abergavenny. Her eyes moved across the capital letters of its name on the map, and she tried to imagine what it was like. Had she and Len stopped there on their honeymoon? She couldn't remember. Surely though, it would be a big enough town to be able to buy things for the baby. She needed a car seat, some toys, and clothes. If she stopped for the night she could find a baby shop, have some time to decide where they were heading, get a good night's sleep and be fresh for the next part of the journey.

It was nearly three o'clock by the time Val drove into Abergavenny. The sky was grey as if threatening rain again. The baby had woken up and was beginning to grizzle. There was a hotel on the main street, one of those old provincial places which would once have been grand and important but now looked rather rundown. The porch stretched over the entire width of the pavement, supported by two huge sandstone pillars. Val slowed the car and peered into Georgian windows that reached down almost to the pavement. A couple were sitting in the window in what looked like the restaurant. Val turned into the car park at the back of the hotel and switched off the engine. She took a deep breath. The noise of the baby was beginning to make her head feel muddled. She lifted her suitcase out of the car along with the baby's tartan bag, the nappies, wipes, and the tin of milk powder. She opened the passenger door to lift out the child. Suddenly she didn't have enough hands. She crammed all the stuff into the tartan bag, heaved the strap across her and cradled the baby's head as she lifted it through the doorway. She walked through the entrance to the car park and round to the front of the hotel.

A breeze was blowing up the main street, signalling rain, but it wasn't cold. It felt refreshing after being cooped up in the car. Val hovered near one of the porch pillars. The baby was crying. Behind her on the road, the traffic churned. The front door was open, and a stone step led down from the pavement onto a huge bristle mat which covered the whole of the lobby. Between the lobby and the reception area was a glass-panelled door. Val peered in. A man stood looking at a computer, his hand moving a mouse on the counter. His face had a blue hue, lit by the reflection of the screen. A teenage girl in an apron appeared in the foyer and spoke to him. He looked up from what he was doing and followed her into the restaurant.

Val stepped down onto the bristle mat and pushed open the door. The foyer had a thick red carpet, and the walls and door panels were covered with pink toile de jouy wallpaper. It smelled of roast dinners. Along one wall was an oak dresser displaying china plates. Val glanced through to the restaurant and saw the man still talking to the waitress.

Come on, come on, said Val under her breath. The baby was wailing. The man looked across and headed back towards the foyer.

'How can I help you?' he said as he scurried through the doorway to take up his position behind the desk. He had a thin face and tiny teeth. His grey hair was cut very short at the sides and the top of it was as flat as a table.

'I haven't booked, I'm afraid,' Val said. 'But do you have any rooms?'

'Let's have a look,' the man said, moving the mouse with his long, thin fingers and clicking around the screen.

'Is it just for you, madam?'

'Yes,' said Val. 'Oh, and this little one, of course,' she said, rubbing the child's back. Its cries were loud in the small space.

The man looked at the baby. 'Doesn't seem very happy,' he said.

'Just needs a feed, I expect,' Val said, and smiled. She tried to read the man's face. Was that a flicker of something? She felt uneasy. Did it seem strange, a seventy-two-year-old woman turning up with a baby and no reservation?

'Yes, we do have a room available for tonight,' he said. 'There are travel cots here. We could provide one in the room if you'd like?'

'Oh, um . . . Oh no, it's alright. That won't be necessary, thank you.' She wouldn't be able to look at a baby in a cot. Not after Duncan.

The man stopped clicking the mouse and looked up. He appeared to flinch, as if the baby's noise was hurting him.

'Your grandchild, is it?' he said.

'Yes, my grandchild,' she said, kissing the side of the baby's head. It was the easiest thing to say. The man tapped on the keyboard. Did it sound odd that she hadn't specified its gender? Do people say 'grandchild'? She tried to distract the baby by turning it towards the speckled reflections of the wall lamps. Its cries began to quieten. She watched its big wet eyes looking at the lights, felt it clutching the lapel of her coat.

The room was on the first floor, overlooking the street. It was decorated in the same toile de jouy wallpaper, but it was a darker shade of pink – almost brown. Thick curtains with deep pelmets framed the two floor-length windows. Uneven floorboards made ridges in the worn carpet. The double bed had a Dralon headboard and next to the bed was an easy chair. The room smelled of plug-in air freshener and was stiflingly hot.

Val lay the baby in the middle of the bed while she filled the kettle. Once it had boiled, she poured the water into the sink. She boiled it again and again until the sink was full. While she was waiting, she sat on the bed and held the baby's hands and moved its little arms this way and that, making funny faces. It was still spluttering, but she was able to distract it. She found Duncan's old rattle in her case and shook it gently above it.

'What's that, Bonny-Boo?' she said, and watched its face as it concentrated on the sound. She put the bottles into the sink

74

to sterilise them, then filled one with boiling water. While it cooled, she could change the baby's nappy.

'I wonder what you are,' Val said, lifting the child from the bed. 'Hmm? Boy or girl?' She swayed from side to side, her body finding a mother's rhythm, her hand cradling its head. 'This is going to be a wonderful surprise,' she said. 'Like unwrapping a present.' She planted a hundred little kisses on the baby's face and when she'd stopped kissing, she still held her mouth against its cheek. 'The best present.'

She wanted to take her time over what she was about to discover. This moment needed to be relished. It felt so huge, so important, almost like when the midwife had told Val the sex of her own babies when she placed them onto her chest after the sublime struggle of birth.

Inside the tartan bag Val found a portable changing mat. She unfolded it on the floor and lay the baby down. One by one, she pulled the poppers on the legs of the babygro apart.

'Pop!'

Slowly.

'Pop!'

One at a time.

'Pop!'

She lifted out its legs – one, then the other. They were chubby, and the skin was mottled and pale. The baby felt smooth and new. It kicked its legs as if glad to be free of the clothing. Val lifted its bottom and tucked the babygro under its back. The nappy was different to what Val had used with her children. She'd only ever changed Terry towels, the ones with liners and pins. All those buckets on the kitchen floor, dragging out the twin tub every day. Already she could see disposable ones were going to be more convenient. Yes, these would make life much easier. It was obvious how to use them; of course, mothers have an instinct for these things. Slowly, she unpeeled the fastenings at the front of the nappy. Then she saw. And she smiled.

'I knew you were,' she whispered, leaning over him and putting her forehead against his. She was filled with such glee she thought she would burst. 'I just had a feeling you were.'

It wasn't that she would have minded either way . . . but a boy! Kneeling in front of him, she closed her eyes and hugged herself. A boy, just like her Duncan. Any earlier doubts she'd had about whether she'd done the right thing now fell away. It was fate that this little chap had been left on that pavement just as she happened to be passing. An unwanted baby boy, found by a woman whose own son had been taken from her. It was meant to be. He wasn't a replacement for Duncan – of course not. He could never be that. But he was a gift, certainly. The best thing she could have found.

She wiped him clean, ensuring he was spotless, then put on a fresh nappy. She fed his legs back into the babygro and started to refasten the poppers: 'One! Two! Three!' She held his little feet in her hands, making them march. His knees were soft and she bent them forward and back. 'Four! Five! Six!' She did up the rest of the poppers, then smoothed the front of his little suit with the palm of her hand. 'A boy!' she said. 'My, my.' When she held her index fingers against his hands, he gripped them, his grin so big it could have turned him inside out. 'Then I'll call you Christopher,' she said. 'There you are, little Christopher, all clean!'

Christopher. She smiled. She liked it. It happened to be the name Elizabeth Taylor had chosen for one of her sons. Well, if it was good enough for Miss Taylor, then it was good enough for Val. Christopher. It suited him. Yes, Christopher was perfect.

He probably wasn't due another feed yet, but they had to find a baby shop and may be gone a while. She rummaged in her handbag for her glasses and read the instructions on the milk powder. She measured out four scoops, just as it said, and tipped them into the bottle of hot water, then added a little cold from the tap. It wasn't ideal to use tap water, but once they reach three months babies don't need everything sterilised. Val remembered that from when she'd had her own. Anyway, once they were settled somewhere she'd be able to sterilise everything. Do it all properly.

When she picked Christopher up from the floor she felt a twinge in her back, reminding her she was no longer a young woman. How easy it had been, carrying and bending when hers were young, but now her body had stiffened with age. The baby took the bottle greedily, sitting on her lap in the easy chair. Val closed her eyes for a moment, worn out from how this extraordinary day had turned out, and consumed with love for her little one.

TEN

Rafe climbed the steps from the beach and headed toward the dark shapes of the bushes. He hated Duke's Mound, the cruising area below Kemp Town on the east side of Brighton. It lay at the bottom of the cliff which carried the main road out of town. It was a desolate piece of land, a labyrinth of paths through dense tamarisk shrubs. Set into the cliff were the remains of a stone temple, crumbling like the statue of Ozymandias, its dark corners providing perfect shelter for sex with strangers. It was a seedy place. Used condoms littered the ground and rats scurried across the paths day and night. Jim used to joke that the salty smell in the air came as much from semen as the sea. Duke's Mound was left to itself, its occasional dog-walker and its men, who waited in the shadows, on the lookout. Far away from the kiss-me-quick thrills of the Palace Pier, Rafe was drawn to other, darker pleasures here on the east of town.

It was dusk now, and the only light came from the orange

street lamps up on Marine Parade. Rafe walked up the incline towards the bushes. Whoever he was about to meet, whatever he was about to do, would only make him feel worse. He knew that from experience, but he didn't care. What was sex if not a relief? Briefly his mind went back to Clem. I bet he'd never been with men in the open air, thought Rafe bitterly, trying to kid himself that he was the one who had fun. Clem looked far too sensible for that. He found himself hoping that Jim and Clem's sex was already flavoured with the dull routine of domesticity. Fuck a stranger, Clem! Live a little! he thought, unkindly. He shook his head, trying to get the image of his ex-lover's sex life out of his mind. Once again, jealousy over Jim was bringing its own kind of madness.

Away from the beach, there was no wind. The stillness was eerie. Sounds were amplified, reverberating across the waste ground. The quiet conversation of two people up on the road carried so that Rafe could make out every word. A man further up Madeira Drive towards the marina shouted to his dog, and his voice echoed off the cliff. Two men were fucking behind the engine shed of the Volks Railway, their grunts as loud as if they hadn't bothered to hide.

A man stood against the trunk of a low tree. Rafe looked over, caught his eye. He was young – no more than twenty – Latino-looking, and short, with black hair and small features. Despite the cool air, he wore a tight white T-shirt and pale jeans. His body was solid, tight. He beckoned Rafe over with

80

a backwards flick of his head. He didn't smile, but kept his eyes fixed on Rafe as he stepped across the stony soil, ducking his head under the branches.

'Alright?' said Rafe.

'Hello. How are you?' The guy's accent was Portuguese. Brazilian, perhaps. 'Just finished work?' he asked.

Rafe nodded.

'Where's that?'

'Shop up there, in Kemp Town. You?'

'Restaurant. Waiter.' He pointed towards town.

They didn't need further introduction. The man knelt on the ground beneath the tree and opened Rafe's flies. The pleasure was intense, thrilling, and as Rafe came he looked across at the twinkling lights and the thudding neon of the pier. When Rafe repaid him, the Brazilian put his arms up and held onto the trunk of the tree. It took ages for him to come. He seemed to be stringing it out, enjoying how his noise was carrying, as if he wanted to draw attention to himself. Rafe considered running off, leaving him hanging on the tree with his trousers round his ankles, but in the end he just tried to speed things up, bring him off faster. Still it went on. Rafe was irritated at the time it was taking, the performance of it all. And that high-pitched noise the guy was making, warbling up through the octaves like Mariah fucking Carey. For god's sake, man, hurry up, thought Rafe. He wanted to go home. He didn't mind a bit of danger, but this bloke was an idiot. When it was over, Rafe couldn't get away fast enough, running up the steps to the main road, the fleeting carnal thrill replaced by self-loathing, just as he'd predicted.

He trudged along the walkway above Madeira Drive towards the town centre. Near the pier he stopped and leaned against the turquoise railings. Vines of brittle black seaweed, pods like dried-up baked beans, lay scattered over the beach. A lone swimmer bobbed in the waves under the steel girders of the pier. Rafe thought of the swimming lessons he used to have from his daddy in the sea at Weston. Although he could never recall the features of his dad's face, he remembered the lifesaving badges on his trunks, and the long walk out to where the water was deep enough to swim. He remembered the little squiggles of sand that lay like spaghetti on the shoreline.

'It's the waste that the lugworms leave behind after burrowing in the sand,' his daddy said. 'Those mounds are actually piles of poo.'

'Piles of poo!' Rafe remembered saying it aloud and laughing. When he was older, whenever he saw the lugworm casts on the beach, he would think of his daddy.

Any child living along the north Somerset coast grew up having nightmares of quicksand. The beaches had a reputation. When the tide went out, they became vast mudflats. Coastguards were on constant alert. Over the years, at Weston as well as further along the coast at Berrow and Brean, countless people became trapped, gripped up to their waists by sinking sand. Some would manage to haul themselves out, some were not so lucky. Stories of people dying in the mud were widespread. Rafe remembered seeing vehicles submerged too, being slowly swallowed by the beach. Despite the tales, Rafe always felt safe on that long walk out to the sea with his daddy's big hand around his. His father was familiar with the tides, knew when it was dangerous.

After he died, Rafe's mum took him to swimming lessons at the sports centre instead. She sat in the spectator seats at the side of the pool, smiling and nodding encouragement when he completed a length, or learned to dive in off the side. She insisted he did all his badges, and after he'd earned each one she would sew it onto his trunks. After a while Suki started bringing her kids too, and she and his mum would sit together watching them all in the pool, his mum in one of those colourful scarves she wore tied around her head like a ribbon, passing Suki coffee from a flask. It became a regular Saturday morning outing. On the way home they stopped at the newsagent and Suki would buy them all Milky Ways.

Rafe watched the swimmer emerge from under the pier's iron legs and climb up the shingle. How many more swimming lessons might there have been in the sea if it wasn't for that day at the lido? He wondered if his dad would have been proud of him now. Suddenly, it felt important to know. Then he laughed at himself. Why ever would he be proud of this broken shell of a man who had wrecked his life because of his own obsessive jealousy, and who believed the way to redeem himself was having crap sex with men in public places? You're a disgrace, Rafe, that's what his daddy would have thought. And he'd be right. A thin drizzle was coming in on the breeze.

ELEVEN

While Christopher was finishing his bottle, Val reached for the remote control and turned on the television. Her heart skipped. Wasn't that Weston-super-Mare on the screen? The entrance to the Grand Pier, the Weston Eye revolving on Beach Lawns? She quickly turned it off. They really had to get a move on if they were to make it to the shops before closing time. Back down in the lobby, when Val asked the hotel manager whether there was a baby shop nearby, she tried to sound as casual as she could. Was that a hesitation before he gave her directions? No, come on, Val, she said to herself. Stop worrying about everything.

She lay Christopher on the back seat of the car while she tried to fix the two parts of the pram together. It was quite easy to unfold the chassis and snap it into place, but it was unclear how to attach the carrycot. Val had to get onto her knees in the car park to study the mechanism from underneath, see which bit fastened where. After a few attempts it finally clipped together and she lay Christopher in and tucked him up with the yellow blanket.

It sounded as though it was going to be a bit of a walk, but it would do them good to have some fresh air. She'd done enough driving for one day, and, anyway, the car was probably best where it was, hidden round the back. She had removed the sparklies from her earlobes and swapped her shoes for her flatties. Even with her full skirt and her high black hair, Val didn't think she looked particularly noticeable. Only young women were visible, after all. Young women and movie stars.

It was nice to be outside, away from the hot room. Rain was no longer threatening and behind the clouds there were swathes of blue sky. As Val pushed the pram along the pavements, she watched Christopher studying the changing facades of the buildings and the rolling shapes of the clouds. She concertinaed the hood down a little so that he had a bigger view. They passed a park and Val stopped and looked through the gates. It was still only just past four, so there was plenty of time for a detour before the shop would close. Val followed the tarmac path down to a pond at the bottom of the slope. She sat on a bench and lifted Christopher onto her lap and put his blanket around him. A little girl and her dad were feeding bread to the ducks. The mallards chortled and quacked, making a din. An exotic-looking duck swam serenely past. It had an orange frill at either side of its beak and two long feathers on its back that stuck up like sails. Val looked at the different species of ducks on the information board next to the bench. It was a mandarin. She thought it looked as though it was wearing one of those fascinators on its head, like women wear at weddings.

'Look at that one, Christopher,' she said. 'It looks like it's dressed up for a party none of the others have been invited to!'

The man turned and smiled at Val's remark. A pintail duck clattered out of the reeds and touched down on the island in the middle of the pond. Christopher was transfixed by it all. Val watched his eyes moving, his curiosity as big as himself. When one of the ducks let out a prolonged comical quack, Christopher laughed and turned to Val to share his delight. She pulled him closer and lay her cheek on the top of his head. Already, she loved him.

The shop was on a small industrial zone next to a roundabout at the other end of the town. Val pushed open the door, but it shut on the pram before she could get through. She turned round and backed in.

'Here, let me help you,' a woman said, coming over to hold the door. 'There's a button outside on the wall that you can press to hold it open,' she said, smiling. She had cropped grey hair and wore an oversized necklace.

'Oh,' said Val. 'Thank you.'

'There's one inside too, look,' the woman said. 'Just so you know for next time.'

There was nobody else in the shop and Val felt self-conscious with the pram. She wheeled it around the displays and looked at the pushchairs and toys and clothes. All the bright colours. She felt the woman's eyes on her, watching. It was quiet inside the shop. The woman coughed. The car seats were up on a shelf along the wall. They all looked so big, like armchairs.

'Is there anything I can help you with?' the woman said.

'I need a car seat,' Val said. 'But I've no idea which one.'

'Of course,' the woman said, bustling over. She appeared pleased to have something to do. Val relaxed a bit, realising she'd only been staring at her because the shop was so empty.

The woman smiled into the pram. 'How old is he?'

Val liked how she knew her baby was a boy.

'Five months.' She'd revised Christopher's age since seeing him with the ducks. She didn't think a child could laugh like that until they were at least that age. Although she wasn't exactly sure. Was that right? How old had Rafe been? She couldn't really remember. She hoped Christopher did look five months. The woman would be an expert, working in a shop like this, seeing babies every day. Val was glad she didn't pursue it, and was lifting car seats from the shelf, making an *ouf* sound each time she bent down to put one on the floor. They looked so fiddly with all the harnesses and clips.

'Will it be easy to fix into my car?' Val asked. 'My daughter's gone on holiday, you see, and taken the seat with her. I'm not

used to all these new things. It's years since mine were small.'
As with the police officer, she found the lies coming easily. She
thought about the encounter with him at the side of the road.
Was that only this morning? It seemed like days ago.

'Of course.' The woman smiled and showed Val where
to feed the seatbelt and adjust the straps. Val chose a seat with
a blue checked fabric and the woman took it over to the till.
Val looked through the rails and held up baby clothes, trying
to picture the length of Christopher's body.

'There should be sizes on everything,' the woman called
over.

Val smiled at her. Labels were no help. In the end she chose
six babygros in two different sizes. She draped them over the
handle of the pram along with three vests, some pyjamas with
an astronaut design, a pair of red quilted trousers and a
cardigan with rabbits on the pockets.

She spent a long time at the far end of the shop, browsing
the toys. She found them enchanting. She squeezed and shook
all the soft toys and rattles, showing them to Christopher and
selecting the ones he seemed to like best: a plush tortoise
with a shell that made a scrunching sound; a Peter Rabbit
rattle; a music box with a little screen showing an animation of
a girl dancing on a bridge and which played the tune of 'Sur
le Pont d'Avignon'. Val took them over to the counter, along
with an activity arch with mirrors and animals that dangled
down from the frame.

'He's just the right age for that,' the woman said. 'They seem to love those. Might give you a bit of peace, too.' She caught Val's eye and smiled. Val had forgotten those knowing looks shared between women with children. Perhaps once she and Christopher became settled somewhere, she could join mother and baby groups. Be part of all that again.

There were some baby slings hanging up behind the counter. Val never had one for her own children, but wherever she ended up she might take the baby for walks away from the roads.

'Can I have one of those?' she said, pointing.

'A carrier? Yes, of course.' The woman showed her where to feed the baby's legs and how the straps crossed over and clipped at the sides. Val was pleased she'd thought to get it. They could have some lovely walks, wherever they were going.

She piled the things into the basket underneath the pram. 'It's so handy having this,' she said, trying to sound as though she was familiar with it. The boxes for the car seat and the arch were enormous.

'Oh,' said Val. 'I wasn't expecting them to be as big as that.'

'Have you not got the car with you?' the woman said.

'No. I didn't think . . .' Val said. She balanced them across the pram, one on top of the other. They were so high she couldn't see Christopher anymore.

'Are they going to be alright, like that?' The woman looked alarmed.

'Don't worry, I'll manage,' Val said, pressing the button to open the door.

Outside the sky had darkened, and cars had their lights on. It was difficult walking with the boxes like that on the pram. Val had to steer with one hand and press down on them with the other to stop them sliding off, all the while negotiating kerbs and crossings. She didn't like not being able to see Christopher and she stopped from time to time to peep in the pram. He seemed happy enough, lying there looking up at the boxes and a slice of sky. By the time she got back to the hotel, her arm ached from holding onto the boxes all that way. It was a relief to get in the lift.

Once they were in the room, Val untucked Christopher's blanket, slid her hands under his little body and lifted him out of the pram. She held him against her chest, her body finding its natural sway. She hummed the tune of 'Bye, Baby Bunting', putting her chin on the top of his head and feeling the soft down of his hair. Something inside her was appeased. She turned to look at him. His face was as round as a penny, his hands like little suet puddings. Everything about him was round. His great wide eyes, the curve of his cheeks, his button nose. She fingered the wooden buttons on his cardigan, the cuffs turned over on the sleeves. 'You're beautiful, aren't you?' she said. 'My gorgeous little boy.'

She laid him on the floor, pulled the toys out of the bag and cut off the labels with her nail scissors. She scrunched the tortoise's shell and shook Peter Rabbit and watched as Christopher listened to the sounds. They lay together on the floor, Christopher on his back and Val on her side curled around him. She wound up the music box and they listened to 'Sur le Pont d'Avignon' over and over again and watched the girl dance on the bridge. Val moved onto all fours to get up, feeling the nag of age.

'Mama will make you all clean and nice,' she called to the baby from the bathroom. The sink in the ensuite was the perfect size for a bath, and she ran the water and added some of the hotel's Orange Blossom bubble bath. She lay Christopher on the bed to get him undressed because it was easier on her back. Then she held him in the sink with one hand and with the other smoothed white bubbles over his belly, his arms and his chest. She dipped cotton wool into the water and gently wiped each eye, out from the nose and across his cheek, just like the nurse had shown her when Rafe was born. Then she wiped his ears, his neck, his hands. 'Rubadubdub, put baby in the tub, rubadubdub, let's give him a scrub!' she sang, putting her words to a tune. He looked up at her with his big trusting eyes and she felt his legs kick under the water. 'Rubadubdub, let's give him a scrub!' she sang again. She scooped up a mass of bubbles and blew them across the bathroom, put some on her nose and her chin. She scrunched up her face and made it pop open in surprise, her eyes wide, her mouth the shape of an

O. Christopher beamed. Val wrapped him in the hotel's big white towel, and he looked like a cherub peeking out of a cloud. 'Peepo!' Val sang. 'Peepo, Bonny-Boo!' She put her nose against his shoulder and smelled all his freshness. Then she patted him dry and put on a clean nappy and his new astronaut pyjamas. She gave him a bottle and when it was finished, she felt his body go limp with sleep. Pulling back the duvet, she laid him in the middle of the bed with Rafe's giraffe next to him and placed a pillow on either side. She switched off the main light so that the room was lit by the soft glow of the wall lamps. For a time, she sat on the bed and watched him sleep. He was lying on his back, his arms aloft, his fists clenched next to his ears. Dreaming, perhaps, of the ducks they'd seen in the park, of his bath time, of his new mama singing that funny song. He looked so contented and well fed and it made her feel proud. She picked up the giraffe, remembering the time Rafe had lost it in town. All afternoon they'd spent retracing their steps, trawling along Weston high street to revisit every shop, Rafe inconsolable in his pushchair. Eventually they'd found it in Walker & Ling, amongst the balls of wool in the haberdashery department. Typical of Rafe, making a song and dance. He was always difficult.

Val smiled absently, ran her hand down the giraffe's fluffy mane and tucked it in next to Christopher. He was her everything now. Everything she held dear. She sat on the bed for nearly an hour, watching the little movements of his mouth while he slept, the rise and fall of his chest. It was hard to leave him. The last time she'd taken her eyes off a baby while it slept . . . well, she wasn't going to let this one out of her sight. How could that have happened to her own baby when she'd taken such care of him? All she'd done was put him to bed. She couldn't have loved him more, yet somehow she'd failed to look after him. She put her hand on Christopher's little arm, felt the soft cotton of his pyjamas. She would make sure she looked after this one. She'd be his protector now. She'd be his mama.

However sharp her memories of the day Duncan arrived in the world, they would never be as vivid as the day he left it. She could tell something was wrong as soon as she opened the bedroom door. It was like a change in the air. A minor chord. She stood in the doorway for a moment, unable to let go of the handle. When she finally dared to look in his cot, the sight of him stopped her heart.

He was lying on his front, face towards the wall. Still swaddled in the waffle blanket Val had tucked tightly up to his neck and down the sides of the cot a few hours before. But it was all wrong. She knew he wasn't breathing even before she picked him up. She tore back the blanket and lifted him out. He felt the same: the noble weight of him, the suppleness of his body, his limbs that hung towards the floor. The only difference was that his skin was stone cold.

Val heard her lungs fight for air. Rapid, panicky gasps of terror. Instinctively, she rocked her baby in her arms – to soothe him, to placate herself.

'No no no no no no.' She knelt on the carpet and his little arms swung with the motion of it, then lay limply across her lap. She looked at the barely perceptible hairs of his lashes, the tiny veins under the translucent skin of his eyelids. His startling black hair. The smell of Johnson's powder from last night's bath. She clutched him and a noise started deep down in her womb. It rose out of her in one continuous base note, like the bellow of a sick animal. It echoed the low moans she'd made when she'd pushed him out of her body not three weeks before, as if the birth and death of a child was expressed in the same way. The sound filled the room, filled the whole house.

Suddenly she felt a violence inside her, a bitter sting in her throat. She put her baby down and grabbed the nearest thing to hand. Duncan lay next to her on the carpet in his blue sleep suit while Val retched and retched into Rafe's old potty, her stomach turning itself inside out.

She'd always found it strange, the phrase 'lost a baby', as though she'd put him down somewhere, then forgotten where he was. She hadn't lost him. She'd known exactly where he was. In the weeks that followed, her mind shut down. The pills they gave her to dry up her milk she swallowed in a haze, never remembering when she'd taken the last one. She pulled sauce-pans from the cupboards with no idea what she was going to put in them, stared at plates and dishes on the table. She gathered up dirty clothes from Rafe's bedroom and left them in piles on the landing, unable to face pulling out the twin tub. Sometimes she would sit on the floor with Rafe to play Lego, but instead found herself just staring, holding the bricks between her useless fingers. The grip of her grief was physical. Despite it being mid-summer, she couldn't get warm. She lay on the sofa like an invalid, shivering under a blanket, too sick to move. It felt as if her belly was being ripped out; her womb hurt like after-pains.

In those first terrible days, she would leave Rafe with Len and pace along the seafront. Some days she would tear down the promenade, charge all the way to Uphill Beach as if trying to outrun her own grief. Other days she walked more slowly, her shoulders drooped, her head bent forwards, dragging her body along like Marley's chain. Back at home, Len just seemed to sit, always so quiet, his emotions pushed somewhere deep down.

'I wish you'd let it go,' she would say, kneeling beside his armchair, her hand on his knee. 'It'll eat you up. If we could just share it . . .'

But he would simply get up and brush past her, tramping upstairs for one of his long baths. He started agreeing to all the overtime offered at the station, calling in at the staff social club after his shifts. Once or twice he'd got so drunk that Terry had to bring him home, worried he wouldn't find his way.

The coffin was barely bigger than the box Val's winter boots came in. It only needed two pallbearers. She and Len sat at the front of All Saints' Church enclosed in their separate vacuums of sorrow. Val reached across the pew to her husband, but he didn't take her hand. He just sat there staring at the tapestry kneeler in front of him, his fingers picking at the flannel fabric of his trousers. Familiar people in the church were incongruous – startling – in their black clothes. While the mourners sang 'All Things Bright and Beautiful', Val stared at the blurred words on the Order of Service. Nothing felt real. It couldn't be real. He was three weeks old. Most of these mourners hadn't met him. Some of them hadn't even known she'd had him. They held a wake in the back room of the Monaco Hotel. The quiet murmur of conversations, the sympathetic looks and weak smiles; it was more than Val could bear. She pretended to go to the ladies then left through a side door, crossing the car park and running up towards Anchor Head, her heels clacking on the pavement, her handbag under her arm. She clambered down the rocky cliff that dropped down to the sand below Birnbeck Pier. On a snaggled ridge, she hugged her legs into her chest and expelled her despair as if it were the last breath of air in her lungs. The tide smashed into the barnacled columns of the pier.

Val pinched the bridge of her nose to stop her tears spilling. That same old thick ache. She'd had a lifetime of crying. She might be happier, now. Christopher would give her a new lease of life. She hovered the back of her hand over his mouth and felt the trace of his breath. She fancied a bath, but didn't want to leave him. Perhaps if she left the door open, she'd see him from the bathtub. That would be alright. She edged away from the bed with her eyes still on him.

The bath crème foamed under the tap and made the water silky. Everything was so sparklingly clean. It was such a treat to be staying in a hotel. Val took off her clothes and folded them into her suitcase. Lying back in the bath, she could see Christopher under the low lights, asleep in his nest of pillows. She wondered how long it had been since she'd felt this content.

With her skin warm and soft from the bath, she slipped on her dressing gown. She lifted her negligée from the case, pulled out the feather mules. She lined up her make-up on the dressing table, ready to puff her face with powder, twist the beauty spot into place and spray her neck with L'Air du Temps. Then she stopped. Where was the need? That urge – that maddening 'Elizabeth' itch she normally felt – had gone. She didn't need to do it. Christopher completed her. She tidied the make-up away, put her negligée and fluffies back in the suitcase, and put on her nightie.

She sat in the easy chair next to the bed and ate the sandwich she'd bought at the garage, and the bar of chocolate. She opened the road atlas. Her eyes moved across Wales, from Abergavenny over to the west. Tracing the coastline with her finger, she looked for Aberdovey. Fifty years since she was there with Len, she still remembered the vast expanse of sand, the dunes that lined the beach, the pastel colours of the Victorian terraces along the seafront. Her finger continued northwards. Ah, there it was: Aberdovey, on the mouth of the river. She remembered the estuary and how the river spilled out onto the beach. Didn't Len get his shoes wet? And what was the name of their guesthouse? Something about the sea . . . Turning Tides? Yes, that was it! Funny how she could remember the name after all this time. Maybe it was still there. The more she thought about it, the more convinced she was that Aberdovey was the place to go with her new baby. Small and quiet and tucked away from the world, it would be perfect. Her eyes flicked forward and back, contemplating the distance from Abergavenny. She held her thumb against the scale line at the bottom of the page and estimated the distance, moving it across the map and counting. She followed the course of the roads, studied the colours and contour lines, trying to visualise the journey. So much of the land was coloured green – the route passed right over the Cambrian mountains. She'd never driven that far before, and never on those sorts of roads. Would they climb up very high? Would her little Peugeot even make it? At least she'd be away from that awful motorway. She and Christopher could take their time and wouldn't be intimidated by all that traffic whipping around them on all sides. She divided the journey into chunks, road number to road number, town to town. It began to look better. She moved her thumb across the map again to calculate how long it might take.

'Four hours I'd say, Christopher,' she said. 'Do you think we can manage that?' She studied him while he slept. How tiny little humans are, she thought. How awe-inspiring. She looked back at the map. 'Yes,' she said. 'I'm sure we can manage that.'

TWELVE

Of the many routes Rafe could have chosen to walk home from Duke's Mound, he always seemed to pick the one that took him past Florence Road. Yet again he found himself lumbering up his old street, glancing at the huge Victorian villa he once shared with Jim. The new owners clearly enjoyed the name he and Jim had given the place, for the plaque saying 'Gatsby's' was still fixed to the wall next to the front door. Rafe's window boxes were there too, on the sills of the upstairs bedrooms, planted with lavender and trailing ivy. They'd repointed the brickwork and painted the front door a smart grey. He was glad they were looking after the house.

It had been five years since the party, but it was strange how much of it was so clear in his mind. As well as Jim's great big laugh and his quips about Noël Coward, Rafe could remember a lot of the little details too. The black-and-white geometric design of Susannah's dress, her big yellow resin earrings; the peonies Louise had brought, wrapped in brown paper. The 'graffiti' cake Rafe had ordered as a centrepiece for the table – a grungy, distressed affair with white icing and red fondant roses, hand-painted with Brighton landmarks and cartoon lettering.

Someone put on Boney M. Louise's husband Marcus, who'd once trained as a ballet dancer, was performing Russian Cossack kicks to 'Rasputin' in the sitting room and when Jim's brother Simon tried to copy him, he fell on his backside and split his trousers. Rafe even remembered the conversation he'd had with the guy who ran the florist's next to Kemp Town Gallery, about which plants to buy for the window boxes he was planning to put along the front. He remembered the laughter, the buzz of conversation. They were such an interesting and gregarious bunch of people. They were his friends. While he stood in the kitchen watching them all, it crossed his mind how far he'd come since his claustrophobic childhood in Weston-super-Mare. It had been a relief to escape that town, but also to escape his mother, who lived out her grief through some bizarre Hollywood fantasy.

The most vivid memory of that night was Lucas. Beautiful, bewitching Lucas, with his smooth olive skin, the sheen of his black hair, his belt with its silver buckle slung round his slim hips. Everything about him sparkled. A few weeks before the party, Jim and Rafe had taken him on as an intern at the gallery. They were spending more and more of their time travelling between Brighton and London, and visiting Europe to buy art. They needed someone to staff the gallery and keep track of the paperwork when they were away. Immediately Lucas became an asset to the business. Twenty-three, with an art degree and an impressive knowledge of artists as well as the industry, he talked about current exhibitions, trends, the next big thing. A gifted photographer, he took black and white images of underground culture – tattoo conventions, East End boxing clubs, gang violence. He could show movement in his work like no other photographer Rafe or Jim had ever seen. His images were gritty and raw. Jim had decided to take a risk and put on an exhibition of his work. It was a busy time for the gallery, and he was excited by the dynamic Lucas' work might bring to the business.

At the party Lucas was taking pictures of people as they chatted in the kitchen or danced in the living room. Rafe watched him twisting the dial of his lens as though it were a part of him. He knew that the mood of the party would burst from every one of those still, two-dimensional images. There was a politeness about Lucas that everybody liked. He was charming yet unobtrusive, and he knew how to get people to respond to the camera. He was magnetic. So magnetic, in fact, that Rafe could see that Jim was completely enchanted by him. He observed them that night, when they appeared to have found a moment alone together in the dining room. He hovered by the door and listened to Lucas admiring the Mapplethorpe above the piano. Jim was asking him about his own portraits, and he talked about the importance of light. What was paramount though, he said, was the personal relationship he made with his subjects. Rafe watched Lucas hold Jim's eye while he talked about shutter speeds and exposure and apertures. He watched the way he leaned into Jim to show him the camera, the way he put his fingers on Jim's to move the zoom in and out. As Rafe lingered, he imagined Jim's heart beating faster. Insecurity was getting the better of him again. He knew he was being ridiculous. He knew what Jim would say: 'I love you. How many times do you need reassuring?' But he couldn't help himself. They'd been arguing recently about his possessiveness. The more successful Jim became, the more attractive Rafe believed he was to others, and the more his jealousy began to eat him up. He'd started scrutinising the way men behaved when they were around him. It was becoming an obsession. He wished he could stop it. It was as if he loved him too much. It was intolerable. Despite his attempts to hide his feelings, he knew it was beginning to drive Jim mad.

'D'you mind if I . . . ?' he heard Lucas say from the dining room, and he watched him pull a wrap of cocaine from his pocket.

'Sure, go ahead,' Jim said.

Their parties weren't generally druggy affairs. Beers, champagne cocktails, only ever the occasional line of coke. Lucas chopped two lines out on the coffee table, sniffed one up his nostril with a rolled-up banknote, then passed it to Jim.

'Oh, I don't as a rule,' Jim said, putting his hands up in front of him. 'My days of hedonism are long over. Partied too hard in the nineties!'

'Really?' Lucas said, grinning at him. 'Wouldn't have had you down as a raver.'

'I had my moments,' Jim laughed. 'Under the arches down on the seafront back in the day.'

Oh shut up, Jim, Rafe thought. I can see what you're doing. You're trying to impress him, hoping he won't see you as an old prude. It's pathetic. Inside, he felt that familiar panic. It was all he could do not to storm over and tell Lucas to go home, not to clasp Jim round the waist, make him promise never to leave him.

Jim took the bank note from Lucas. 'Oh, why the hell not?' he said, and snorted the remaining line off the table. He sniffed heavily and wiped his nostrils with the back of his hands. He put his palms against his temples.

'Woah,' he said, grinning at Lucas. 'Oof. Nice.' He sniffed again. 'Thanks.'

Rafe stood in the doorway and seethed. When Jim was heading back to the kitchen Rafe followed him and grabbed his arm.

'What d'you think you're doing?' he said, his heart thumping.

'What?'

'All over him like a rash. Oh yes, Lucas, I'd love some of

your cocaine. Oh yes, Lucas, you're so incredible. Oh yes, Lucas, I'd love to go to bed with you.'

'What the fuck are you talking about?'

'Taking drugs with him. I saw you.'

'It's just a line of coke,' Jim said. 'Chill out, will you?'

'No, it's a line of *his* coke, with *him*,' Rafe said.

'Oh, here we go.'

Even though their guests were beginning to notice something was wrong, Rafe couldn't help himself. 'I can see what you're doing, Jim. You're trying to convince him you're some carefree spirit, make sure he knows you've had a wild past. You're not twenty-three, for god's sake. You're overweight and nearly fifty. You like *Antiques Roadshow*. It's childish.'

'Childish? Who's being childish?' Jim spat, his eyes blazing. 'You're the one who's behaving like a teenager.'

'Are you *trying* to make me jealous?'

'I don't need to try, Rafe. You do it to yourself. If I even look at someone, you're jealous. You've got a massive problem, and I'm sick of it!' Jim's voice was booming now, and there was a lull in the conversation. Someone turned the music down.

'Hey, hey, you two, no need for a domestic,' Louise said, standing between them with her arms out like a referee in a boxing ring. 'Don't say stuff you're going to regret.'

Rafe couldn't leave it. He could only see Lucas' fingers on Jim's, the way their shoulders had touched. Their hips together.

'You were giving him the come on, I saw what you were doing,' he hissed.

'Oh, shut up. I wasn't giving anyone the come on. He was showing me his fucking camera. We're putting on an exhibition of his work, remember, you absolute wanker.'

Lucas had appeared in the kitchen and made a face to the guests to show how awkward he felt. They shrugged and shook their heads at him, as if to reassure him it was nothing he'd done. People were trying to pick up conversations again, trying to distract attention away from the argument which had soured the mood.

Simon opened another bottle of champagne. 'Anyway, let's move on,' he said, throwing his brother a look. 'Who wants a refill?' he said, as the cork hit the ceiling. He moved around the kitchen, but people put their hands over their glasses and were starting to look for their coats.

'I'm really sorry, everybody, that Rafe's being an utter *prick*!' Jim said. Someone was calling a cab. 'Oh, please don't go,' he said.

'I'm sorry if I've been the cause of something,' Lucas said, grimacing. 'I really didn't mean anything.' He looked confused. 'I was only showing Jim my camera, Rafe,' he said. 'It wasn't a big deal.'

'Oh, really?' Rafe said. 'No, no, you're right. It wasn't a big deal. Not a big deal at all. You carry on. You rub up against my partner all you like, with your cool black clothes and your perfect little arse. Go on, you fondle away – that's absolutely fine. It's not a big deal at all.' Rafe spat out his words. He was aware of everyone looking at him, but he couldn't stop now. He'd lost control. 'Tell you what, Lucas, why don't you cut all the bullshit and just put your dick in his mouth? That's obviously what you both want.'

Lucas picked up his coat and scarf from a stool tucked under the kitchen island. 'Oof,' he said. 'Not enjoying the vibe, I gotta say.' He looked at Rafe. 'You've really got this wrong,' he said, and walked out.

By ten everyone had gone. The graffiti cake was untouched, and Boney M was still playing quietly in the living room.

'Look what you've done!' Jim shouted. 'You total *fucking* loser!' He thumped upstairs and slammed the bedroom door.

Rafe spent a sleepless night in the spare room, knowing his jealousy had just cost him his relationship. He couldn't control it; it was like an illness. Deep down he knew they were only being friendly. A bit of harmless flirting perhaps. Why couldn't he be rational about it? In the early hours he went downstairs and sat at the kitchen table. He rested his head against the wall and watched the sun come up over the house at the end of the garden. Around eight, he heard Jim's feet on the stairs. He stiffened.

'You still here?' Jim said, scuffing into the kitchen in his slippers, his voice thick from last night's excess. He put the kettle on, dropped two slices of bread in the toaster and slammed the metal lid back on the bread bin, making Rafe flinch.

'Well?' Jim said.

Rafe couldn't meet his eye. He looked down at the table and traced the curve of a wood knot with his finger.

'Funny,' Jim said. 'You had plenty to say last night, when all our guests were here.' He made himself an instant coffee, smeared butter on his toast and took a huge bite. 'Alright, here it is,' he said, talking with his mouth full. 'You made us look ridiculous last night and you actually need to leave.' He gesticulated with his toast. 'Go on. Get out.'

Rafe felt himself buckle. 'I'm sorry,' he mumbled. 'I promise I won't do it again.'

'Bollocks. You're always doing it,' Jim said. 'This has been coming for ages. I hope you're happy now. Congratulations – your insecurity has finally destroyed us. And you need to go.'

'But, Jim, I—'

Jim put out his hand to stop Rafe speaking. 'There's nothing you can say that'll make me change my mind. Now you're doing this in public, it's actually humiliating. You crossed a line last night.' He leaned against the worktop and rubbed his eyes with the balls of his hands. 'I need you to go, and it needs to be today.'

'I'm so sorry,' Rafe said again. Tears needled his eyes. He felt his world caving in. 'I'll change,' he said. 'I can change.'

'No, you won't,' Jim said. 'You can't. You're getting worse. You're doing it all the time. Interrogating me when I speak to another man, looking for my reaction if we happen to pass some fit guy down the seafront. You've even started watching my fingers as I type my passcode into my phone. Don't deny it – I've seen you. I can't even leave my phone around anymore because you'll be snooping. And d'you know the sickest thing about it, is that there is absolutely nothing on that phone which would upset you.' He held his fingertip to his temple. 'It's all in your head.'

'I know,' Rafe said, his voice cracking. 'I can't help myself. I wish I could. It's crippling me, Jim. I just love you so much and I don't want to lose you.' He sounded pathetic. No wonder Jim had had enough.

'Of course, the irony . . .' Jim said, '. . . is that you're so obsessed with what you might lose, that you've just gone and lost it.'

'I know. I'm sorry,' Rafe said again, although he knew it wouldn't make any difference. It was too late. 'It was just seeing you with Lucas . . .'

'Oh, you really need to get a grip. Lucas is just *some guy*,' Jim said, angry again now. 'He's a good photographer. He's got untold potential. He could have brought us a whole load of business.' He opened the fridge and poured himself a glass of orange juice. 'I'm not about to run off with him. I don't want to fuck him. Yes, he's good-looking and young and sexy.' Rafe smarted at that. 'But so are loads of people.'

Jim slammed the fridge shut. 'And talking of Lucas,' he

went on, 'you do realise you've screwed up the exhibition too? D'you really think he's going to want to work with a couple of squabbling old queens, taking swipes at each other in public? Not very professional, is it? You saw how he was when he left last night. Clearly very embarrassed. And he's every right to be.' He swallowed his juice and banged the glass down on the counter. 'It's all so demeaning. So fucking unnecessary.'

Rafe hung his head, unable to meet Jim's eye.

'So well done, Rafe. Nice work. You've succeeded not only in destroying us, but also wrecking an opportunity for the business – which puts this roof over our head, by the way – to explore something really exciting and branch out.'

'I know,' Rafe said. 'Don't think I don't hate myself. I've tried to ignore these feelings, but I can't. I'm just so anxious all the time . . .'

'Why don't you talk to someone?' Jim said, softening a little. 'I've suggested it so many times and you've done nothing about it.'

Rafe shook his head. He knew where this was going.

'I've said it before,' Jim said. 'It's classic attachment theory.'

Rafe felt himself welling up again.

'You lost someone you loved when you were a child, and now you're worried it'll happen again,' Jim continued. 'It's fear of abandonment, don't you see? You could really do with some help. Maybe if you were able to explore your feelings about what happened to your dad . . .'

111

Rafe bridled. 'But that's the problem,' he said. 'If I knew what happened . . . but I don't.' He drew his hand over his face. 'I've just got these images in my head, but no one's ever helped me make sense of them. It's as if I know the context, but not the narrative.'

He'd always avoided talking about his dad's death. It was easier to push it down inside. There was just so much to unpack. His mother had never explained what happened at the lido. Rafe couldn't remember much, only his father lying on the concrete terrace at the side of the pool, the badges on his navy trunks and his legs lying so still. There was an older man, with grey hair and baggy skin that hung off his skeletal body, bending over his father, blowing air into his mouth. The rest of the image was distorted, warped like the walls of the pool in the heat haze of a hot summer. Ever since, it had been as if it were some sort of secret. Whenever his mother referred to what happened, she always used the word 'accident'. Rafe was sure it was a euphemism. Other people, Suki included, talked about Len's 'fall'. Why did people use different words? Had it really been an accident? Nobody had ever discussed anything with him, and he hated his mother for that. He hated her.

'Anyway,' Jim said. 'I can't live like this anymore. Your jealousy is suffocating. It's driving me insane.'

He sat next to Rafe at the table, but didn't touch him. 'Please don't see this as me trying to patronise you,' he said. He was calm now but was already speaking as if they were friends, not lovers. 'But I genuinely think you could do with some help. If you do this to someone else in the future . . . well, you'll drive them away too.'

'But there won't be anyone else,' Rafe said, hearing the desperation in his voice. 'There's only you.'

'No. It's over, Rafe. I can't live with someone who doesn't trust me,' Jim said. 'It's too exhausting. I need you to leave now.' Rafe closed his eyes and pressed his fingertips against his eyelids, but the tears came all the same. He had just destroyed the best thing he'd ever had.

On his way back to the flat, Rafe stopped at the deli on the corner to buy olives. He couldn't afford them, but he wanted to stand in the shop and feel his old life. The olives sat in huge tubs, shiny-coated in chilli oil and garlic and lemon. Home-made pies, prosciutto and hams were displayed on wooden boards, the shelves lined with handcrafted chutneys and artisan gin. When Rafe was with Jim, they used to come in together and buy pizza slices or croissants stuffed with spinach and cheese. They would chat to Emilio, the Neapolitan owner, about their trips to Milan and Turin and Florence, debate where to find the best gelato and why pasta should be fresh, never dried. Without Jim, Rafe didn't chat. Now, he held his head lower. It was only when they broke up that he realised how much he'd ridden on Jim's gregariousness all those years. It was easy to be swept along by it, believe you were two of a kind. Without Jim he was quiet and shy. He found he didn't have much to say. Emilio seemed to treat Rafe differently now, no longer bursting into life when he went in the shop the way he always did when Jim was there. Without Jim, Rafe began to wonder who he was. He didn't seem like anyone, much.

Back at the flat he poured himself a large gin and tonic. The cat padded over and smoothed her flank against his legs. He reached down and stroked her. He loved the sleekness of her fur, her slender body. He was glad Jim had let him keep the cat. They'd split everything fairly and amicably. Florence Road had been Jim's house – he'd bought it outright in the nineties before Brighton prices went nuts. He kept the shop in Portobello and the stall at Spitalfields, but let Rafe keep Kemp Town Gallery. He had plans to open a photographers' studio in Hove. They managed to agree on who got what without any need for solicitors. Neither had the appetite for custody battles.

Rafe put the glass on the piano in the living room and thumbed through his record collection. He pulled out Mahler's 'Symphony Number 5' and eased it from its sleeve. He held the record at the edges by his fingertips, placed it on the turntable and lowered the stylus. All his extravagant possessions from Florence Road – the first edition Mapplethorpes, an original Miró, the colonial sculptures he'd picked up at the Marché de Clignancourt – all were now crammed into his small local authority flat. He sat on the velvet Chesterfield and removed his shoes and socks. He liked the softness of the reindeer hide rug under his bare feet. It occurred to him that he was hungry, but other than the olives he had nothing in.

Every encounter he ever had at Duke's Mound made him feel worse about himself. He was still irritated by that young man and his operatics. A blow job on the Mound was never going to be dignified, but that guy had left him feeling cheap and ludicrous. He thought of when he'd bumped into Jim at the cafe and cringed. He thought of Clem and his oh-so-Brighton spectacles, the way he'd been leaning against Jim when they were looking at the phone. He hated him, although he guessed he was probably a lovely guy. He thought of Lucas too, just a bright young thing trying to make his way in the art world. He'd never been interested in Jim. Rafe was still embarrassed by the way he'd behaved that night, although something still twisted inside him when he thought of them holding that camera, the way Lucas had offered Jim the bank note, how he was so impossibly handsome. Stop being bitter, Rafe, he said to himself. Stop destroying yourself. He lay back on the Chesterfield, his head at one end and his feet up at the other, drinking his gin and listening to the exquisite beauty of Mahler. The cat jumped up and settled on his lap.

THIRTEEN

It was one in the morning when Christopher began, protesting about something Val couldn't fathom. She walked him up and down the room, tried to get him to settle, but his cries echoed round the walls.

'What is it then, dearie? Tell Mama,' she said. 'Tell Mama all.' She tried to feed him, but he contorted his mouth and rejected the bottle, his little face crumpled into a hot ball of rage. Val held him to her and rocked him, but nothing she could do would pacify him. After two hours of it there was a sharp knock on the wall. A door opened, and Val heard a woman's voice in the corridor. 'Really?' she said, her voice raised. 'Two bloody hours! I need some sleep!' Val heard her go back into her room and slam the door, then listened to the angry tone of the muffled voices on the other side of the wall.

It was nearly four o'clock by the time Christopher settled. Val couldn't sleep though, still wanting to watch him, check that he was breathing. She watched his little chest rise and fall, held her ear near his mouth to feel his faint sweet breath. She was so tired. It was all coming back to her, how hard it was looking after a baby. She remembered how Rafe used to keep her up all night, how she would sleepwalk through the whole of the next day. It didn't matter how much gripe water she gave him, he'd still yell the house down half the night. It never made one jot of difference. Even his birth had been a twenty-hour battle to separate mother and child before they hauled him out like a calf from a heifer. For days his head was a funny shape. The marks from the forceps on either side of his skull made him look as though he'd been branded. And that's not to mention what he'd done to her down below. The less said about that sorry mess the better. Duncan's birth had been very different. A few quick sucks on the gas and air and he'd slid out as easy as winking. And as for sleep, virtually from the day he was born he seemed to sense the difference between day and night. He never kept her up all night like Rafe. As soon as Val brought him home from the hospital, he fell into a pattern completely in sync with hers. She hardly knew she had him, that one. Such a good little boy. She reached over to Christopher and put her arm across his tummy as he slept, smoothed his tiny hand with her thumb.

As she lay there staring into the darkness, she thought about Christopher's mother for the first time. Val had no doubt that she would be having the best night's sleep she'd had for months. Relieved, finally, of the burden that led her to leave him on the pavement like that. Who would be so desperate to do such a thing? A young mum struggling to cope, most likely. Perhaps it was one of those secret teenage pregnancies. Or a young girl who hadn't even known she was pregnant until she'd felt the sudden, startling violence of labour, the astonishing sting of a head crowning between her legs? You always heard about those sorts of stories. Whoever it was, the responsibility of looking after a child had clearly been overwhelming. It wasn't wicked, what she'd done. It was hard with babies. There was no blame. Whoever she was, thought Val, she'd done the right thing leaving it in a prominent place like that for someone to find. No one would leave a baby on a pavement unless they were asking somebody else to take care of it. It was a plea for help. And what a stroke of luck that Val had been there at the right place at the right time, as though the stars were aligned. She hoped the girl didn't feel too guilty. It was a selfless act, really, what she'd done. Christopher was in better hands now. Sleep well, thought Val, whoever you are.

Her own head fizzed from lack of sleep. She couldn't fight it any longer. As she began to drift off, she heard the sound of the observation wheel turning, the giggles of a child, the sing-song voice of a woman in the pods above her head.

In those few short hours, she dreamed of Len coming home from his shift at the station. She ran from the kitchen as soon as she heard his key in the lock. 'I've found something,' she said, pulling him up the stairs to where Christopher lay sleeping. 'You'll love him, Len,' she said, 'I know you'll love him as much as I do.'

FOURTEEN

The map was in the footwell below Christopher, open on a section of Wales. Val had memorised the road numbers which would lead them out of Abergavenny and was pleased how straightforward it had been to find the right route. She was beginning to feel more confident in the car. It was much easier pootling along these roads than being on the motorway with everything screaming past. A few miles on from Abergavenny was the little market town of Crickhowell. As Val drove towards its centre, the familiarity of it made her catch her breath. She pulled over in the main square and opened the car door. This was where she and Len had stopped for lunch on their honeymoon. She would never have remembered unless she'd stumbled upon it like this, but now here it was, looking virtually the same as it had in 1969. The market cross in the middle of the road junction, the row of shops, the bakery near the zebra crossing. They'd bought pasties there, from a man they'd joked looked like Christopher

Lee in *Dracula*, and then eaten them sitting between the colonnades of the market hall.

The clarity of the memory was startling. It happened like that sometimes. Recollections so strong they were tangible, the years suddenly falling away. The previous morning, she and Len had spilled out of the porch of All Saints' Church in a blizzard of confetti, his fingers laced in hers. She knew that from then on, whatever happened, she'd always have him beside her. He looked so smart in his morning suit, his waistcoat and tie. Shiny black shoes. His broad smile didn't leave him for a moment. In his speech he told the guests that Val completed him, and she thought it was the most beautiful thing he could ever have said. Val had modelled her dress on the one Elizabeth Taylor had worn at her first wedding to Conrad Hilton in 1959. She'd taken the photograph to a dressmaker in Bristol, asked her to copy it exactly. It was made of the whitest satin with an off-the-shoulder bodice covered in pearl beading. It had a huge skirt of crinoline and net, and a boned corset that cinched her waist to eighteen inches. At the reception, Len joined the span of his hands around her waist, and she'd felt so proud and happy she thought she would burst. After the reception Val changed into a pale-green two-piece with a pill hat and pearls, and a spray of Lily of the Valley pinned onto her swing coat. They set off for Wales in Len's new Marina, the tin cans that the lads from the station had tied to the bumper clattering behind them on the road.

Of course, Val had had to give up her job in the bank when she got married. Back then, it wasn't expected that married women had careers. But she didn't mind too much. She liked looking after the house. She made sure she always had something nice in for Len's tea when he came home from his shift at the ticket office at Weston station. His best friend Terry and some of the others usually went for a pint at the railway club after work, but Len rarely did. He told Val he preferred spending his evenings with her. Sometimes in the summer he'd stop at the lido for a swim, but he always hurried straight home afterwards. While they were having their tea in the kitchen, he would tell her about his day. Late trains, the grumpy stationmaster, the items in lost property. 'You'd never believe some of the things that are handed in, Val,' he'd say. He told her about the laughs they had with Terry's weekly sweepstake, taking bets on how many customers would moan about having to change at Bristol, or ask why a return was more than twice the price of a single. Then they'd watch television or go up to the Odeon on Alexandra Parade. Thursdays was classic film night. Katharine Hepburn, Elizabeth Taylor, Cary Grant, Gregory Peck – they saw them all. The films weren't their era, but they were Len's favourites. 'Proper cinema, that,' he would say as they walked back to Palmer Street arm in arm. Val used to get so caught up in the films she often came out giddy, floating out of the cinema imagining she was the star. She was Audrey Hepburn clinging to the back of

Gregory Peck's Vespa in *Roman Holiday*. She was Doris Day in brown suede on the Deadwood Stage. Whip Crack Away! She was a problem called Maria, striding out of the convent with her guitar and carpet bag, or spinning across an Austrian mountain. That night they sang 'Do Re Mi' all the way home, Val dragging Len by the hand to run with her around the fountains on Royal Parade and jump up and down the steps of the Winter Gardens. In Val's mind she was touring Salzburg in an open-top carriage accompanied by seven singing von Trapps. Sometimes, when she went to the station to meet Len from work, she would go out onto the platform and pretend to get soot in her eye, and Len would play along and kiss her the way Trevor Howard kissed Celia Johnson in *Brief Encounter*.

Val stood with the car door open and her elbow on the roof. 'Remember this place, Len?' she said, looking up. 'Fancy me stumbling across Crickhowell after all these years.' The yearning for him was a physical ache. She cast her eyes around the square again, trying to reach for more, but there was nothing left to grasp. The memory had escaped, flitted out of reach, like butterflies from a box. She patted the roof of the car with the palm of her hand like he used to do, started the engine, and pulled back out onto the main road.

They pressed on. The roads were quiet, and Val's nerves had disappeared. Enchanted by the beauty of the landscape, she began to enjoy the journey. The trees were avenues of crimson and copper, and the River Wye sashayed through the valley, bright and alive, tumbling over centuries-old rocks. So different to the brown River Parrett which sidled through the centre of Bridgwater, or the grey tides at Weston. Val felt invigorated. It was as if she'd been given another chance at life. Each town they passed felt smaller and more remote than the last. Rather than frightening her as they had the day before, the Welsh place names now excited her, like a great adventure.

They pulled into a car park at Clywedog reservoir. Val sat on the wall of the dam and gave Christopher his bottle. The sun had come out and the breeze drew ripples across the surface of the water. Autumn had not yet turned cold. The water slurped against the wall of the dam and lapped the reservoir's edge like waves on a shore. Out in the middle, a rowing boat sat motionless, its occupants at either end leaning back against the gunwale, letting the boat drift. Val thought of poor Shelley Winters in *A Place in the Sun*, telling Montgomery Clift in that boat about her dreams of their future happiness, not realising he is in love with Elizabeth Taylor, wants rid of her and knows she can't swim. Val chuckled to herself. Whoever it was out on the reservoir, it was unlikely to end in a man being sent to the gallows like it did in that film. She was struck by the greenness of the hills and remembered them from her honeymoon. 'Welsh Green' should be the actual name for this colour, she thought. There's no other green like it. It was only now that she wished she'd come back to Wales these past years. Sitting on the dam bridge with her baby, looking at the clouds reflected on the surface of the water, she was struck by how much life she'd missed since hers had stopped in 1976.

Christopher was taking it all in. There was an intelligence about him. He had such curiosity in those endlessly watching eyes. Val held him a little tighter, smoothed her hand over the soft skin on his scalp. She was consumed by him, her heart so full of this baby she could weep. She'd forgotten what it felt like, the love you have for your own child.

Back in the car park as they were about to set off, a flock of chaffinches – twenty or more – flew onto the car, scrabbling on the bonnet and pecking at the windscreen. A flurry of dusky pink breasts and maniacally flapping wings. More and more arrived, covering the windscreen, their wings beating and their beaks tapping the glass. Val had never seen anything like it. For a moment it was pure Hitchcock: the climbing frame thick with crows; gulls dive-bombing the telephone box; Tippi Hedren pecked half to death in that frenzied attack in the attic. But there wasn't any horror here. These chaffinches were joyful rather than murderous. 'Look, Christopher!' Val said. 'Look at them all!' She was as excited as a child. It felt like a sign somehow, of life being re-energised. Despite her lack of sleep, Val had never felt more alive.

FIFTEEN

Rafe was going through the clothes rails, separating the hangers, fastening belts and buttons, checking the labels were facing outwards. He'd displayed the fur coat on a mannequin in the middle of the shop, styled it with a mini dress, silk scarf and sunglasses, and given it a fat price tag. It must be worth a fortune. He thought about his mother and felt angry. He always felt angry when he thought about her, but in the five years since they'd last spoken it had got worse. The older he became, the more he realised she was a big part of the reason he was the way he was. His insecurity hadn't come from nowhere. Why hadn't she told him the facts about what really happened that day with his dad? It's hard to grieve when your memory is one mangled mess. Why had she never tried to explain? And all that stuff she'd say about what he'd been like when he was a baby hadn't helped. He'd always been difficult, she used to tell him. Wouldn't wean, wouldn't settle, wouldn't sleep at night. If only he'd been a little angel like Duncan. The perfect brother who'd only lived long enough to *be* a perfect child. How could Rafe possibly compete with a newborn baby? If only she'd bothered to find out why he wouldn't settle at night, he could have told her about his dreams, about the hot sun on his head and his daddy lying at the side of the pool with a skinny man blowing into his mouth. He didn't think his mother would want to hear about the dreams. After all, she was too busy dealing with her own heartache.

He gritted his teeth as he thought of all the times she'd tried to contact him over the years. Her number always came up on his phone. When she couldn't get hold of him on his mobile, she'd ring the gallery, but he couldn't bring himself to pick up and he never rang her back. He had enough on his plate, what with him and Jim breaking up, having to leave Florence Road and move into a shitty local authority flat. Anyway, it wasn't just his relationship that had fallen apart – he had too. He caught the reflection of himself in the mirror next to the hat stand and ran his hand over his hair that was long overdue a cut. Sometimes it was enough to have a shower and get through the day, let alone speak to his mother. She left messages. She offered to come to Brighton. 'All those free tickets from your dad working on the railway,' she would say on his voicemail, 'and I never use them.' But he didn't want her there. The mention of his father angered him too. How dare she refer to him so casually like that, when there was so much she hadn't told him about the way he died. Had he done it on purpose? Did he mean to end his life? The questions buzzed in his skull like a trapped wasp. Why had she never discussed that day at the lido with him? It was all too late now. Weeks had turned into months had turned into years. It had gone on too long. It was easier like this. He winced as he thought about all that Elizabeth Taylor nonsense. One whiff of L'Air du Temps and he would be back at those awful evenings at Palmer Street with his mother parading around in a strapless ballgown, cooking his tea in a tiara, her black hair teased up like a bearskin hat. It was hard enough growing up gay in Weston-super-Mare in the eighties without your mother dressing up as some washed-up movie star, sitting in her armchair by the gas fire in a fur coat and jewels night after night. 'It's Mama's little secret,' she used to say, touching the side of her nose with her index finger. 'There's nothing wrong with it, Rafe,' she would add. 'But we don't need anyone to know, do we?' Even now, all these years later, it still made him feel sick.

He should have told Suki. She'd always been kind to him. She knew he liked painting, and whenever he was next door she would rummage in the cupboard of her Welsh dresser for the watercolours. She arranged bowls of fruit on the table for him to copy, gave him orange squash and custard creams, pegged his paintings up to dry on the clothes rack that hung from the kitchen ceiling. His mother seemed to drop him next door more and more to go on her 'walks'. 'She needs to walk off her grief,' Suki would say, even though he didn't understand what that meant.

Rafe used to dread his mother's 'evenings'. He hated all the make-up – the way her eyebrows looked like thick black caterpillars and that fake birthmark on her cheek. Once, when he was sixteen, he made the mistake of bringing one of his school friends home for tea. He'd picked the wrong evening. There she was staggering around in a pale-pink corset and that coat of dead animals, puffing on a cigarette. He never knew she smoked. As soon as he saw her through the kitchen window, he did an about-turn, ushering his friend out the back yard before he spotted her. Later, when Rafe came home, she could see he was upset, and she beckoned him over and murmured that sickening phrase 'Tell Mama all,' in her sham LA accent, moving her double row of pearls from side to side with the hook of her finger. He finally found the nerve to confront her and exploded. 'What *is* it with all this shit?' he yelled. 'Why the hell d'you dress like this? What are you *doing*?' His mother burst into tears then, said his dad used to tell her she had Elizabeth Taylor's eyes. She ran upstairs crying, and he could hear the wardrobe opening and closing and the sound of her heels walking around on the bedroom floor.

It was the inconsistency he found so confusing. Often, she'd be her usual self – regular clothes, genuine smile, kind eyes. When Rafe came home cold from swimming, she would run a hot bath and soap his hair and sing that 'Rubadubdub' song and make hot chocolate and Marmite crumpets. Then she would squash up in his single bed with her arm around him and read him a story. When they read *The Enchanted Wood* she did all the voices. Rafe could still hear the way she made Silky's voice so lispy and sweet. Sometimes, when she was being really funny, she'd bring pots and pans upstairs and clatter them when there was a chapter about Saucepan Man. Even when he was a teenager they'd enjoy stories together, watch old films on TV, their feet up on the pouffe, tea and Jaffa cakes on the trolley. Over time though, his mum seemed to fade further and further into the background, overshadowed by a freak who thought she belonged in Hollywood, until he couldn't stand it any longer.

As soon as he was eighteen, Rafe packed a bag and moved to London. He squatted at first, then rented a flat in Camden and found a job in a gallery in Marylebone. He reshaped himself, changed his name from Ralph to sound more refined – avant-garde, even. His mother wouldn't have understood it was her who pushed him away.

He'd only been back to Weston once since. He was twenty-three and had been having a low spell after breaking up with a boyfriend. The usual feelings of inadequacy, of never being good enough. He was beginning to do well in his career, had been given a lucky break at an art valuer's, but his personal relationships were plagued by his insecurity. That day, his mother tried her best. As his train pulled into Weston station, Rafe saw her on the platform checking every window for him. She looked pretty, not garish, in her flowery dress and pearl cluster earrings. It was one of those April days that held the promise of summer, and when the sun came out they felt the warmth of it on their faces. They walked the whole length of the promenade, talking easily about his new life. They sat on the sea wall eating 99s, watching the donkeys being tugged by their bridles along the sand. Val said she felt sorry for the animals, that they all seemed to sag in the middle. Rafe said it was because of the overweight children they were expected to lug up and down the beach all day and that it was cruel and should be banned. Val told him how much she'd missed him. Back at Palmer Street Val cooked them a shepherd's pie and they watched a Bond film on the television. For a few short hours, Rafe was happy to be back in Weston. It felt normal, visiting his mother and his family home. But then while he was in his old room getting ready for bed, he glimpsed a long tulle gown hanging on the wardrobe in his mother's room, saw her powder puff on the dressing table, and there was that same suffocating feeling, that same discordant chime inside him, and everything felt wrong.

He stood in the middle of the charity shop amongst the tea sets and egg poachers, the glass cake stands, the boxes of jigsaw puzzles with missing pieces. The stink of unwanted clothes, musty curtains and washed-out duvet covers was sometimes overwhelming. All those mothballs, that dirty fabric and human sweat. It made him think of electric bar heaters, non-slip bathmats, black mould on rubber seals, stale farts. All that decay in one airless shop.

SIXTEEN

Beyond the reservoir, Val's journey had begun to feel endless. Occasional hamlets with unpronounceable names, greater distances between them each time. The road just seemed to go on and on. Up hills, round corners, then down again. The motion of the car, the up and down and the sharpness of the bends was making Val feel sick. Crossing the Cambrians, the climb went on for so long she wondered if they'd ever make it to the top. Just when she thought they'd reached the summit, the road climbed again, higher still. There were no markings, no signs, only an everlasting strip of grey tarmac cutting the green in two. The weather changed. A thick hill mist meant she couldn't see very far ahead and had to drive slowly, leaning closer to the windscreen, peering into white murk. Although it wasn't raining, the fog was so wet she needed the wipers on. Once, she had to slam her foot on the brake, surprised by a sudden sheep in the road. It gaped at her with a vacant expression, then leaped across the verge and trotted off onto the moor.

By the time they reached Machynlleth, the lack of sleep had caught up with Val. Her eyes were heavy; her head buzzed with tiredness. Five hours on the road and it felt as though her hands were welded to the steering wheel and her back would never bend again. She began to fret. What if all the guesthouses were full? She should have booked ahead, but how could she without a phone, and not knowing how to use the internet? Christopher was starting to complain. His head was moving from side to side, his little legs rubbing up and down on the fabric of the seat.

Val switched on the car radio. Perhaps if she could find some music it might distract him. Instead it was the news that blasted on, making her jump out of her skin. Something or other about a missing baby. Val swiped at the controls, trying to change the station, turn it down, turn it off. She didn't want the news; that was hardly going to soothe Christopher. The last thing she needed was voices in the car, making her flustered, breaking her concentration. She had enough to contend with, negotiating her way along these unfamiliar roads. She twisted knobs and jabbed at buttons, until finally the radio fell silent. Darned thing. She'd never got used to it.

She tried to get Christopher to grip her finger again, but his little hands were splayed and rigid. The radio had made him angrier.

'Alright, dearie,' she said. 'We'll stop again. Just let me find somewhere.' She heard the anxiety in her voice.

She pulled into a parking bay on the high street and looked again at the map. On paper it wasn't far to Aberdovey now, but when she looked back at the reservoir, it also looked close, yet it felt like ages since they were there. Distances were not what they seemed. The roads were so windy and slow that an inch on the map felt like an eternity behind the wheel. Val leaned down to put the map back in the footwell and smelled that Christopher needed a clean nappy. For the first time she felt tears prick her eyes. She was tired and there was nowhere to change him. Suddenly she felt out of her depth, like it was all too much. She took a deep breath and tried to gather herself. To make room on the back seat, she lugged the suitcase and the carrycot onto the pavement. She pulled the things she needed from the tartan bag, lay Christopher on the back seat on his little mat. 'Oops, poops!' she said, just like she used to say to her two when they needed a change. She tried to sound cheery. The poo had gone everywhere – up his back, all down his legs. He needed a whole change of outfit, and his clothes were in the case. She clicked it open out on the pavement while Christopher twisted and yelled on the back seat. A few passers-by gave Val sympathetic glances. One woman said: 'Oh dear, someone's not very happy, are they?' which irritated Val. Talk about stating the obvious, she thought. You try changing a dirty baby on the back seat

135

of a car – it's not easy you know. Then immediately she felt upset that she'd had such unkind thoughts. The woman only meant well. It was just that Val was so tired. If only Len was here to help her. Another pair of hands and someone to take over the driving. Someone to share all this with. By the time she'd found some clean clothes, Christopher had managed to roll into the crease between the seat and the back rest and had smeared poo on the upholstery. Val wiped everything as best she could – his bottom, his back, the seats. Still he yelled, his little hands punching the air in rage. Val was becoming overwhelmed with it all – the mess, the smell, Christopher's screaming. Her nerves were frayed.

She wished then that Suki was with her, and realised how much she'd missed her all these years since their children were small. She was disappointed in herself now that she'd never got in touch with Suki despite having her new address. How could she have let everything from her past that was good slip through her fingers? If Suki was here, she would take the baby off Val's hands like she used to when Rafe wouldn't settle. It didn't matter that she had four of her own. 'Pass him here,' she'd call over the garden wall. 'Have half an hour to yourself, Val.' Then she'd come in through the back gate and pick him out of his pram. 'Here, let me take him,' she'd say. 'You need a break when they're griping like that.'

Once Christopher was clean and changed, Val felt so stiff

from being hunched in the small space that she could barely sit up. She backed herself out onto the pavement and straightened up, feeling her back twinge. Despite her weariness and desire to reach Aberdovey, she clipped the pram together, then lifted Christopher out through the car door. He needed a change of scene. She held him at her shoulder and let him look around, then laid him in the pram, tucked his blanket around him, and walked through the town. A little way up the street there was a chemist shop, and she manoeuvred the pram through the doorway. It might be as well to buy Christopher's milk while she could; it was anyone's guess when she might next find a shop selling baby products. On the shelves next to the powdered formula were cartons of ready-made milk. Val never knew there was such a thing. How convenient. It would save so much trouble making up feeds. She filled a basket with cartons and took it over to the counter. While she stood in the queue she noticed a camera on the ceiling and looked away. Funny how there were cameras everywhere nowadays, even in chemist shops.

Back outside, she pushed the pram hood back so that Christopher could see the sky and the tops of the buildings. It was doing them both good to be out of the car. Val also needed some fresh air and to change her posture from sitting at the wheel. Christopher began to settle, enjoying the trundling motion of the pram and having new things to look at. They passed antique shops, a bookshop, a ladies fashion boutique, a bakery. Someone had stopped a policeman on the other side of the road, and they stood in conversation outside the Co-op. Val glanced over, but they weren't looking at her. She bought a pasty and sat on a bench next to the war memorial. While she ate, she wheeled the pram forward and back, forward and back. She'd forgotten how utterly exhausting it all was. Pulling the pram alongside her, she smiled down at Christopher and made faces at him, opening her eyes wide in surprise, making popping sounds with her mouth, clicking her tongue. He watched her transfixed, his little face angelic, inquisitive, trusting.

As she walked back along the main street, her hands felt snug around the handle of the pram and her feet found a natural rhythm on the pavement. She was like any mother out pushing her baby, as if she did it every day. He was Rafe, or he was Duncan. For those few minutes it was 1975 and Len was due home anytime from the station.

Back at the car there was a parking ticket stuck on the windscreen. The sign next to the bay said thirty minutes. Val hadn't seen it, hadn't even thought to check. She looked up and down the street for the parking attendant. If she explained about the baby, surely he'd let her off. She peeled the ticket from the glass and put it in the pocket of the door. How was she supposed to pay a fine with only cash in her handbag? She couldn't do things online, and her chequebook was at Palmer Street, in the drawer of the sideboard. As she drove off, she wondered when she'd be back home so that she could send off a cheque. Maybe she wouldn't be home for months. Maybe she'd never be home again.

From Machynlleth, the road was lined with a tall bank on one side and deciduous forest on the other, making it feel as though the car was in a tunnel. Val put on her headlights and they lit up the trees, casting shadows. It began to feel as if they would never reach Aberdovey. Christopher was unhappy being back in his car seat and was wailing again. It was so difficult concentrating on driving when his noise was prodding her nerves. 'Won't be long, Bonny-Boo,' she said, putting the back of her fingers against his cheek. 'As soon as we find somewhere to stay, you can have a nice kick about and one of Mama's bathtimes. Won't that be fun, eh?' Anxiety crawled up her back.

Finally, the bank gave way to a low wall, and she could see the estuary off to the left. The tide was out, and the sand was pink in the late afternoon sun, streaked with vast golden puddles. Boats lay scattered across the flats, their hulls listing as if waiting for the tide to put them right. Sea birds picked across the fluted sand or wheeled above it. The road descended quite sharply so that it was no longer above the estuary but alongside it. At last, Val saw the tall terraces of Aberdovey that lined the road opposite the sea. They seemed so familiar in their Victorian grandeur and rainbow of colours. She drove slowly along the front, scanning the guesthouses. There it was – Turning Tides

– just as she remembered. The facade was a different colour – she was sure that back then it had been white with a black front door. Now it was a pale grey-blue, the windows and woodwork painted white. She remembered the huge fanlight over the front door. Opposite the guesthouses was a row of parking bays. There was one space available between two other cars. Val stopped alongside it and considered its length. She couldn't parallel park, or at least she'd never tried. She drove past the space, then looked down for reverse. She crunched the car into gear and began to turn the wheel, braking nervously as she went. She ended up too far back in the space, as if the car was about to bump into the one behind. She pulled forward and tried again. She made several attempts, each time having to drive out and start again. Eventually she got her car in, although it was miles from the pavement. She daren't try again; it was probably the nearest she would get it. Besides, Christopher was screaming now, and she needed to get him out of the car. She lifted the pram chassis from the boot and clipped the carrycot onto it, then lay him in it.

'I'm so sorry,' she said while he raged. 'I promise you won't be in here long.'

As she walked up the path of the Turning Tides Guesthouse, she wondered why she'd bothered to put the pram together at all. Why hadn't she just carried him? Her head was jumbled. It would seem very odd turning up so late in the day with a screaming child and no reservation. She tried to imagine how it would look, but she could scarcely think straight. The front door was pinned open, and she pushed Christopher into the entrance, then leaned over the pram to open the inner glass door. It flung open violently, clattering against the wall as she bumped into the reception area. Oh, why had she brought the pram? Christopher was already making a din – she didn't need to draw any more attention to them. Val lifted him out and held him to her shoulder but still he screamed. After a while a woman emerged from the stairs and asked Val if she could help her.

'I know it's short notice,' Val said. 'But I wonder if you've got a room.'

'For tonight?' The woman looked astonished.

'Yes.'

'No, I'm sorry. We're fully booked tonight,' she said.

'Oh.'

'We've been inundated lately,' the woman said. 'Even during the week.'

Val was crushed. She didn't know if it was a weekday or not. She didn't know what day it was. When had she had her hair done? Was that only yesterday?

'Do you suppose there might be somewhere else?' she asked. Christopher's crying was drilling into her. If only he would just settle down while she sorted this out.

'You could try The Sandpiper, a few doors that way,' the woman said, pointing.

'Oh, alright. Thank you,' said Val. She seesawed the pram round in the tight space and reached across for the door.

'Here, let me,' the woman said, holding it open while Val pushed the pram with one hand and clutched the baby with the other. 'Sorry we can't help. I hope you find somewhere,' she said, looking at Christopher with concern.

'Thank you, I'm sure we will,' Val said, trying to sound casual even though her heart hammered.

Out on the pavement she took some loud gasps to try and calm herself down. She held Christopher tighter, rocked and jiggled him. 'Shhh,' she said. 'Please, little dearie. Shhh.' But he wasn't going to settle now, not until they found somewhere to stay. He needed a new environment with different things to look at. He needed a bottle and a warm bath. Val told herself she mustn't cry. There must be somewhere with a room. She pushed the pram along the pavement, looking up at the lights in the tall windows of the terrace. The Sandpiper was four doors along. She stopped for a moment and looked back at her car, wondering whether to put the pram back in the boot so as not to make such an entrance. But that would mean having to lie Christopher on the seat again, and he was upset enough as it was. The Sandpiper was set further back and had a larger front garden. On the lawn was a stone bird bath, and feeders hung from posts in the flower beds. She pushed the pram up the path to the front door.

The hall was warm and smelled of lamb tagine. The walls

were painted cream, with red-and-white-striped wallpaper below the dado rail. A reception desk ran along one wall. On a side table was a collection of ornaments: glossy china statuettes of milkmaids and shepherdesses, a coloured glass dolphin, a ship with paper sails and rigging made of cotton thread. A woman appeared from the archway. She was short and plump and not much younger than Val. Her blond hair was cut into a blunt bob, and she wore bright-red glasses.

'Oh dear,' she said, looking at Christopher and pulling a sad face. 'What's the matter, pickle? Have you had a long journey?' Her voice was a Welsh melody.

'You could say that,' Val said, grateful for someone to acknowledge it. 'I don't suppose you have a room, do you?' She didn't know what she'd do if the woman said no, but she tried to hide her desperation.

'We've only got one. Room Five. It's on the second floor at the back. Only thing is, there's no ensuite. But there's a bathroom along the corridor on the same floor. Is that any good for you?'

'Yes, that'll be fine,' said Val. 'Thank you.' She felt such a sense of relief she could have burst into tears.

'I'm Pamela,' the woman said brightly. 'You can leave the pram there for now,' she said. 'Here, let me.' She wheeled it against the wall. 'Don't worry about it for the moment. We can sort it out later. Get yourself settled in first.'

The woman's kindness and the way she took over and

helped made Val want to hug her. It was too hard doing this on her own.

'It's this way,' Pamela said, beckoning Val to follow. In a recess halfway up the stairs there was a photograph of Princess Diana in a silver frame. She was wearing a hat with a fanfare of fluffy feathers at the back and was looking up and to the side the way she did with her eyes. Next to the photo was a vase containing an artificial pink rose.

The room on the second floor was painted pale green with a floral border around the walls. The duvet cover had a pattern of spring flowers and there were scatter cushions on the bed in velour and satin and broderie anglaise. It wasn't a big room, but it was bright and there was enough space on the floor for Christopher to lie and play. It felt clean and warm.

'The bathroom's just along here,' Pamela said, bustling along the corridor while Val followed with the baby. Pamela stood in the doorway and smiled, sweeping her hand into the bathroom as if she were a hostess on a 1970s game show.

Val ducked her head to look under Pamela's arm. 'It's lovely,' she said. 'This will do us nicely, won't it, Christopher?'

Christopher was still fractious but had quietened a little.

'Your grandchild, is it?' Pamela said. Something in the way she was smiling at him – wistful, remembering – made Val think she must have children of her own. Mothers could sense these things.

144

'Yes, this is Christopher,' she said. 'He's not normally so cranky. He's just tired of being in the car, I think.'

Pamela smiled. 'Of course he is. I'm sure he'll be fine once you're settled in. Oh, talking of which, you must have things in the car you need bringing in. Can we help you with that? If you give me the key, I'll get my husband to bring it up for you.'

'Well, if it's no trouble,' Val said, passing Pamela the car key.

'Come to think of it, I'm sure we've got a baby bath somewhere,' Pamela said, walking back towards the stairs. She stopped and turned. 'Oh. And we've got a cot. Would you like Tony to put that up for you?'

'Oh, no, I don't need a cot,' Val said. 'I can manage without.'

'Oh.' Pamela hesitated for a moment, a look of concern on her face. 'Are you sure?'

'We'll be fine,' Val said. She went into the bedroom and stood at the window looking over the little garden at the back. Down on the patio was a blue bistro table and two matching chairs, and flowers in terracotta pots. It looked quite a nice place to sit out. Val cuddled Christopher and kissed the top of his head.

'I hope you don't mind,' Tony said, as he bustled into the room with her bags and the baby arch. He wore green corduroy trousers and his glasses were pushed up on his bald head. His eyes were kind. 'I tucked your car in a bit nearer the kerb. It was sticking out a fair way into the road. I didn't want anything to clip it.' His accent was as strong as his wife's.

'Thank you,' said Val. 'I'm terrible at parking. My husband used to do all the driving.'

'No problem at all,' Tony laughed. 'Now, Pamela's found the baby bath, so I'll just go and get that for you. She says you don't need the cot though?'

'No. We'll be fine without,' Val said.

'Alright then,' he said, although he looked a bit puzzled. He stood with his hand on the doorframe and hesitated a moment. 'Right. I'll bring up the bath and leave it across the landing for you,' he said. 'What about the pram down in the hall? I'd love to say you could keep it where it is, but it might be in the way a bit in the morning when people are coming and going. Is it alright if I put it back in the car for you?'

'Thank you so much,' Val said. 'There are two clips underneath – you have to pull them at the same time.' It was such a relief to have someone help her like this.

'OK. I'm sure I'll figure it out.'

Val hung her clothes in the wardrobe, arranged the four purple dresses she'd brought with her in order of light to dark. She held the fur coat against her and smoothed the pelt with her hand. It was still as soft as the day Len had brought it back from the station. They'd only been married a few months. He stood in the kitchen doorway, grinning, his hands behind his back.

'You'll never guess,' he said. He looked back over his shoulder, at whatever he had in his hands.

'What, Len? What is it?' Val felt a stab of excitement. Whatever could it be that he was so delighted about? She shook the suds off her hands and wiped them on a tea towel.

'I told you I'd never be able to afford to buy you a Krupp diamond,' Len said, still beaming. 'But I've got you the next best thing.'

Val tried to look behind his back to see what he was holding, but he moved this way and that, blocking her view.

'You'll never believe it, Val. This is pure class. Total luxury. If it's good enough for Liz Taylor, it's good enough for my lovely wife.' At this he whipped out the fur coat like a matador swishing a cloak.

'Oh my! Len! Where did you get this?'

'Left on a train,' he said. 'Just lying there on a seat. There wasn't a soul around. I'd got on the train as soon as it had pulled in and it was all on its own in an empty carriage. So it can't have been someone who'd got off at Weston. I waited a moment, had a good look around. It didn't belong to anyone.'

'Oh but, Len. It must belong to someone. What about lost property? Shouldn't you have handed it in? Somebody may want to claim it.' Already she was glad he hadn't done that. It was her dream to own a coat like this.

'I could never afford this, Val, not on my wage. But it's

147

what you deserve. You already look like a movie star. Now you've got the coat of a movie star.' He held it out to her. 'Go on, try it on.'

'Oh, Len.' She took the coat and held it against her cheek. 'Feel that,' she said. 'So soft. Is it real mink, d'you think?' She opened it and felt its silk lining.

'I reckon it is. Here, hold your arms out.'

He took the coat from her and slipped it over her arms. She pulled it round her, turned a full pirouette. 'How do I look?' she asked. She couldn't stop smiling.

'Like Elizabeth Taylor herself,' he said.

Val ran her hands up and down the sleeves, spun round again. 'It feels so light, Len. They say that about real fur. It's weightless.' She walked up and down the kitchen, her hands on her hips, grinning. 'It feels like a cloud.'

'It suits you,' Len said, admiring her.

'Oh but, Len. Are you sure you shouldn't have handed it in? It's worth a fortune.'

'Exactly. And it's what you deserve. How could I put that in lost property when I know someone who would have to wait her whole life to afford something like that? Whoever left it on the train was careless. They can't have wanted it that much. You'll appreciate it far more.'

They exchanged a look of guilty glee.

'You're right,' she said. She paraded up and down again, running her fingers through her hair. 'It would probably just be sitting at the bottom of the lost property box in the station,' she said. 'D'you think?'

'Absolutely,' Len said. 'It would only live in some dusty old office for years.' He shrugged his shoulders. 'You might as well have it.'

'Oh, I don't know, though . . .' Val said. She spun again. She couldn't stop spinning, watching the coat move in the light.

'I know I should have handed it in, love,' Len said again. 'But. Well. I knew how much you'd love it. I just couldn't resist.'

She bit her lip. 'Oh, Len, we can't . . . can we?' She looked at him with wide eyes, wanting to be convinced.

'Course we can. Anyway, who's going to know?'

She turned the collar up and held it against her cheeks. 'But I feel bad . . .'

'Don't,' Len said. 'It's yours. Sometimes you've just got to grab something when the opportunity arises. If it's just left there and nobody wants it. Don't feel bad. Nobody's going to know, anyway. It can be our little secret.' He touched the side of his nose. 'Finders, keepers,' he said.

'Alright then. Finders, keepers.' She held the collar up around her face and beamed. 'Oh, I love it. Thank you so much. Thank you!' She threw herself around his neck and kissed him in the doorway and felt the silk lining slide up her arms.

*

149

Once changed and fed, Christopher was much happier, and Val sat on the floor with him on her lap. They played with all his toys and listened to the tinkling melody of 'Sur le Pont d'Avignon' and watched the girl dance on the bridge. Val made the tortoise march up his legs, his tummy, then tickle him under his chin. She hid Peter Rabbit up her sleeve and shook her arm, listening to the rattle and pretending she didn't know where it was coming from. 'There he is!' she said, watching Christopher's delight. She lay him down so that he could move his legs on the carpet. 'Kick your legs and make them grow!' Val sang, and she was taken back fifty years to when she used to sing it to Rafe and Duncan. She reached for the arch and placed it over him. She pushed each of the hanging animals and mirrors in turn with her index finger and watched his eyes follow their movement.

The room was cheerful with its bright bedlinen, its pretty tie-backs that matched the curtains, the lamp on the wall above the bed with its little pull cord. It made Val feel safe, enveloped in the guesthouse's old-fashioned comfort.

It was still only half past five and not yet dark. Val was hungry, and a bit of sea air would do them both good. She fed Christopher's legs into the baby carrier and lifted him onto her, putting the straps over her shoulders and clipping them into place like the woman had shown her. The weight of his little body against hers felt comfortable and perfect.

Outside, the sky was orange, the late afternoon sun bleeding along the tops of the houses. Val walked along the terrace, past the guesthouses, the apartments and gift shops. Past restaurants and pubs and a chapel. She could hear the caw of the gulls and taste the sea. She stopped at a fish and chip shop and waited in a queue along the sticky counter while a woman in a blue baseball cap and huge hoop earrings shovelled chips into cones. On the counter was a jar of pickled eggs, white and blubbery behind the glass. Wooden forks spilled out of a cardboard holder. High up on the wall a television was tuned to the six o'clock news. Nobody was paying much attention to it, but Val heard the newsreader say something about a baby having been stolen from its mother and a police search. How terrible, she thought. She put her hands on the carrier and pulled Christopher closer. No one was having her baby. She wasn't going to let him out of her sight. She asked for plenty of salt and vinegar on her chips and ate them as she walked towards the harbour. They were hot on her tongue. She stood near the railing and looked down at the boats. She heard the low thrum of a fishing boat heading out to sea, the metal rattle of a flag on a mast, the ever-present whine of the seagulls. One gull flapped heavily above her, then settled on a post between the railings. She clasped her cone nearer and covered it with her hand.

'They're mine!' she taunted the gull, laughing. 'You're not having them!' Obediently, and seemingly out of character, the gull took off from the post and flew away over the boats, resettling on the harbour wall. Val finished her chips and walked along the cobbles to the pier. It was a wooden structure reached by a concrete walkway. It didn't stick out into the sea but instead ran parallel to the harbourside, with a stretch of water in between. Sea moss covered the lower timbers like sleeves. The wood looked old, gnawed by the winds and waves of time. Something about its solidity, its endurance, made Val feel calm. Weathered, yet still standing. She smiled. When was the last time she had felt this free? After all the years of being stuck, she finally felt she had something to look forward to. Her skin tingled as she thought of Christopher's first steps, his first words. Birthday parties, friends round for tea, nativity plays. Grass-stained knees from football in the park. His first day at school in little grey shorts and knee-high socks, his PE kit in one of those drawstring bags. The name labels she'd have to sew into his uniform, sitting under the standard lamp late into the evening while he slept the sleep of the just upstairs in the back bedroom. All the little rituals, all the traditions and surprises. She would be Santa and the Tooth Fairy. She would help him learn to read, sitting side by side on the settee with Rafe's old Janet and John books, moving her finger under the words. She would run along behind him holding the saddle of his first bicycle. She would bring him up to be a fine man. And unlike Rafe, he wouldn't run away to London the first chance he got. He would stay with her. He could live at home, even when he was grown up. They could sit and watch television together, have their tea on trays. Maybe he could get a job on the railway, follow in Len's footsteps. She hoped he'd always call himself Christopher, not shorten it to Chris. She hoped he wouldn't go changing his name like Rafe had done. They could even have their holidays here, she thought, as the black shape of a cormorant sped low across the water before turning inland through the mouth of the Dyfi river.

Back at the guesthouse, she gave Christopher a bath and sang their 'Rubadubdub' song and watched his face open in surprise when she blew the bubbles around the bathroom and piled them on her head. She carried him back to the bedroom and sat him on her lap, all wrapped up cosy in his towel, and cut his nails with the scissors from her vanity bag. She held each tiny finger and followed the curve of the nail, peering through her reading glasses. It took all her concentration; she didn't want to nip his skin. She named each of his fingers and greeted them: 'Hello, Tommy Thumb! Pleased to meet you, Peter Pointer! How d'you do, Finger Tall! Hello, Ruby Ring! Good evening, Baby Small!' She was pleased she could remember all the names from the song she used to sing to her boys when she wiggled their fingers and made them happy. When she dressed Christopher for bed he grizzled a bit, but it was just tiredness. Mostly he seemed as content with his new surroundings as Val. He drank his milk sitting on her lap while she smoothed his head. He smelled of bubble bath and clean pyjamas. 'Good boy,' she said. He was such a perfect little chap. Of course there would be times when he cried – it's what babies do. Most of the time he was good as gold. How well they were adjusting to their new lives together. Perhaps somehow Christopher knew he'd been saved.

SEVENTEEN

The door of the charity shop rattled open, and a woman struggled in with a pushchair. Rafe hastened over and held the door while she manoeuvred herself through. She went over to the children's section and unfastened her little boy so that he could look at the toys. He chose a plastic digger and the woman picked up some books and they brought them over to the counter.

'They look like nice stories,' Rafe said, ringing them into the till. 'Nothing like snuggling up together with a good book, is there? Enid Blyton, Roald Dahl – my mum read them all to me.'

He was right. She'd been a perfectly normal parent much of the time, when she wasn't imagining she lived in Hollywood with Richard Burton. Why couldn't she have been like that all the time? Those evenings from his childhood still plagued him. She was creepy. When he'd studied *Great Expectations* at school and his teacher asked him to read aloud the description

155

of Miss Havisham, a quiet horror ran through him. He had his own Miss Havisham at home.

The little boy in the shop was pushing the digger along the corduroy lines in his trousers and making engine noises. Rafe smiled at the way his lips vibrated, the dimples on his chubby hands. 'How old is he?' he asked the woman.

'He's four.'

Rafe watched him. The same age I was, he thought, when I lost my dad.

The woman put the books into the shopping bag that hung from the handle of the buggy. She had that air of busy mums. It seemed exhausting, looking after children. Rafe held the door open and watched her push the buggy up the hill.

On the wall near the door hung a portrait of a young woman. It was a modern painting, but it felt charmingly old fashioned, as if the artist was trying to capture the tropes of European works from the 1800s. The woman was sitting on a ladder-backed chair and staring stiffly, as if she mistrusted the artist, or didn't want to sit. Rafe leaned forward to study it more closely. He observed the softness of the brush strokes, the way the artist had captured the sun shining through the window and how the light heightened the folds of her blouse. Light. It was always about light. What was it about the way an artist captured it that made one yearn? Rafe wondered why he never painted anymore. He'd had a summerhouse in the garden at Florence Road where he used to go and work when the mood took him. Since he moved out, he'd lost his appetite for it. Somewhere in the flat there was a box containing his watercolours and brushes, but he wasn't sure where.

To the right of the portrait was a large canvas. It had been in the shop for months. Nobody appeared to want such a brazen, violent abstract, although Rafe loved it. The oils had been thrown on in uneven clumps and smeared around with a palette knife. A section along the bottom of the canvas held a series of heavy scores like cuts in skin. He loved the contrast between the textures, the richness of the brilliant yellows, the swirls of scarlet and burgundy. For a moment he was caught up in its sublime beauty. Just for a moment, everything he'd lost was forgotten.

He locked up the shop and walked through Kemp Town, past the butcher's, the bookshop, the Doorstep cafe. He turned towards Edward Street, a wide thoroughfare that formed the northern boundary of Kemp Town and walked down the hill. The Jobcentre was a brutalist structure: three storeys of pebble-dashed concrete set behind a high brick wall. Rafe showed his appointment card to the security guard and went inside.

It was a large open-plan office with a waiting area at one end and a line of desks at the other, each staffed by a 'work coach' whose remit it was to get clients off benefits and into employment. Rafe sat down on one of the red chairs. Under a poster about how to write a CV, a teenage girl in leggings and a denim jacket picked at the rubber trim of her Vans trainers.

On the other side of the room, a woman in a long skirt balanced twin babies on her knees, reading them a story from the pages of a cloth book. One of the babies began to fret, and she lay one in the double pram while she breastfed the other. She looked down at it as it fed and blew a strand of hair out of her face. Now and again another woman looked up from her phone to make half-hearted attempts to stop her son running around. In the end, exasperated, she swiped at his legs with the back of her hand, which looked as though it hurt her more than him. A man in his fifties with a red, puffy face sat staring at the carpet. The rest of him was grey – his hair, his jacket, his jeans. He seemed lost in himself, crushed by being out of work. He looked the same as Rafe probably had four years before, when the gallery folded and he found himself unemployed. After Jim had given him his share of the gallery, he'd quickly lost the will with it. He couldn't manage things. Suddenly he was jobless, his confidence shot to pieces. When his relationship ended, his self-worth crumbled with it. He didn't have the energy or the capital to set up anything new, so he began looking for jobs even though he knew he wouldn't be able to cope with them.

Next to a large orange sign saying Zone A, a young lad in baggy jeans and a baseball cap kept standing up to look towards the interview desks, then sitting back down and sighing loudly to signal his impatience. Rafe hated this place. It was a congregation of the beleaguered, the downtrodden, the weary. A collection of people whose tenacity required to keep their worlds turning was slowly draining away. At one of the interview desks at the other end of the room, a man raised his voice. 'This is a *fucking* joke,' he said, pushing his chair violently so that it fell backwards onto the floor. He kicked the door as he walked out. Rafe hunched his shoulders and put his head down. All the times he'd been in here and it never got any easier.

After a while his name was called, and he followed a young woman to a desk.

'My name's Chelsea,' she said, gesturing for him to sit down. 'So . . . Mr Hinsby . . .' she said, looking at his records on her computer screen rather than at him. Each of her long fingernails was painted a different shade of pink. They clacked on the keyboard as she typed.

'You're still doing three days a week at the charity shop?'

'Yeah, that's right.'

She paused. 'That's all very well, but you do need to be making the transition into paid employment.'

Rafe nodded along.

'Can I ask how much time you've spent looking for paid work this week?' she said, finally looking up at him.

'Three or four hours,' he said. He wasn't lying. He always answered truthfully, even when it was likely to mean a sanction.

She pulled a face to show that clearly wasn't enough. 'You know you're in the "work-related activity group" category, and you need to be spending at least fifteen hours actively looking for employment?' she said. Her script was well rehearsed.

'There's nothing out there suitable for me,' Rafe said.

Truth was, he didn't even know where to start. He wasn't lazy – he would have loved a real job. But there were very few curating jobs in Brighton. He couldn't stand the thought of working in any old gallery, not after he'd run one so successfully with Jim before he let it go down the pan. He'd be prepared to do something else, but truth was, he'd lost all his confidence. Why would he put that much time into finding a job he wouldn't be able to do? Volunteering at the charity shop was all he could manage. The thought of paid employment, with a boss scrutinising everything he did . . . well, it was overwhelming. Sometimes it was enough just to get through the day.

'And have you any proof of what you've done to find employment this week?' Chelsea asked.

'A bit,' said Rafe. 'Mostly I've scrolled through adverts. Although I've got a screenshot of a job I applied for. Here.' He opened a page on his phone and turned the screen towards her. It was true he'd applied, but like all the jobs he went for, he was hoping he wouldn't get a reply. Even the thought of completing an application form filled him with dread.

'And have you heard anything on that one?' Chelsea asked, looking from his phone back to her screen.

'No. Not yet.'

Chelsea's nails draped over the mouse, and she clicked it with the middle of her index finger.

'And are you applying for every job that matches your skill set?'

Rafe snorted at that. His skill set. What was it? He could write a thesis on Jackson Pollock and Abstract Expressionism. He could curate a private collection or make bids for millionaire investors at Sotheby's. He could probably spot a genuine master from a fake. Although he'd never got a degree and didn't have a private school background, he'd worked his way up as high as any History of Art graduate, landing a top job at the Courtauld Gallery by the time he was twenty-four. What could he do though, with all that experience? There was nothing for him in Brighton's Jobcentre Plus, or on Indeed.com.

'I'm not sure anything would match my skill set,' he said.

Chelsea looked up at him with a mixture of confusion and impatience. She clearly had a time target for each client.

'What about any clerical skills? IT? Customer service?' she said. 'There are nearly always jobs available in call centres.'

'I'm not sure I'd be capable of those sorts of things,' Rafe said. He wanted to leave.

'You might need to widen your search,' Chelsea said, writing his next appointment onto his record card. She held the pen awkwardly in her fingers to protect her nails. 'So, I've put all that onto your record, Mr Hinsby, but I have to let you know that you will be receiving a sanction due to you not putting enough hours into your job searching,' she said. 'Have you had a sanction before, and do you know what that means?'

'Yes,' said Rafe. He'd had dozens of them. If people didn't meet the government's expectation of the amount of time they should spend looking for work, their benefit was reduced for twelve weeks. 'I'm sorry. I'm . . . I'm trying my best, I promise you I am. It's just . . .' His right leg was bouncing up and down like a piston.

Chelsea had stopped tapping on her keyboard and was looking at him with what seemed like genuine sympathy.

'Is there any medical reason why you can't work, Mr Hinsby, or that prevents you looking for employment or training?'

'I'm not sure . . .'

'Because if you have limited capability for work, we can help you with that, but we'd need proof from your GP.'

Rafe wondered if he did need to go and talk to someone. But to what end? Could a doctor piece a man back together? Heal a broken heart, block out the regret that ate away at him like a cancer? They'd only try and give him pills. He didn't want pills. Part of him wanted to remind himself what he'd done, not blot it out. Punish himself for his idiocy.

Whatever his issues, he didn't want to go into them with Chelsea. 'I don't have limited capability,' he said. 'I just haven't

162

done enough to find work this week. I understand what a sanction means, and I probably deserve it.'

Chelsea flashed him a smile, then carried on clicking her mouse and tapping her keyboard.

'So, next time you are paid you'll notice a reduction in your Universal Credit. The reduction will last ninety days. In that time, you can apply for a hardship payment if you can't meet your basic needs such as rent, heating and food.' Again, she knew the words off by heart. 'If you feel you've been sanctioned unfairly, you can challenge it,' she said. 'Just go to the website.'

Rafe shook his head.

'That's all then, Mr Hinsby,' Chelsea said. 'Next time I'll need to see more evidence of your job searches if you want to avoid another sanction.' She stood up, signalling for him to do the same, then walked out into the waiting area and called her next client.

EIGHTEEN

Howard was taking breakfast at his usual table in the bay window at The Sandpiper. One of the reasons he had such a fondness for this guesthouse was the bird feeders in the front garden. Periodically he would pick up his binoculars from the table and raise them to his eyes to examine something in more detail: the glossy black head of a great tit, the purple sheen on a magpie's wing feathers, a fieldfare's barred breast. From behind the binoculars, he watched two sparrows pecking at seeds whilst clutching the wire feeder with their twiggy feet. There was a politeness to the way they fed, not like the blackbirds that thrashed about, making the seed spill all over the lawn. A goldfinch flew in, blazes of rape-yellow along its wings and its face an astonishing red. It really was the prettiest of garden birds, Howard always thought. Its long fine beak meant it could extract the most inaccessible seeds from deep inside the feeder. Howard liked how it could get one over on the other birds. The goldfinch had one of Howard's favourite calls too – long liquid notes and quivering trills, repeated in seemingly random patterns. No musician could match the speed of those trills. A pigeon, fat as a squire, landed on the edge of the stone bath, causing the smaller birds to scatter. It hopped in and dipped down, making the water run over its back and revealing the whole of its underside, which was the palest of grey. Its tiny feathers hugged its breast, tight as a pullover.

The waitress was a girl of eighteen or nineteen. She wore a black waistcoat over her white blouse and her hair was tied in two short plaits which didn't quite reach her collar. She had a habit of asking, 'Everything alright for you?' in her canorous Welsh lilt whenever she passed a table. Despite this over-insistent auditing of the guests' satisfaction, Howard enjoyed seeing her at breakfast each morning, and admired the way she balanced plates up her arm and moved around the tables with practised efficiency. A few guests were still having breakfast. A young couple held hands across a table. The woman had a ponytail sprouting from the top of her head like a bellpull and rings tattooed on her middle fingers. Her partner wore a mustard polo neck and had a beard as thick as a seaman's. A plump couple in their sixties were tucking into a full Welsh, each staring over the other's shoulder as they chewed. Above their table on the wall was a painting of the bridge across the estuary at Barmouth. A young family sat at the back of the restaurant near the door, the father exasperated at one of his children for not eating their breakfast and insisting there would be nothing else till lunchtime. Meanwhile his wife stared at her phone, her thumbs moving in sudden flurries over the keypad at the bottom of the screen.

Howard liked to imagine the intricacies of people's lives, where and how they lived, the dynamics of their relationships. What tragedies they might be carrying, what anxieties they were hoping to escape by staying in a guesthouse in north-west Wales. He wasn't a busybody; he just liked people and was interested in their stories.

Although Howard still owned a house in Sheffield, the noise and bustle of the city wearied him now. He preferred the sea's energy. Since his wife left him, his spells at The Sandpiper had become longer and more frequent, until he seemed to be spending more of the year here than he was at home. Recently he'd concluded that for all the time he stayed here, he might as well sell the house and move into The Sandpiper permanently. Why not? Aberdovey was far more invigorating than Sheffield, and the room he always requested on the first floor at the front had a huge window that ran from floor to ceiling. What better way to see out his days than by watching the ever-changing view of the sea, walking out on the beach, listening to the slap of the waves and the music of the birds? At seventy-five, he hoped he still had some years ahead of him, and he'd calculated that the money from the house would cover the cost of living in the guesthouse for at least the next twenty years. He had no dependents. He and Cheryl hadn't had children – a source of sadness for them both, and perhaps in the end part of the reason she left him. Both had imagined their lives full of family, but it had never happened and when they were approaching their seventies it was clear neither of them would be able to fill that gap for the other. It was no coincidence that the man she'd left Howard for had children and grandchildren in abundance.

They say the most successful marriages are those where one person loves their spouse a little more than the other. It hadn't made a success of theirs, however. Howard had always been more devoted to Cheryl than she to him. He'd known it, she'd known it, and so did their friends. For the most part he accepted it, but there were times when it hurt, like when she used to say in public that he was 'too nice', or when she was offhand with him because she knew she could get away with it and that he'd never think less of her. He knew he got on her nerves, but the more he tried not to, the more he would see her rolling her eyes or laughing quietly under her breath. The slap of his backless slippers on the tiled kitchen floor, the fuzzy hairs that grew on the back of his neck below the natural hairline, the way he read aloud the more interesting obituaries from *The Times*. He knew it all irritated her, but none of them were things he could change, not really. It had crushed him when she left, but it had been eight years now, and it's true what they say: time heals, at least enough to find

enjoyment in life again. Howard still counted his blessings –
he had good health; he was not plagued by the illnesses that
had struck some of his friends. Although he was on his own a
lot, he rarely felt lonely. The guesthouse was a hubbub of
life, for a start. Often, rather than spend the whole evening
in his room, he would sit in the Queen Anne chair in the back
room to watch television, talk one of the guests into a game
of Scrabble, or chat to the staff while they prepped the tables
for breakfast.

There was a new lady in Room Five. She was sitting having
breakfast two tables away. Howard watched her spread
marmalade on her toast, clutching the baby on her lap. She
was angling her spoon so that it caught the reflection of the
light for the baby to see. Between mouthfuls of toast, she
rested her lips against the baby's head and kissed it, or blew
raspberries on its cheeks and hands. She was clearly a doting
grandmother. Howard was rather charmed by her. He'd
seen her arrive yesterday afternoon while he was taking tea.
She had intrigued him with her pram and her old-fashioned
glamour. She must be around his age – in her seventies – and
was dressed rather elaborately. The full skirt she'd been
wearing under her swing coat was reminiscent of the fashions
of the 1950s. Today her clothes were plainer, but her hair
was still trussed up in big black curls. The style reminded
Howard of the way Cheryl used to do her hair back in the days
when she had those heated rollers.

168

The woman had appeared flustered when she arrived, crashing in through the front door, the baby screaming and screaming. Likely they'd had a long journey. Howard had wanted to help her, but felt rather shy, as he always did with women. As it was, Pamela had it all in hand. He overheard the woman asking about availability. Odd that she hadn't booked in advance it occurred to Howard, seeing as she'd brought her grandchild with her. He wondered where she'd come from, how long she was staying, why she'd turned up like that without a reservation. He found himself wondering whether she was married too, where her children lived, what interested her. She looked like one of those people with rich lives and interesting friends, who went to the theatre a lot and had dinner in smart restaurants.

He picked up his binoculars again. It was a clear day, and he could see all the way past the pier, beyond the beach huts and dunes and the mouth of the river. All the way to Tywyn in fact, two miles up the coast. The tide was on its way out, the best conditions for birdwatching, and a group of oyster-catchers had just touched down on a spur of sand beyond the shoreline. Plenty of bounty out there today. With the bino-culars Howard was able to pick out the oystercatchers' pink legs and the vivid orange of their bills against the dull grey of the sand. He watched them hammering mussel shells, prising them apart with their beaks. He loved how their high-pitched call sounded like the gleeful shrieks of children in a playground.

He went for a walk every morning, studying the birds out on the estuary or in the nature reserve behind the beach, depending on the tide. In the afternoon he would sit in the window in his room and note in his diary all the species he'd seen. During the months he'd been staying he'd managed to spot most, although he was yet to see an osprey.

Cheryl hadn't shared his love of birdwatching. It used to bore her. 'What's the point of me talking to you, Howard,' she used to say, 'when you've always got those bloody binoculars on your nose? How do I know if you're listening to me?' It grated on him how she called them 'binoculars'. He preferred 'field glasses'. He also preferred the word 'ornithologist' to 'twitcher', thinking of himself as the former. Although he'd never studied birds for a profession – he'd been an account-ant before he retired – he was proud of how much he knew about their behaviours and habitats. How he could recognise them not simply by their appearance but also by their song.

Gradually the other guests left, and Howard and the glamorous woman and the baby were the only ones in the restaurant. It took a bit of courage, but in the end he made himself speak to her.

'Not such a bad-looking day, is it?' he said. 'A bit of a fresh breeze by the look of it, but the sun's trying to come out, I think.'

'Oh, it looks super,' said Val. 'Just what we need to blow the cobwebs away.' She bounced Peter Rabbit gently along the edge of the table while the baby followed it with his eyes. 'I expect a walk in the sea air will knock this one out.'

Howard smiled at him. 'He's bonny,' he said. 'Is he your grandson?'

'Bonny. That's a lovely word,' Val said, beaming. 'Actually, I sometimes call him Bonny-Boo.' As soon as she said it, she thought it sounded silly and wished she hadn't.

But Howard was smiling. 'Bonny-Boo! That's enchanting.' He looked at Val. 'What's his real name?'

'Christopher.' She liked hearing it out loud, liked the way it sounded.

'Are you on holiday?'

'Yes,' she said. 'I'm not sure how long we're staying. My daughter and son-in-law are abroad, and it sounds as if they're going to be away longer than they thought.' It was a shame to have to lie, but it was the easiest thing to do.

'Have they gone far?' said Howard.

'Oh . . . abroad.' She didn't elaborate; she couldn't think of anything quickly enough. 'I'm not exactly sure where. Here and there,' she added, then regretted it. It sounded even more vague.

Howard didn't seem to have noticed. 'I say,' he said. 'Would you like to join me for coffee? It's rather lovely sitting looking over the sand.'

Val looked at Christopher. 'Oh . . . well,' she said. She could see the huge view of the bay from the window. 'Yes, that would be lovely.' Something about this man's manner made her feel at ease. There was a gentleness about him. And goodness knows she could do with some company.

'I'm Howard,' he said, standing up and reaching across the table to shake her hand as she sat down.

'Val,' she smiled.

The coffee arrived in a cafetière with a jug of hot milk. Val liked the way Howard offered to pour her coffee and didn't expect her to do it the way some men would. It meant she could sit and relax with Christopher on her lap. It was only a little thing but after all the exhaustion of the previous day, it felt wonderful for someone to be taking care of her like that.

'Look,' said Howard, pointing at a speedboat carving across the bay, its wake a white streak on the surface. 'I've always fancied doing that,' he said. 'How about you, Val?'

It felt strange someone taking an interest in her. It had been so many years she'd been on her own. It was delightful.

'I think I would, yes,' she laughed. 'Why not?'

Why not indeed? She felt a lightness, as if realising for the first time since losing Len that it wasn't wrong to enjoy herself. Why not zip across the ocean in a speedboat? Why not live a bit? All these years she'd been stuck inside herself, her life shaped by two unthinkable events which had happened while she was still a young woman. Had she wasted all this time?

A yacht was anchored further out.

'Here,' Howard said, passing her his binoculars. 'Have a closer look at those people on board.'

'Oh yes, I can see them clambering around,' she said. 'Now they're looking down into the water.'

'Perhaps they're hauling up a treasure chest. Or disposing of a body,' laughed Howard. 'We'd never know, would we?'

Val looked at him, realised he was joking. 'I suppose not,' she said. 'They could be up to anything!' How long had it been since she'd laughed? It was as if the weight she'd been dragging around all this time was being lifted.

'Is that what these are for?' she asked, handing him back the binoculars. 'Spotting marine murderers?'

'Oh yes, I could spot all kinds of crimes with these.'

Val swallowed. She bounced Christopher on her knee.

Howard smiled at her. 'No, they're for birdwatching,' he said.

Val smiled, relieved somehow. She told Howard about the chaffinches that had flocked around the car at the reservoir.

'Ah, they're known for that,' Howard said. 'They're pretty tame. They hang around car parks looking for scraps. Also, if they were attacking your windscreen, it would be because they could see their own reflections. Still, that must have been quite a sight.'

'I've never seen anything like it,' said Val. 'It was most extraordinary.'

Talking to Howard was easy. She felt as if she'd known him for years.

'You seem to know a lot about birds, Howard.'

'Yes, I'm a bit of a twitcher,' he said. 'But that's a terrible word. I prefer ornithologist. Sounds a bit more serious.'

'Oh yes, that sounds very professional!' Val said. 'It makes you sound like a scientist or something.'

Howard laughed. 'Well, I'm certainly not that, but I do take the study of them seriously. Oh, that makes me sound very boring. I hope you know what I mean.'

Val nodded. 'If you know a lot about something, you should feel proud of it,' she said.

Howard poured her another coffee. 'Well, thank you,' he said. 'That's very respectful of you.'

Val turned Christopher around and lay him in her lap. She picked up the binoculars again and leaned forward, putting her elbows either side of the baby so that she could adjust the vision. She watched some paddle boarders in the shallows.

'So, I take it Aberdovey is good for birdwatching?'

'It's the best.' He hesitated, tried to gather the courage to ask her. Then he said: 'Actually, I'm planning to walk out to the nature reserve this afternoon. The osprey is still eluding me. I know there are a few here, but I've not been lucky enough to see one yet. Would you like to come?'

'Oh,' said Val, lowering the binoculars and looking across at him. 'Well, I'd like that very much.'

'Only thing is,' said Howard. 'I'm not sure how Bonny-Boo will be in a pram. It'll be tricky in the dunes with wheels.'

'Oh well, that's not a problem,' Val said. 'You see, I've got one of those carrying things. I can just strap him onto me.'

'Oh, I know what you mean. Yes, that's just what we need.'

Val liked how he said 'we'. It made her feel as if she wasn't on her own anymore.

NINETEEN

A text made Rafe's phone ping. 'Alright m8? Shall I come round your gaff?' It was Robert, a man Rafe had met a couple of weeks before at Duke's Mound. He was a builder. Their encounter had been rather sweet – none of the usual tugging at zips, none of the tiresome impatience. It had ended in a long kiss, and Robert had run his finger along Rafe's cheek, stopping to gaze at him. When Robert suggested they exchange numbers, Rafe began to imagine every kind of fairy tale. Maybe this was the beginning of something. He didn't normally give out his phone number so readily, but Robert could have it. Robert could have anything he wanted. As Rafe walked back to his flat that afternoon, he touched his fingers to his lips, feeling the place where Robert had kissed him.

Ever since, Rafe had been wondering how long to wait before he should text. He hadn't invited a man round to the flat before, but there was a tenderness about Robert. Despite Rafe's low mood and diminished self-worth, he had to start again somewhere. Over the past fortnight he'd written and rewritten the same text a hundred times, rearranging the words, changing the tone from 'laidback' to 'keen', before losing his nerve and deleting the whole thing. Who was he kidding? Robert had probably forgotten all about him.

Rafe stared at the text. He wasn't sure what the '8' meant. It must be a typo. The tone seemed very casual, but Rafe told himself that texts were easily misconstrued. He remembered Robert's subtle touch. He clicked 'Reply' and started composing. Should he offer dinner? Perhaps he could cook his famous moules marinières. He hadn't made them since Florence Road. Maybe he could stretch to a bottle of Chablis. It wouldn't take him long to nip up to the deli. To hell with the benefit sanction. He imagined the two of them sharing a romantic meal, refilling each other's glasses, talking about important things with full mouths. Then afterwards, shirts strewn along the hallway, lying together in Rafe's bed and watching the light coming up across the rooftops of Brighton. For the first time since Jim, Rafe began to imagine another relationship. Perhaps it would be him next time in the Doorstep, all cosied up with Robert, his new love, smirking at pictures on a phone, their thighs touching. Strolling through the Lanes on a Saturday afternoon, a double bill at the Picturehouse, dinner out, then back home for telly and bed. Rafe looked at the text again. M8. Ah, he saw what it was now. *Mate*. He felt a twinge of disappointment. He texted

Robert back his address, told him he'd be in all afternoon and was looking forward to seeing him.

An hour later, Robert was standing in the hallway of Rafe's flat, staring at his Lucian Freud self-portrait with a look of disdain. In it, the artist is standing with a palette knife, wearing nothing other than a pair of boots. His body is that of an old man, his saggy skinn painted in smeared oils in shades of brown and grey. Defiant in its raw honesty, it is a startling depiction of the human form.

'Who the fuck is that?' Robert said.

'It's Lucian Freud.'

'Never heard of him. Wrinkly old fucker, isn't he?'

'There's something unapologetic about the way he's standing though, don't you think?' Rafe said, regretting his words as soon as they were out of his mouth. *Shut up, shut up*. It was clear Robert was no art lover, and it already felt wrong, talking so intimately about human flesh when he was barely through the door.

'It's such a declaration of the authentic self,' Rafe went on. *Oh stop. You're sounding like an arty wanker.*

Robert seemed like a different person. He was the same height and build as Rafe remembered, but his hair looked greasy, and his mouth was small and ferrety. Rafe couldn't imagine it kissing him now. He didn't want it to. Robert's jeans and steel-capped boots were covered in builder's dust.

'I can't stay,' Robert said. 'We're waiting for a timber delivery that hasn't turned up, that's all. Probably arrive anytime and I'll have to get back on site.' He went to kiss Rafe on the mouth. Horrified, Rafe leaned past him to shut the front door.

Robert followed Rafe into the sitting room. It was mild outside and Rafe wished he hadn't put the heating on early; it had made the room unbearably hot. At least he hadn't cooked. How ridiculous that seemed now. Even the thought of it brought on a wave of embarrassment. All the scenarios Rafe had imagined since Robert's text, and this was already worst case. The strangeness of having a man in his flat, the unbearable expectation of what was about to happen in the dull calm of his front room made him so uptight he could snap. Suddenly, he didn't know what to say, how to behave. It seemed silly to make small talk now. Pointless. He couldn't think of a single word to say. Robert wasn't speaking anyway; he was already pulling Rafe towards him, running his fingers down the front of his legs, fiddling with his belt.

'Hang on,' Rafe said, tugging the curtains across, alarmed they might be seen.

Then Robert was on him again, his tongue all over his neck like a wet flannel. There was none of the gentleness of their first encounter. The kisses Rafe had remembered so fondly were now making him nauseous. He should never have agreed to Robert coming here. He was too used to his own solitude,

179

his intimate space, and Robert's presence had made it so charged with expectation, he felt as if his head was caving in. It had felt appropriate on the Mound, but here in his living room, with the possessions that had filled the house he'd shared with Jim – their art, their books – it was a crude intrusion on his privacy, on who he was. What he'd imagined as romantic now just felt predatory.

Robert took Rafe's shirt off, his mouth all over his chest. Rafe felt as if he was just being licked. Robert undid the catch of Rafe's trousers, and they fell to the floor. But instead of being aroused, he just felt humiliated. All he could think about was when he'd be able to shut the front door and be on his own again. It was stifling in here; he could barely breathe. Roughly, he pushed Robert away, moved to the window and threw it open.

'What's wrong?' said Robert. 'Thought you were up for it.'

'I'm sorry. You'll have to go,' Rafe said, pulling up his trousers and doing up his belt, already heading to the hall.

'What?'

'You need to go. I should never have—'

'Whatever.' Robert followed him along the hall. 'Weirdo.'

'I'm sorry. I just can't . . . I just feel . . .'

'I've driven all the way across town to get here,' Robert said, all kindness gone. 'What a waste of fucking time.'

TWENTY

Up in her room on the second floor, Val tried on each of her outfits. She wished she'd brought more clothes. She had her old polyester trousers and her dressing up clothes, but nothing in between. She could hardly wear these old trousers now she was going out with Howard. They were what she wore around the house. It had all been such a hurry when she left Weston; there'd only been time to throw a few things in a case. She studied the dresses hanging in the wardrobe and chose the lilac one with the full pleated skirt and lace trim around the pockets. She held it up against her. It was rather fancy for a walk on the beach, but what choice did she have? Perhaps if she didn't put on any jewellery and wore her flatties it would look alright. She rolled on her stockings, slipped the dress over her head and zipped it up at the back. She slid on her flat shoes. It would look better with her heels, but they were completely unsuitable for the beach. Howard would think she was crackers. She looked in the mirror, turned this way and that and decided the flatties didn't look too bad. Luckily the swing coat fell to a nice length to skim the pleats of the skirt. It would have to do. She changed Christopher and then fed his legs into the baby carrier, lifted him onto her front and fastened the clips. She liked the feeling of him strapped to her like that, their bodies connected. Christopher seemed to enjoy the closeness too, hanging there looking up at her with his inquisitive face and his little legs dangling down.

She met Howard in the lobby at two. They crossed the road and walked through the boat yard towards the beach. The hulls of the sailing boats rose up high as houses around them. Rigging clanged against aluminium masts. Lobster pots lay piled against a low wall. Above them, the ever-insistent cries of gulls. A skiff was being towed out to sea by a fishing vessel and it bumped and bounced from a rope. Behind the coloured terraces and the hotels and fish and chip shops along the seafront, the green Welsh mountains towered over the town.

They walked out onto the huge sweep of beach, their feet kicking up sand like fine powder. The vastness of the beach reminded Val of the scene in *Lawrence of Arabia* where Omar Sharif appears from the horizon like a shimmering mirage, riding a camel and toting a rifle, his black cloak billowing in the Saharan wind.

'I can see why you spend so much time here,' Val said. 'It's beautiful.'

'There's nowhere like it,' Howard said. 'You can keep your

Greek villages, your Thai paradise islands. For me, north Wales is the most beautiful place on earth.'

Val thought of Weston and the bleak greyness of the north Somerset coast; the flat marshes behind rundown seaside towns; the hulk of the nuclear power station across the bay. How the sand was packed down hard as tarmac, gradually turning to black mud at the shoreline. The sand was much softer here.

'It's certainly nicer than the coast where I'm from,' she said.

'Oh, where's that?' Howard asked.

Val paused for a moment. Then said, 'Weston-super-Mare. It's nothing like as pretty as this.' She wondered whether she should have been so honest, but at that moment she felt as though she could tell him anything. Everything. She wanted to tell him how her life was a case of merely moving through days, watching the time pass, dressing up sometimes in the evenings to escape it all. She wanted to tell him how lonely she was, how Christopher wasn't her grandchild and how she never saw her son. How callous it would sound though, if Howard knew she hadn't seen Rafe for most of his adult life. It wasn't as if she'd wanted it that way. It wasn't as if she hadn't tried to fix things – she had. But here she was, estranged from her son without really knowing why.

A flock of birds flew in and landed on a strip in the middle of the estuary.

'Look at that!' Howard said. 'Lapwings. It's rare to see

them in a group as large as that.' He passed Val the binoculars. 'Did you know that the Latin name for them is *Vanellus Vanellus*? Isn't that funny?'

Val laughed. 'No, I didn't! Oh, and listen to that sound they make,' she said, peering at the black and white birds out on the spit. 'Can you hear it? It's like a penny whistle.'

'Yes, the other name for them is a peewit,' Howard said. 'It comes from the cry – *Pee-wit! Pee-wit!* It's just how it sounds, isn't it?'

'There seem to be several birds named after the noise they make,' said Val. 'The cuckoo . . .'

'The chiffchaff,' Howard added. 'Um . . .'

'I remember something we learned in school,' Val said. 'About the yellowhammer. It sounds like it's saying: "A little bit of bread and no cheese!"' She sang the words. How uninhibited she felt!

'Ah yes! I'd forgotten about that one,' Howard said. 'By the way, did you know . . .' he turned to her, 'that the collective noun for a group of lapwings is a *deceit*?'

Val felt her stomach turn over. Had he paused before that last word? Why did she feel uneasy suddenly? She passed him back the binoculars and bounced Christopher gently and rocked him in his carrier. They rounded the bend at the funnel of the estuary and walked east along the beach, past the sand dunes and the caravan parks. The breeze coasted across the dunes, skittering loose sand and tugging gently at the marram grass. Val's hair was buffeted this way and that. She was glad she'd had her hair dyed Cleopatra Black so that Howard wouldn't see the grey roots of an old woman. Near the shore the sand was smoother, and they followed a line of human footprints which at intervals converged with those of a dog. Val watched as each wave gathered itself into a small peak and then fell onto the shore with a lazy slap, followed by the hiss and suck of the backwash.

She could feel Christopher's little feet knocking against her with the rhythm of her steps. She smoothed her hand over his soft hair. Before long, when the weather became colder, she would need to buy him a hat. She dipped her head to check if he was still asleep. His eyes were closed, his dark lashes perfect half-circles against his cheeks. Val smiled at how he could sleep so soundly whilst vertical. She laced her hands around the baby carrier, pulled him closer. He was her little miracle.

'Lost to his dreams,' Howard said. Val relaxed again. The kindness in his smile made her feel as though the three of them belonged together, like a family. Howard seemed so steady and dependable walking next to her, his hands clasped behind his back. The word 'mainstay' kept coming into Val's mind. It felt as though that's what he was, or could be. Her mainstay.

They climbed the slipway by the lifeboat station and walked along the harbour. Stacks of skiff boats lay upside down at the end of the jetty. A fishing boat clunked against the struts of the pier, crabs scrabbling over each other in plastic crates on deck.

A fisherman, his navy-blue waders held up by braces, clambered around the buckets and crates. He threw a rope up onto the harbour, climbed the iron ladder built into the wall, and tied the rope around a bollard. The air smelled of his catch. A group of children stood on the opposite wall, dangling pieces of string into the water, not taut enough to catch anything. It reminded Val of when she used to take Rafe to Clevedon to fish for crabs off the sea wall. Fine orange line on a spindly wooden reel, pieces of ham torn from sandwiches and used as bait. His sandcastle-shaped bucket with tiny shells in the turrets. How she used to run the corner of a towel between his not-quite-dry toes.

Howard stopped on the harbour, leaned against the railing, and put his hand on Val's arm.

'Can you see that, under the pier?' he said, pointing.

From the wooden supports beneath the pier hung a cast-iron bell. Moulded in the shape of an egg timer, its colour weathered into verdigris.

'It chimes when the tide comes in,' Howard said. 'Twice a day, the force of the water makes it ring.'

He took his hand off Val's arm and gestured out at the whole of Cardigan Bay. 'The story goes,' he said, 'that there is a forgotten world out there. Under the waves, a whole kingdom is submerged. The sea level was lower back then, of course,' he continued, 'and the kingdom of Cantre'r Gwaelod was protected by sluice gates. Legend has it there was a watchman named Seithennin whose job it was to study the tides and close the gates when the sea was rising. One night there was a huge storm and the waves surged. It's said that Seithennin was fond of a drop or two, and he'd got drunk at a party at the king's palace. When he got home, he fell asleep.'

A seagull flew across the jetty, settled on the rail near where they were standing.

'Of course, Seithennin hadn't shut the sluice gate,' said Howard.

'And so the kingdom was flooded?' said Val.

'That's right. The water burst in, and Cantre'r Gwaelod and its people were overwhelmed.'

Val loved the way Howard pronounced the Welsh words. She looked out across Cardigan Bay and imagined the lost city under the waves and the people who must have perished. She looked at Howard.

'Then everyone drowned, I suppose?'

'So they say.' He wrapped his fingers round the railing. 'The bell under the pier tolls every time the tide comes in to commemorate all those who lost their lives.'

'Is it a true story?' Val said, looking at the bell.

'I think it is,' said Howard. 'Actually, when the tide is very far out, strange tree trunks appear in the sand. There's a huge pile of boulders out to sea too, off the coast of Aberystwyth. They say it marks the location of the king's palace.'

Christopher had woken up and was making soft cooing

sounds. Although Val barely heard them, she could feel the vibration where their bodies met. She glanced down at the child's face. His wide eyes were staring towards the ocean in the sky's pale light. She turned slightly, angling him so that he could see the boats bobbing in the harbour, tugging on their moorings.

'There's something else about the bell, of course,' Howard said. He paused, ran the rail through his hands. 'They say that if couples hear the bell together,' he cleared his throat, looked at Val. 'They might find happiness.'

Val turned towards him now, and for a moment they held each other's gaze before shyly looking away again across the bay. Val felt as if her heart was clattering against her chest, a sensation she hadn't had for forty-five years. Howard's words hung in the space between them. Indeed, they filled the whole of the harbour.

Val waited, then dared herself to say it: 'Well, perhaps we should wait for the tide to come in, then.'

She couldn't believe she'd been so bold. It wasn't long before she felt a prod of guilt, however, being so forward with another man in sight of the place she'd stayed with Len on their honeymoon. She felt for Christopher's little feet and rubbed the bumps on the rubber soles of his pram shoes with her thumbs.

Howard was quiet for a moment, then looked at her. 'Yes, perhaps we should.'

They glanced at each other again, then looked away.

'I wonder . . .' he said. 'I'd be delighted if you'd have dinner with me this evening. Round off a lovely day.'

Val felt her heart surge. Typical of Howard to put her at ease when she felt she may have overstepped the mark. She loved his lack of presumption, his old-fashioned manners. It occurred to her that Len would have liked him too. They would have got on very well.

'I'd like that.' She looked down at Christopher, put her hand round the carrier. 'I hope this one will behave himself,' she said.

'You may find they've got one of those baby monitoring machines,' he said. 'Or they might even offer a babysitting service. Worth asking.'

'Oh, it's alright,' she said. She couldn't bear the thought of being parted from Christopher. The last time she'd left a baby alone was when she closed the door on Duncan. 'I'll bring him with me if you don't mind,' she said. 'I don't like to let him out of my sight, you see.'

'Of course.' Howard smiled. 'Whatever's best for you both.'

TWENTY-ONE

Rafe switched on his computer and forced himself to click through his emails. The cat lay snoozing under the desk and Rafe crossed his legs and tickled her belly with his bare foot. He opened an email from the council, another reminder about the overdue rent. He scrolled through the rest: an insurance quote and an electricity bill that would clean him out for the month. Universal Credit was barely enough to feed himself and the cat at the best of times, let alone now he had another sanction. Back in the 80s, when he'd first gone to London, it seemed you could be in arrears with the council for months – years – before anyone came knocking on the door. Not these days. Now they'd evict you as soon as any private landlord. He doubted the council would put up with another month of missed rent. It was all beginning to weigh on him. He was going to have to do something about money.

He crossed off his emails and looked around the living room. The answer was staring him in the face. He'd have to sell some of this art. It was going to break his heart, but what choice did he have? He walked across the room in his bare feet and studied the Mapplethorpe and wondered how much it would fetch. Out in the hall he stared at the Freud. Whatever that heathen Robert had said, Rafe loved it. He'd been so thrilled when he'd bought it at a London auction that he'd taken Jim out to dinner at The Delaunay to celebrate. He wandered around the flat, looking at each of the pieces, trying to imagine what they would fetch, his heart heavy. Everything was Florence Road. Everything reminded him of Jim. How could he part with any of it?

He began scrolling through websites that would help him value the works. He wondered how best to sell them. Auctions often took months, and even then there was no guarantee of sale. He needed funds sooner than that. There was always eBay, he supposed, but he couldn't bear the thought of having to list every item, buy all the packaging, take everything to the post office or arrange a courier. Then the inevitable complaints when things were damaged or went missing. Worse still, people turning up at the flat to collect. Imagine that. He couldn't face any of it. He thought about the pop-up shops in the North Laine and the disparaging remarks Jim had made about them in the cafe. Jim was right, of course. A bunch of amateurs not knowing the first thing about art, flogging off any old tat. Whatever would Jim think of him, selling his soul like this? Part of him couldn't even bear to enquire about them, but at the same time they appeared to be a relatively easy way to sell a lot of stuff quickly. It would save the long wait of auctions and the hassle of eBay. He tried to convince himself it was a positive step. Chatting to people about art – it used to be his bread and butter. Come on, Rafe, he thought, you might even enjoy yourself. Make some new friends. He trawled the internet, found a contact email address and sent an enquiry about renting a unit in the Lanes. Within an hour he had a reply. There was one left, and it was available for the following weekend. The rate was extortionate. He'd have to sell quite a lot just to break even, but it had to be worth the risk. He needed to do something unless he wanted to be homeless. Next weekend was ideal. He'd noticed posters around town for a big antiques and collectables fair up at the racecourse which would bring plenty of potential customers into Brighton. He could swap his shift at the charity shop, hire a van, and get everything to the shop in time to open first thing Saturday morning and catch the weekend trade.

For the rest of the day, he sorted through his collection. Many of the prints and canvases were leaned against the walls, one in front of another. In all this time he'd not put them up – this flat would not do them justice, and anyway there wasn't enough space on the walls. He pulled them out one by one and assessed their value. He slid posters out of cardboard tubes, unrolled them and lay them on the floor with books on the corners to hold them flat. He photographed everything, then printed out the images and stuck them on the tubes to show customers what was inside. He dusted the gilt surround of a mantelpiece mirror, polished the glass, and bound it in bubble wrap. With a damp cloth he wiped each of his sculptures and figurines, even the carved walking stick he'd brought back from South Africa. Some market seller in Johannesburg had told Rafe it used to belong to Nelson Mandela, and Jim had howled with laughter on the plane on the way home, telling Rafe he had 'Gullible Tourist' tattooed on his forehead and that the guy must have seen him coming a mile off. Ah well, it happens, Rafe had said, chuckling and looking down from the plane window onto the sunlit clouds below. It was part of the fun of travelling. It became quite a joke between them after that, Jim making a point of hobbling around with it the time he twisted his ankle during a short-lived running phase.

As Rafe worked, he listened to Chopin and Rachmaninov and Górecki, turning up the volume from time to time until the music blared from the speakers. Every time a record ended, he paused from his work and selected another one from his collection, sliding it from its sleeve and placing it carefully on the turntable.

He eyed the art books that lined the shelves and were stacked in piles on the floor. Why ever had he spent so much money on coffee table books? Who needed this much stuff? He realised how much of his old life had been about material gain.

Perhaps if he sold some of this lot it might actually be therapeutic. Clear out the clutter, pare it all back. Wasn't minimalism better for the soul?

He thought about Clem with his designer glasses and expensive shirts. Clearly Jim was still caught up in that indulgent lifestyle. Sloshing around in 'stuff'. It wasn't healthy. Far better to have a good detox. Rafe took the books down from the shelves, dusted each one in turn, making a note of its title and author, and writing a brief description. Before long he was lost in them – turning the pages, looking at the images, skimming some of the text. They were beautiful. He'd not even read most of them. Perhaps he'd have got more out of life if he stayed in his flat reading these books instead of wasting his time down at Duke's Mound.

Once he'd sorted through everything he compiled a spreadsheet, cataloguing each volume, each artwork. He made price tags out of card and string. He wrote a short piece about each item with information about the artist, the medium, a little of its history. Once he was happy with the words, he handwrote them onto postcards which he thought he could prop next to the items once they were in the shop. It was important, he felt, that whoever acquired these works should know something of their history. He wanted people to appreciate them beyond the monetary. It was interesting indexing everything like this, choosing the wording for the cards. He might even have found it fulfilling, had it not been so upsetting.

Many times during the afternoon, he left his desk to study a piece of work, agonising over whether he could let it go. He returned to the hall again and again, trying to decide whether he could part with the Freud. There was a sculpture on the side table of a man's head carved from black limestone that he'd picked up at a *vide-grenier* in Burgundy on one of their first trips to France. Jim had found it rather ugly, but Rafe could see a truth in its contemplative face, in its sorrowful eyes. He thought about Jim and wondered how he'd feel, knowing Rafe was selling off so many of the pieces they'd chosen together. Oh, but why would he care? He'd had his share of the artworks when they split up. He had his new life with Clem now.

Rafe poked around for other bits he could sell, pulling out drawers and opening cupboards. In a cardboard box at the bottom of a kitchen unit he found the glitter ball he used to put up in the sitting room at Florence Road for their parties. It still had the ribbon attached. It had stayed up for a few days after that final party; both he and Jim were too drained to bother with it. He held it up by the ribbon now and let it spin. If he hung it from the ceiling in the shop it would probably sell in no time. At the back of the drawer in his bedside table he found a box containing the watch his mother had sent to him for his fortieth birthday. It had a silver bracelet and a tiny window displaying the date. He slid it over his wrist. He'd never so much as tried it on. He put it back in its box and carried it into the sitting room. Might as well put a price tag on it. He didn't need any reminders of her lying around. The cat climbed out from under the desk and padded through to the kitchen. Rafe opened the back door for her, and she slunk into the yard.

TWENTY-TWO

U p in Room Five, Val felt like a teenager on a first date. She tried on all the outfits she'd brought with her and decided on the taffeta dress. It was the colour of the wrapper on a Cadbury's Dairy Milk.

Christopher lay on the floor under his arch. Val had been wondering how to take him into the restaurant, whether to put him in his pram or just have him on her lap. In the end she fetched his seat from the car. It wouldn't be in the way like the pram would, but she'd still be able to see him.

'He's nice, Howard, isn't he?' Val said to the baby. She sat on the floor in her dress and pushed the animals on the arch so he could watch them swing. She studied his pale, unblemished face, his neat little nose, his almost-there eyebrows and smiled. So lucky they were to have found each other. 'Finders, keepers,' she said aloud, smoothing her hand over his forehead. 'For both of us, eh, Christopher? Finders, keepers.' She prepared his milk and gave him a bottle. As she held him on her lap with a linen square draped across her shoulder to protect the dress, she said: 'Now, I'm hoping you'll be a good boy tonight. If you could let me and that nice man have a chat, well, that would make me very happy.' She kissed his cheeks then clipped him into his car seat and carried him down to the restaurant. 'Don't forget – be a good boy,' she whispered. 'For Mama.'

Howard was at the same table as at breakfast. All the tables had been laid with white cloths for dinner and there was a bud vase on each one containing a single pink gerbera. 'The Girl from Ipanema' was playing quietly in the background.

'He's awake,' Val said, looking down at Christopher when Howard stood up to greet them. 'But he seems quite settled, so hopefully he'll give us some peace.'

'He'll snooze off, I expect,' Howard said, pulling out Val's chair for her to sit down. 'He must be zonked after all that sea air.'

'It was certainly a good walk,' Val said. She put the car seat on the floor and angled it so that she could see Christopher.

'That's a very striking dress. You look lovely,' Howard said, passing Val the menu. 'If you don't mind me saying,' he continued, 'you really do have the most wonderful style.' He felt daring saying it, but it was true. What was the point of hiding things at this age? Something about this woman made him feel joyful and carefree in a way he hadn't since long before Cheryl had gone.

198

'Thank you,' said Val. How long since a man had paid her a compliment?

'It has a rather nostalgic feel about it,' Howard said. Then, realising he might be misconstrued, held his hands up. 'Oh, I don't mean old fashioned, you understand! No, I meant chic. Dapper.'

'Don't worry, I know what you mean,' Val laughed. 'I love the glamour of the old styles. People looked so smart back then.'

'Yes, didn't they? Hats! Why don't people wear hats anymore?'

They laughed.

'I think you look beguiling,' Howard said. He paused. 'You make me feel . . . I don't know . . . a certain wistfulness. For the past, I mean.'

'Hmm,' said Val. 'Well, perhaps we all yearn a little for the past.'

'Yes, I suppose we do,' Howard said. 'Although we should always look forward too.'

'Oh.' She looked across at him, his warm face, the way his eyes smiled. 'Yes, I suppose we should.' It was the first time, she realised, that she'd started to look towards her own future without a sense of dread.

'Now,' Howard said, looking up at the menu board, 'I'm considering myself very lucky because not only do I have wonderful company, but they've got my favourite Special on this evening. I'll *try* and say it,' he laughed. 'It's a Welsh dish – "Cqthi Salmon", I think. It's baked salmon in a sauce with sautéed cucumbers. I can recommend.'

'Sounds wonderful. I love fish,' Val said. 'And I'm happy to trust your judgement.' She felt as though she could trust him with anything. Even a secret.

'Well, we'll have to try our luck pronouncing it to the waitress. Who knows what she'll bring us? We could end up with all kinds!'

They perused the wine list, deciding on Howard's suggestion of a Mâcon-Villages. It was as if they were a proper couple, choosing things, discussing together. While they were waiting to order, they looked through the other dishes on the menu and talked about the different flavours, of capers and fennel and dill. Val used to enjoy trying new foods. Len had introduced her to curry when the first Indian restaurant arrived in Weston. She was so stuck in a rut now, with her coddled eggs and corned beef sandwiches and her lonely little life. Suddenly new opportunities were opening up. She glimpsed a whole new existence in Wales with Christopher. She ventured to think Howard might become part of it too. Everything seemed possible with him. Easy, even. She imagined, fleetingly, how it would feel to be with him all the time. So much talking and fun. Her mind began to run away with itself. It was so exciting. The way he took charge of things yet at the same time was gentle and respectful and unassuming. She hadn't felt this comfortable with a man since Len. She wouldn't have thought she could be. The waitress came over, her pencil hovering over her notepad.

'Now, forgive me, but I'm going to attempt it,' Howard said. 'We'd like two of the Cqthi Salmon.' He looked up at her with a playful, quizzical expression. 'How did I do? Is there any chance that my appalling Welsh will mean that what arrives on the table will be what I think I've just ordered?'

'Don't worry, it was close enough!' the waitress said, repeating the name of the dish a couple of times for him to practise. Howard said it again, enjoying rolling the consonants, putting his all into the Welsh pronunciation.

'How's that?' he said, smiling.

'Not bad at all!' the waitress laughed. Val loved the way Howard was so charming with the waitress, so good-natured and polite. It wasn't just for Val's sake, she was sure. He was the sort of customer who made people's jobs worthwhile.

When the waitress had gone, Val and Howard practised the word together.

'Ah, you're far better than me,' Howard said. 'You've got it spot on, I'd say.'

The waitress brought the wine and showed the bottle to Howard and he smiled at her and nodded.

'Would you like to try it first?' the waitress asked.

'No, no, we can just pour it,' Howard said, smiling at her. 'I'm sure it'll be fine.'

He could have been pretentious, thought Val. He could have asked her to pour a little in his glass and sample it, but he didn't. He seemed so honest, never pretending to be something he wasn't. He poured them each a glass of wine and held his up.

'Here's to finding something – someone – when you're least expecting it. And to new adventures and happy times.' They chinked their glasses.

'Cheers,' they said.

Howard reminded Val a little of James Stewart. He was tall like him, with the same big hands and features and that kind, hangdog expression. One of those old-fashioned men – honest and hard-working, with strong values, just like George Bailey in *It's a Wonderful Life*.

'What do you enjoy doing most, Val?' Howard said.

The question rather caught Val off guard. Did she enjoy anything? She just ebbed along day to day. There were no highs or lows.

'I used to love going to the movies,' she said. 'I went all the time when I was younger.'

'Oh I do, too! What are your favourites?'

'Probably the old romances.'

Howard smiled. 'Me too. Who's your favourite pairing? Mine would have to be Sophia Loren and Cary Grant in *Houseboat*. It's a terrible film – utter nonsense. But Cary Grant is at his most debonair. And Sophia Loren in that gold dress. She's so mesmerising she isn't really believable as a character in that film. It's not that she was a bad actress – she wasn't. It's just that she's too radiant for me to be able to notice anything else. How can you conceive she's the nanny, cook and cleaner on that boat, when her beauty overrules everything on the screen?' He smiled. 'Oh dear, does that sound terrible? I don't know if I'm allowed to talk like that nowadays,' he said. 'But there you are. Beauty is beauty.' He swallowed a mouthful of wine. 'How about you? Who d'you think is the greatest Hollywood double act?'

'That's easy,' said Val. 'For me, it's Elizabeth Taylor and Montgomery Clift in *A Place in the Sun*. The best-looking actors of their generation – possibly ever – together on screen. She never looked finer. And I'm afraid I would have her white strapless gown over Sophia Loren's gold lamé any day of the week!' She laughed. 'When they dance on the veranda, and Elizabeth whispers "Tell Mama All" in his ear, it's so . . . powerful, you know?'

'Ah yes, I remember that scene. Those spellbinding close-ups. It's as if we're being invited to experience the euphoria of falling in love with someone.'

Val smiled, suddenly bashful.

'So, what did you do before you retired?' she asked.

'I was an accountant.' He paused. 'There. That was a swift exit out of Hollywood, wasn't it? Always a conversation stopper,' he said, laughing. 'The dullest of occupations.'

'Not at all,' Val said. 'I like numbers and figures and things.'

'Really?'

'I used to work in a bank, years ago before I was married.'

The waitress brought over their plates and put them on the table.

'I loved it, actually,' Val said. 'I loved the handwritten ledgers, writing in the columns and trying to line up the digits all neatly, one above the other.'

'Yes, I agree. There's something satisfying about seeing your calculations in ink.'

'I did like those old adding machines too, though,' said Val. 'The clunky noise they made when I punched the numbers in, and the strip of paper jerking out of the top.'

'I'm with you,' Howard said. 'I much preferred all the manual stuff before computers came along.'

'My friend Marion worked in the bank up the road, and we used to meet for lunch and sit on the sea wall with a bag of chips,' Val said. 'It seemed to always be sunny back then. Don't you think?'

'Yes,' Howard smiled. 'I think it was.'

'Of course, I had to give it up when I got married. That's how things were, then.'

'Gosh, I remember that,' Howard said. 'My wife was asked to resign from her job in the civil service when we were married in seventy-two. The Marriage Bar, isn't that what it was called?'

'Oh, I don't know,' Val said. 'I didn't know it had a name.'

'Yes, I think so,' Howard said. 'It's unbelievable really. They were such different times, weren't they? Feels like another era.'

'I suppose it was,' Val said. 'I was right to trust you on the salmon, by the way. It's delicious.'

'Isn't it?' Howard said. She watched him while he poured them both another glass of wine. Somehow he put everything into perspective. He brought out a confidence in her she'd forgotten she had. He made her happy. 'So, what brings you to Wales, Howard?'

'Oh, my wife and I used to come every year. She was brought up not far from here, in Barmouth. We used to pop in on her family, but mainly we came because of our love of the countryside, and the sea. West Wales is one of the best places in the UK for birds, too. That wasn't the draw for Cheryl, but, well, she was happy for me to sit at the window here with my binoculars. At least I thought she was. We always stayed in this guesthouse. The views are the best, I think.'

'Oh, absolutely. I'd forgotten how beautiful Wales is. It's the colours that I find so stunning. The hills are such a bright green.'

'Aren't they? I always think everything looks enhanced, as if it's been projected through a colour filter.'

Christopher had gone to sleep. Val leaned down and rocked his car seat. Thank you, my little cherub, she thought. 'Do you mind me asking what happened to your wife, Howard?'

'Well, I was married for forty-two years,' he said. 'Quite happily for most of it.' He sipped his wine. 'But she left me, oh, eight years ago now.'

'I'm sorry.'

'Believe it or not, for a good friend of ours.'

'Oh! That must have been difficult.'

'It was rather,' Howard said quietly, looking down at the table. 'It felt like a double betrayal, if you know what I mean.'

'I'm sure.'

'I survived though.' He dotted his mouth with his serviette. 'It was a long time ago. I was pretty low for a couple of years, but then told myself I just had to get on with my life.'

The waitress brought over the dessert menu and they both chose ice cream and ordered a pot of tea.

'How about you, Val?' Howard looked over the table at Christopher. 'Am I right in thinking you were widowed?'

'Yes. Len died back in 1976.' She paused. 'It was a very hard time. I'd lost my baby son the year before, you see.'

'Oh, I'm so sorry, that's terrible,' Howard said. There was such concern in his eyes. Val could have told him more, but she didn't want to become upset. Even after all this time, she didn't trust herself not to cry.

Howard appeared to sense it and didn't ask any more. There was a vulnerability about her. She made him want to look after her.

'You'd think I'd be ready to talk about it after all this time, wouldn't you?' Val said. 'It's been nearly fifty years after all. But I still can't.' She traced the base of her wine glass with her finger. 'I'd like to think I could tell you sometime though. In the future, you know.'

'Of course,' Howard said. 'Perhaps you'll tell me when we know each other a bit better. But only when you're ready.'

Howard paid the bill. Neither of them questioned it. It was simply how things were done with two people of their age.

'Well, he's been a superstar,' he said, looking at Christopher asleep in his seat.

'He's a good boy, isn't he, my Bonny-Boo?' Val said, leaning down and running her hand over his blanket. 'I think the world of him.'

'I can see you do,' Howard said, pulling a note from his wallet and leaving it on the table for the waitress.

'It's been a really lovely evening, Howard,' Val said. 'A lovely day. Thank you.'

'I've enjoyed myself immensely,' Howard said. They stood facing each other, neither sure of the rules of dating after all this time. Howard looked at the clock above the sideboard. 'Look at that,' he said, suddenly shy and not sure whether to kiss her on the cheek. 'Getting on for ten. I'll go up and catch the news before bed.' He couldn't summon the courage to kiss her and instead made a little bow and shuffled his feet. 'Perhaps we could do it again, Val. I hope so.'

'Me too.'

207

Back in her room, Val lifted Christopher from his car seat and lay him in a nest of pillows on the bed. His limbs were heavy with sleep. What a good boy he'd been to give her time with Howard. Not to fuss or cry, just to nod off in his chair. What a wonderful baby. She thought about Howard and how charming he'd been. She never would have believed she could have been that comfortable with another man, let alone one she'd only just met. There was this unquestioning ease between them. When she thought about him her stomach turned over. She couldn't stop smiling. It had been the most perfect day.

She sat on the bed next to Christopher and pressed the red button on the TV remote. The sound blasted into the room on full volume, making her heart leap. Christopher's arms jerked upwards, his hands open in alarm. Panicking, Val searched for the volume control and watched the white bars on the screen decrease. Christopher spluttered a little, but then relaxed again, his hands lowering back down and resting on the pillows.

On the news was the story of the baby abduction she'd seen the night before in the fish and chip shop. A CCTV image of a woman pushing a pram flashed onto the screen. It was black and white and very grainy. Val didn't recognise herself. It was just a shape. It could be anyone. It's a good job my little one's safe, she thought.

'Mama will never let you out of her sight,' she whispered, looking at her baby. 'Never.'

She jabbed the Off button on the remote. Suddenly she felt unsettled. She held Christopher's little hand as he lay there contented and fast asleep to the world. Unlike that baby on the news, Christopher had been unwanted. Why else would someone leave him out on the pavement like that, unless hoping for him to be rescued and taken care of? Why else?

Still, something nagged inside her. All the happiness she'd felt from being with Howard had fallen away. She felt hollow. Troubled. It was silly, but there was that urge again. That familiar itch to become Elizabeth. She tried to suppress it, tried to tell herself she was tired. Why did she feel the need, after the delightful day she'd had? Howard was wonderful. She had Christopher now. Why not just get into bed? But something was still making her uneasy. She looked at her vanity bag on the dressing table.

Downstairs, Howard sat in his armchair and put the television on for the news.

'Avon and Somerset police are still urgently trying to trace a woman they believe may have taken five-month-old Noah Cavanagh from underneath the observation wheel in Weston-super-Mare yesterday,' the newsreader said. Howard remembered Val telling him about her son's death earlier, and he thought how losing a child must be something from which you never recover. 'Officers have now named a local woman they would like to speak to in connection with the baby's disappearance. She was captured on CCTV walking with a pram along the seafront and turning into Palmer Street where she lives.' A black and white image appeared on the screen. It was hard to make out much, but Howard could see it was a woman with short black hair and a full skirt. 'She was last seen going into her house with a baby at around one o'clock yesterday afternoon, but has not been seen since. It is believed she may have taken the baby somewhere in her car.' They showed a photograph of a red Peugeot 108, along with its registration number.

Howard turned the sound down lower with the remote control. He didn't need to hear the world's bad news blaring out at him when his head was full of Val. He bent down to pull off his shoes, then took off his jacket and hung it back in the wardrobe. In the en suite he loosened his tie and undid the top button of his shirt, then looked at his face in the mirror and imagined how Val would have seen him. He didn't look so bad.

The TV report was showing pictures of the seafront and the 'Weston Eye'. There was an interview with a man standing outside the ticket kiosk, his face wracked with worry. Once or twice he snatched away tears with the back of his hand. 'I said I'd keep an eye on the pram,' he said. 'Next thing I knew it was gone.'

Howard cleaned his teeth, then went back into the bedroom. The report cut to the police officer leading the inquiry.

'The person we are looking for in connection with the disappearance of this baby is named as Valery Hinsby,' he said. 'Mrs Hinsby is described as medium height with short black hair. She is known to enjoy the fashion of film stars of the 1950s and is sometimes seen dressed in the style of that period. We are urging anyone with any information as to Mrs Hinsby's whereabouts to get in touch with the police.'

Howard sat down again. The report had switched to an appeal by the mother of the baby. She was shown walking into a room in a police station, flanked by two officers, one female and one male. She was a tall woman, and her hair was tied back in a short, neat ponytail. She wore a white T-shirt, a coral-coloured cardigan and dark-blue jeans. Her eyes were sunken and tired, her face etched with despair. The three of them sat at a desk behind a cluster of microphones, the press cameras clicking like firecrackers.

'Noah is only five months old,' the mother said, her voice reedy with emotion. 'He needs me. If anyone knows anything about Noah's disappearance, anything at all, then I beg them – please – to get in touch with the police.'

Her voice cracked, but she carried on, looking straight at the camera.

'If you are responsible for this, if you have taken Noah, I beg you to hand yourself in. He's everything. He's my world.'

She lost her composure then, taken by a wave of despair, and broke down into sobs. The WPC led her back through the door, arm around her shoulders.

Upstairs in her room, Val took off her dress and hung it in the wardrobe. She rummaged in her case for the conical bra and swapped it for the one she was wearing. She ran her hands over her breasts and felt their tapered shape. She popped her lace negligée over her head, then opened the wardrobe again and slid the fur coat from its hanger. Slipping it over her arms, she felt the cold glide of the silk lining on her skin, the soft pelt around her neck. She put on her 'fluffies' and picked up her vanity bag. She hesitated, looking over at Christopher asleep on the bed. She'd only be a few minutes. The bathroom was just across the landing. She opened her door a crack and looked up and down the corridor. There was no one around. She closed the door quietly behind her and wiggled down to the bathroom in her heels.

TWENTY-THREE

Howard turned off the television. He'd barely listened to a word of the news; his thoughts kept drifting to Val and how nice it had been to spend the day with her. She had left him with a warm glow, a silly excitement he hadn't felt since he'd first met Cheryl. He hadn't imagined he could feel so comfortable with someone else. Although he'd only met her that day, it felt straightforward and easy. No pretence. Probably how it needed to be at their age. There wasn't time for games. It was clear Val had been buried in her grief for a very long time, but Howard could sense she was a caring soul, and with a keen sense of humour too. He liked her quirky dresses and the way she was with her grandson. She seemed kinder than Cheryl, less self-seeking. Perhaps he could help her rediscover herself.

He wished he'd arranged to see her the next day before they'd said goodnight. He hadn't wanted to be pushy, but now he was kicking himself. What if she wasn't at breakfast? What if she was intending to leave early? She'd been quite vague about how long she was planning to stay. Suddenly he couldn't bear the thought of not seeing her again. If he didn't arrange something now, she might be gone in the morning. Act now, Howard, he thought. You've always been too timid. Far too wet with Cheryl – that was the reason she ran rings round you. If you want something, then you should reach out and grab it when the opportunity arises. You're seventy-five. It's not like you've got time to waste.

He sat in his armchair turning it over in his mind. It was so long since he'd had to think like this. Forty-five years he'd been with Cheryl. This was all new. He thought about Val again and his stomach turned over in anticipation. Was it too late to go up? It had only been half an hour since they'd gone to their rooms. Would she be in bed already? Would he disturb Christopher? Oh come on, man! Carpe diem! He got out of his chair, filled with determined energy. He hurried down to the entrance hall, selected some tourist leaflets from the sideboard and climbed the stairs to the second floor.

On the shelf above the sink in the bathroom, Val leaned the photo against the mirror. Without her heated rollers, it was hard to get her hair just right, but she built in some curls with her big round brush and then gave them some height by backcombing the roots. She covered her head in a haze of hairspray and puffed a mist of L'Air du Temps at either side of her neck. She powdered her face, smudged a line of smoky grey along her brows and painted her lips bright red. Then she twisted the beauty spot in place on her right cheek. She looked at her reflection. More gaudy than usual, but it was probably the harsh strip light above the mirror casting shadows. She pulled back the bolt on the bathroom door and checked there was no one around. In her kitten heels she wiggled down the corridor, hands on her hips, head thrown back in front of imaginary cameras. When she reached the top of the stairs, she turned around and walked back the other way. She loved the weight of the coat, the way it moved, thick and fluid as oil. Lost in the moment, she paraded up and down the landing, catching the glances of imagined passers-by, holding her head a little higher and putting more swing in her hips. A world away from Val's slow trudge, Elizabeth's strut was pure catwalk.

'Val?' Howard appeared at the top of the stairs.

'Howard? Oh. Um . . .' Embarrassment shot down Val's arms.

'Val?' Howard said again. His mouth had dropped open and she could see his confusion, his face etched with enquiry.

'Oh. I—'

'I was just bringing you these.' He held out the tourist leaflets. 'I thought we might go a bit further afield tomorrow. There are some lovely beaches up the coast. I'm happy to drive. We can fasten Christopher's seat in the back and away we go.'

'Oh, yes . . . that would be nice. I'll have a look at them.'
She click-clacked towards the top of the stairs and took the
leaflets from him. She could feel his eyes on her, standing there
in her negligée and high-heeled feather mules, hair puffed up
like a pompom and full Elizabeth make-up. She felt so crass.
She wanted to die. She turned her face back towards the
bathroom and swiped at the make-up with her fingers. Without
the mirror, she was probably making it look worse. Why did
he have to see her like this? This was her private thing.

'Perhaps I'll see you at breakfast?' she said, itching to get
away. 'We can talk about it then.'

Howard looked baffled, as if watching the ending of a film
he didn't understand. She looked like a garish version of some
old film star. She reminded him of Bette Davis in *Whatever
Happened to Baby Jane?*

'You look completely different,' he said, aware how
inadequate he sounded. 'What's all the . . . ?' Nothing was
adding up. Where had the elegant woman from dinner gone?

'I have to go now, Howard,' Val said, looking towards her
door. 'Christopher might be awake.' She raised the leaflets.
'Thank you for these,' she said. 'I expect I'll see you in the
morning.' She smiled, but couldn't meet his eye.

'Goodnight,' Howard said, and he watched her hobble
down the corridor in her nightie and fur coat, the mules
slapping against the soles of her bare feet.

Val could feel his eyes burning into her back. She shut the

door and leaned against it and stared across the room in horror. Whatever did he think, seeing her like that? Why did he have to come up? She wanted to crawl into a hole. What on earth had made her dress up, just when life was turning wonderful? Why hadn't she gone to bed? Only an hour ago she'd been in the restaurant, so excited by her new friendship, daring to believe there might be a promise of something more. And now here she was, everything collapsing around her. To be caught out like this, by Howard, of all people. It was preposterous.

Suddenly, she felt cross with him. Why couldn't he have left things as they were when they'd said goodnight after dinner? Wasn't she entitled to some privacy? Couldn't a grown woman be allowed to pamper herself without somebody snooping around watching her? It felt like an intrusion. Elizabeth was *her* secret, *her* guilty pleasure, and he had ruined everything. Just when she'd found the perfect place to be away from the world and have some time with her baby. She couldn't stay here now. The thought of bumping into him in the morning was unbearable. How could she ever look him in the eye again?

Howard stood on the top step staring at Val's door. He thought about the way she'd sauntered up and down the landing in that fur coat, make-up pancaked on her face and her hair teased up like a mushroom cloud. And that beauty spot drawn on her cheek! She'd looked lovely at dinner, but just now . . .

well, she looked monstrous. It was very peculiar. Whatever she'd been doing, it was clear from the expression on her face that she was mortified when she saw him. Like a child caught with their hand in the sweetie jar.

He wondered if it was some sort of private ritual. Or whether she'd been caught up in a flight of fancy, enthralled by the happiness of the moment. Perhaps she'd fallen in love with him! Perhaps he should be flattered. Don't people do foolish things when they're in love? He felt his heart surge, a welling of excitement. They'd had such a connection – he was sure she'd felt it too. But there was something very unsettling about what had happened there on the landing. Maybe he should try and talk to her about it. But he pushed the thought away. Best not to get embroiled. He didn't know her well enough. He realised he barely knew her at all. He thought back to the wonderful day they'd spent together and felt crushed. Cross with himself too, for getting carried away. Racing ahead of himself, imagining some fairy tale ending. In his mind he'd practically had them standing at the altar! What a fool.

He turned to go back downstairs but then stopped abruptly. Hang on. That story on the news. Didn't they mention something about film stars? The fifties fashion, the baby . . . it all tied in. He stared at Val's bedroom door, his mind racing. Could it be her? Who was he kidding? Of course it was her. He stood at the top of the stairs, unsure what to do. Should he confront her, ask her outright? No, he couldn't go barging into a woman's bedroom, accusing her of kidnapping. That would be inconceivable. And what if he was wrong?

Perhaps he should just call the police. But no, not yet. He needed to be sure. He owed Val that, at least. Although it was late, he'd have to talk to her again. Perhaps he could do some gentle probing, ask a few questions about the baby, see if her answers matched what she'd told him before. Hadn't she told him Christopher was her grandchild? And where had she said the parents were? Why bring the baby to a guesthouse rather than just keep it at home? He tried to think back through their conversations. Had she really told him anything about herself? He wasn't sure anymore. He stood on the top stair running his hand up and down the banister rail. Yes, that's what he would do. A few casual questions, see if her answers rang true. Then if he was still suspicious, he would call the police. He thought again about how she'd looked just now, the exquisite embarrassment between them. This was going to be awkward.

Christopher was still asleep. Val had put the television back on, punching the buttons on the remote through the channels, trying to take her mind off what had just happened. She started watching something about a man restoring an old E-type Jag, although she couldn't concentrate on it. She tried to settle, crossing her legs and letting her 'fluffy' dangle from her foot.

A knock on the door.

'Val?'

Oh god, him again. Why couldn't he leave her be? She thought of the way he'd looked at her while she stood in her heels and pointy bosoms. Why the hell hadn't she changed again, taken off all this greasepaint? She should have known he'd come back. She might have been able to put things right if she'd gone back to being plain Val. Maybe he'd have forgotten what he'd seen. Maybe she could have made a joke about her beauty routine. She uncrossed her legs and sat with her elbows on her knees, her head in her hands. Please go away, she thought. Please go away. She shut her eyes and flinched when he knocked again.

'Val?'

Oh, why doesn't he go? Still she sat frozen, the heels of her fluffies digging into the pile of the carpet. Another knock. She looked over at Christopher. For god's sake, did he want to wake the baby and disturb all the neighbours too? She imagined the person in the room next door coming out on the landing to see what all the fuss was about. That would be all she needed, more people seeing her like this. She turned off the TV and hurried over to the door. She opened it a crack and stood with her face in the gap.

'Val, I need to come in and speak to you,' Howard said, his face suddenly serious.

'I haven't had time to look at the leaflets,' Val said. 'But I was thinking maybe we could go up to Portmeirion.'

'It's not about the leaflets.'

'Then . . . What?' Val said.

'Val, please let me in.'

'What is it, Howard? I'm afraid I'm rather tired.'

'I really need to ask you something.'

Val could see he wasn't going to go away. Reluctantly, she opened the door. They stood facing each other, her in her negligée, fur coat and feathered high heels, with her heavy black eyebrows and lipstick smudged across her face.

Why hadn't she just gone to bed? They'd had such a lovely evening – where was the need? She imagined how she must look. She hoped to God he hadn't seen *BUtterfield 8*. A mink coat over a silk slip, just what Elizabeth Taylor wore in that movie playing a prostitute. She must look so cheap, such a slut. At least the coat covered the negligée. At least it hid her a little. The sight of him standing looking at her while she clutched it around herself was intolerable. She pulled again at her make-up with her fingers, but it was far too late for that.

Howard wore an intense expression. 'I'm sorry to come into your room like this,' he said. 'But I've seen the news. And now I've had a moment to think—'

'The news?'

'I wouldn't have twigged, but they said something about fifties fashions and film stars, and then I came up and found you like this.'

'What do you mean, film stars?'

What can possibly have been on the news that had led him to jump to such conclusions? Val remembered the baby abduction story she'd seen in the fish and chip shop, the headline on the news just now and the grainy image of a woman with a pram. But that baby had been *stolen*. Christopher had been left. No one had wanted him. Nobody would be looking for him.

'What did you say your surname was?' Howard said.

Val looked down at the floor. Her blood thumped. It was so hot suddenly in the room. Suffocating. She noticed her bunions. They'd become so bad and the plastic straps of her fluffies were cutting into her feet and her toes pointed out at a funny angle.

'Why do you want to know my surname all of a sudden?' she said. She glanced up at him. He was waiting for an answer. What could she read in his face? Whatever it was, she'd blown it. How could he bear to be with her now, seeing her like this? She felt such a fraud. Why had she dressed up tonight when she'd been so happy?

'Where did you say you came from?' Howard went on.

Val pulled the coat around her, pushed the furry buttons into the buttonholes.

'What is this?' Val said. 'All these questions. You're making me feel like a criminal.'

'Well, are you?'

'What?'

'Are you a criminal?'

'No!' Tears pricked her eyes.

Howard looked at her. The desperation in that poor mother's face on the news flashed into his mind.

'Did you steal Christopher?'

Val ran over to the bed towards Christopher. 'What d'you mean? I'm his mama!' She realised how absurd it sounded and tried to correct herself. 'I'm his grandmother. I told you my daughter is in the Cotswolds with her husband.' As soon as she said it, she knew she'd confused it with the lie she'd told the police officer back in Weston. She froze, wondering if he'd spot her mistake.

'The Cotswolds? I thought you said she was abroad.'

Suddenly Howard knew. He was absolutely certain. Of course this was the woman on the news! You didn't need to be Inspector bloody Clouseau to piece together the clues that were staring him in the face.

'I know what you've done,' he said.

She looked at him blankly. 'What I've done?'

He didn't say anything then, just stood staring at her. She fastened the top button of the coat and tried uselessly to pull the three-quarter sleeves further down her arms. Nothing she could do would make her feel less ridiculous.

Neither of them spoke for a while. It was unimaginable now that only an hour before they'd been in the restaurant, filled with hope for the coming days, both daring to dream

223

they might see more of each other beyond Aberdovey. And now here they were, everything blown apart.

'You need to tell me the truth,' Howard said. 'You took him, didn't you? From under the observation wheel.'

'No one wanted him. He's mine, Howard.'

Howard shook his head, then looked across at the baby.

'But he isn't, Val, is he?'

'He was just left there, near the pavement, on his own . . . There was no sign of a mother. No sign of anyone.'

'Alright. We need to get Noah back to his mother, Val.'

Noah? Her baby wasn't called Noah. She didn't even like the name; it was far too biblical. She put her hands into the pockets of her fur coat and felt their silky lining.

'Let me take him, Val,' Howard said, looking over at the baby.

'No!' It came out so violently, almost like the primal noise she'd made when she'd found Duncan in his cot all those years before. She sat on the bed and leaned over her baby, putting her hands on either side of him.

'In which case, Val, I'm going to have to call the police.'

She looked up at him. Police. What was he talking about? Christopher was hers.

'I tell you what,' Howard said. 'Why don't I take him downstairs, let you get dressed, and then we'll go to the police together.'

'No! I don't let him out of my sight, Howard,' she said.

'You know that.' She felt a tightness in her throat, tears beginning to brim in her eyes.

Howard smoothed his hair back, trying to think. He would have to do this delicately.

'OK, I tell you what,' he said. 'Why don't I leave you to get changed, then we'll call the police together, eh? Don't worry, Val. I know how difficult this must be. I know you lost your own child all those years ago. I can see it all, you know.' He took a step towards her. 'We can do this together if it helps.'

Val looked up and nodded, trying not to cry.

'I'll give you a moment,' Howard went on. 'Get yourself changed, and I'll wait for you in the lobby.' He moved back towards the door and reached for the handle. 'Have ten minutes to get yourself sorted out, and then come down and we'll take Noah to the police. And don't worry, I'll be with you every step. I'll wait downstairs.'

He closed the door and Val heard his footsteps going down the landing. She wiped her eyes and stood up. Howard was wrong about the baby. Christopher had been abandoned. It was a different baby on the news. How can a mother leave her baby on its own on the seafront hoping it would be found by someone kind like Val, and then appeal for it to be returned? It didn't make any sense.

Quietness filled the room. Downstairs, the tables in the restaurant would all be laid for breakfast; the evening staff would have gone home. Val picked up Christopher's tartan bag and stuffed his things in – nappies; baby clothes; the bottles and cartons of milk; the tortoise with the scrunchy shell; the music box with the dancing girl. From the bedside table she took the photograph of her with Duncan in his pram and Rafe behind them on the sea wall with his bucket and spade. Everything else she left – her clothes, her make-up, the activity arch. The photograph of Elizabeth Taylor was still in the bathroom. She lifted Christopher off the bed and held him against her shoulder. He let out a half-hearted wail of disapproval, but still hung heavy with sleep.

'It's alright, little one,' she whispered, clipping him into his seat. 'We need to be far away from here. Let's see where we end up, shall we? It'll be like another adventure. You're so good at those.'

She opened the door of her room and peered down the corridor. From across the landing came the muffled sounds of a television. She stepped out of her room, holding the door with her foot so it wouldn't slam. She hobbled down the stairs, the tartan bag strapped across her body, her handbag hanging from her wrist, carrying Christopher in the car seat. On the first floor landing she hesitated just long enough to listen for sounds downstairs. She glanced across at Howard's room. The door was slightly open and there was a light on inside. Where was he? If he was down in the lobby Val hadn't yet thought about what she was going to do. Barge past him and tell him he couldn't stop her leaving? That's all she *could* do. She crept

226

down the staircase to the entrance hall. There was no sign of Howard in the reception area. There was no sign of anyone. The front door was closed, and the only light was the glow from the wall lamps above the desk. Val reached into her handbag for her purse and left a wad of banknotes under the service bell. She pulled the front door open and closed it quietly behind her.

'Is everything alright?' Pamela was outside on the path, trundling a wheelie bin down to the road.

Val's heart leaped. 'Oh! You gave me a fright!' She hesitated a moment before following Pamela down the path. 'He's just not sleeping,' she said. 'I thought I'd take him for a drive around to try and get him to settle.'

'Oh.' She saw Pamela look at the baby asleep in his seat.

'Typical, isn't it?' Val said. 'Now we've set out, he's zonked!'

She crossed the road to her car and pressed the button on the key. The wink of the orange side lights seemed bright, and the electronic sound of the central locking was loud in the quiet street. Val could feel Pamela's eyes on her as she bent into the car in her fur coat and bare legs and pulled the belt around the car seat. Christopher had woken up and was beginning to wail. His cries echoed off the tall facades of the guesthouses.

'Shhh,' Val said. 'It's alright, Bonny-Boo.'

She climbed into the driver's seat. Her heart pounding, she

jabbed the key against the steering wheel column, trying to find the ignition. Once she'd started the engine, she realised she'd have to turn the car round. She drove to the end of the terrace, turned in the side road and set off back past the guesthouse. Pamela was on the pavement next to the bins, watching. Val didn't know whether to give her a wave, but thought it might look silly, so instead just gave her a brief glance and a little smile. Her shoulders were hunched. In the rear-view mirror, she saw Pamela coming out to stand in the road, her hands on her hips, watching as the car pulled up the hill and out of Aberdovey.

TWENTY-FOUR

Len died during the hot summer of 1976. It was another day of blistering colour, and sunshine that burnt into your bones. The heat was a tangible thing; you could clutch it in your arms. The air was crimped and corrugated. The lawns of Marine Parade were parched, brown as prairie lands.

Val and Len headed along the promenade with four-year-old Rafe in the middle, holding their hands. It was eight months to the day since Val had found Duncan dead in his cot. A grim anniversary. They swung Rafe by his hands in between them, brandishing their grief. They maintained the veneer of joy for him, always. What was the alternative? They passed the swing boats on the beach, the snack kiosks. Buckets, spades, plastic windmills. Children in socks and T-bar shoes queued on the sand, waiting for donkey rides. A patchwork quilt of trampolines.

They waited in the queue along the high wall of the lido, then clunked through the turnstile and emerged into an otherworld of technicolour and amplified sounds. Kaleido-scopic swimwear, beach towels, arm bands. Bronzed and burning bodies on the concrete terraces. Footbaths, verruca socks, packets of crisps. Excited shrieks of children high-stepping through the shallow end, boisterous youths, splashing, shouts. The shrill blast of the lifeguard's whistle.

They found a space on the sun terrace halfway along the pool. Val laid out their towels on the concrete, made Rafe stand in front of her while she smeared cream on his impatient limbs. She took off her leopard-print kaftan. Underneath she wore a silver bandeau bikini. She lay back and rested her head against her beach bag. Her skin buzzed with the burn of the sun. Above the walls of the pool, the sky was hot blue. Clouds were absent, seemingly forgotten this long summer. A heat haze had turned the sandstone facade into a shimmering mirage. Len lay down next to Val, stretched out on his front. He balanced his chin on two tight fists and stared in front of him, thinking his private thoughts. It irritated her sometimes, this silence. The way he withdrew. It wasn't only him that was hurting. Wasn't she the one with empty arms?

From behind her cat eye sunglasses, she watched Rafe playing in the fountain. Water cascaded over his shoulders like silver beads. She heard his delirious squeals, saw him disappear through the water into the secret chamber underneath. Val remembered being in there as a child, where light and sound were magnified, and you were invisible – king or queen of your own cavern of bliss. Underwater yet somehow, thrillingly, still able to breathe. A magic trick. An optical illusion. Val smiled as she remembered the exhilaration; smiled at Rafe's glee. She turned round to Len.

Len wasn't there. Val glanced past the deckchairs towards the refreshment kiosk. Her eyes scanned the queue of dripping bodies for his navy trunks, but she couldn't see him. She leaned back on her elbows and watched the bathers in the pool for a while. Turned her head again towards the space next to her. She was sure he'd been there only moments ago. Perhaps he'd gone in for a swim. Odd, though. Normally he would have told her. She watched for the relaxed arms of his front crawl, the triangle of his elbow breaking the water. She looked up at the kiosk again, but the queue had gone and there was only a woman with a child on her hip, choosing ice creams from faded photos of Fabs and Rockets and 99s. A family over by the wall were packing up while their little girl whined. A teenage couple wrestled and laughed at the edge of the deep end, trying to push each other in. Val sat back up, leaned forward, scanned the pool again for Len, her eyes narrowing.

Then she saw him. He was on the diving platform, on the steps between the lower and middle tiers. He moved nimbly as if in a hurry, his hand moving up the rail. Despite his haste his movements were deliberate, mechanical. He had reached the second tier, twenty feet up. Already high. Val was puzzled. Diving wasn't allowed on a day like this when the pool was full. A flash of irritation crossed her face. What on earth did he think he was doing? 'Come down!' she gestured from her towel, pulling the air towards her with her hand. But Len seemed to be lost in a world of his own. 'What's come over you?' she said quietly. 'Oh, go on then, Len. If you want to get us banned from the pool. Go ahead with your showboating, you silly man. Get it over with.' Something about Len's face began to alarm her. He had a strange look, expressionless. He had reached the platform to the third tier. Val got up and stood at the side of the pool.

Rafe was by her side now, dripping. 'Daddy's on the diving board!' he shouted, shielding the sun from his eyes.

Val watched for Len to come out onto the third tier, but he didn't appear. Maybe he was going to turn round, come back down the steps. Admit to some weird prank. A joke that really wasn't funny. But then she watched him turn onto the steps to the top. He stepped over the little chain. The sign that said *No Admittance*. What in heaven's . . . ?

'Look, Mummy, he's really high!' Val felt Rafe's arms wrap round her thigh, his little foot on hers. She put her hand around his shoulder. She tried to see the features of Len's face but he was too far away now. She only saw his compact body in those navy trunks, climbing. What was he thinking? She waved again at him. Shouted his name. But her voice was drowned by the noise of the pool. Len was at the top.

'What's he doing, Mummy?'

Val let go of Rafe and ran towards the diving board. The lifeguard blew his whistle. Gestured 'Off!' with his arms. But Len wasn't looking. He walked onto the board. Wandered out over the water. People around the pool were beginning to notice. Conversations stopped and gradually a complete hush fell around the terraces. A prickle of dread burnt up through Val's back. For a time, Len stood at the edge, his toes curled round the end of the board. He teetered for a moment. Moved his feet up and down in tiny steps as if to ready himself. He held his arms behind his back. From around the terraces came a shout of 'Look out!' The pool was quiet. People were swimming on their backs, looking up, moving away. Time seemed to stand still. Val heard herself shout through the silence. 'Len!' It sounded like something out of herself. She heard the crack of panic in her voice. She was suddenly aware of everyone looking at her. Her feet were on the edge of the pool, her eyes fixed on the board. She felt the white heat of the sun on her face. The taut air. Len steadied himself and seemed to lean forward. His body was a diagonal line. As he fell, his arms stayed clasped behind him. Right up to the moment he hit the water. There was a gasp from the terraces. Val froze. She scanned the pool, willing him to come back up. As the minutes went by though, there was only a deafening pulse in her head, a violence in her stomach.

*

233

Six years later, they pulled the diving board down. Despite its listed status and the local outrage, the council was granted permission to raze it to the ground, and the wrecking balls moved in. That day it was cold, and a bitter March wind cut along Beach Road. Val stood on the pavement across the road from the lido and watched the machines dismantle the board section by section. She wanted to watch it crumble. Maybe it would demolish the memory, erase the terrible pictures that never left her mind. All that history, the thousands of visitors over the years, the swimming competitions, the beauty pageants. Laurel and Hardy. All gone, now. She thought about Marion's elbows resting on her shoulders as they queued to go in that hot summer day when she first met Len. The mottled sun on the water, the haze of the heat. Len's legs almost touching hers inside the fountain beneath the silver curtain of water and the space between them, fizzing with electrical energy. She thought of him scuttling up the steps at the back of the diving boards like a gecko up a wall. How small he'd seemed at the top board. The way he fell. The distorted noise of the crowd. The feel of Rafe's little foot on hers, his arms wrapped around her thigh. She wondered how many people would remember now, that day back in the 1970s when someone died falling from the top board. It was probably one of those urban myths that nobody knows whether or not is true. Val stood on the pavement for most of the afternoon, until the upper platform had disappeared, leaving just empty space, the endless grey sky of the Bristol Channel. The iconic diving board that had dominated Weston's skyline for the whole of Val's lifetime was a vast pile of rubble.

Yet even with the board gone, the question would never fade. Why had he leaped? What had been going through his mind? It still tortured her that she didn't know for sure. Had he wanted to feel the water blast the grief from his skin? Let the force from hitting the surface heal him somehow? She remembered what he'd told her the first day she met him. 'Only professionals would jump from that height.' She thought of that word 'kamikaze'. In her heart she knew the truth, but it was too painful to admit.

That evening she sat on her bed and burst into tears. The need to be with Len again overwhelmed her. How could she get closer to him? How could she *feel* him? While she was getting changed, she saw the fur coat hanging in the wardrobe. Since Len died she hadn't worn it. She'd had no need to. There'd been no more cinema outings, no meals at the curry house. Life had stopped. Val took off her dress and stood in her bra and petticoat. She slipped the coat over her bare arms. Her agitation diminished slightly. She felt better. Calmer and happier. 'How do I look, Len?' she said, picking up his photograph from the bedside table. She remembered what he'd said when he'd brought the coat home from the station. 'Like Elizabeth Taylor herself.'

Sitting at her dressing table and peering into the mirror, she smiled, suddenly, and opened the drawer where she kept her make-up. She patted compact powder on her face, lined her eyes in dark pencil, drew in eyebrows, thick and arched. She giggled. She was getting carried away. Oh, but why not? It was a bit of fun. She twisted the pencil onto her cheek with a flourish. Silly, really, but it was making her feel closer to him. The pain had eased a little. She couldn't explain it, but becoming Elizabeth had purged something.

TWENTY-FIVE

Val followed the road back along the estuary. She caught sight of herself in the rear-view mirror: the thick black smudges along her eyebrows, her hair all teased up. She thought of Howard's look of astonishment at the top of the stairs and it made her want to curl up. Goodness knows what he'd thought of her parading around like that, pretending she'd just won a bloody Oscar. And then the way he'd interrogated her. He must have his wires crossed, she told herself. No one was looking for Christopher. That was a different baby on the news, one that had been stolen. Val could imagine what that baby's mother was going through. Poor woman. Val knew how it felt to lose a child. She thought of Duncan, the tiny weight of him hanging lifeless in her arms. She thought of Rafe then, and how she'd lost both of her children, really. Anyway, whether or not Howard intended to call the police, Val certainly didn't intend to humiliate herself any longer by staying in the guesthouse till morning.

Christopher was starting to cough and fuss.

'What is it?' Val said, wearily. 'Tell Mama, eh?'

She tried to push her index finger into his fist, but he punched it away angrily. She wasn't sure she could do this anymore. The relentless feeding and changing and being on the move. It had been tiring enough as a young woman, but she felt the weariness of age. Her back ached from all the bending and lifting and carrying. She was exhausted. It felt as though she could sleep for a month. Come on, Val, she said to herself. Come on. You need to be strong for Bonny-Boo. It's what mothers do – raise themselves, rise to the challenge even when they're worn out.

She stopped the car in a lay-by. She put on the interior light and reached into the back for a carton of milk and a bottle. She'd left her scissors in her vanity bag in the guesthouse, so she had to open the carton with her fingers. Even using her nails, she couldn't tear the cardboard. She started to feel agitated. Something as simple as opening a damned milk carton. Christopher was becoming distressed, screwing up his face, his shrieks jangling Val's nerves. She tried to rip the carton with her teeth, but still she couldn't puncture the packaging. In the end she jabbed the point of her car key into the top of the carton. The milk spurted in all directions, spilling over the upholstery and down the front of her fur coat. She tried to brush it off with the back of her hand. Only half of the milk made it into the bottle. Val climbed into the back of the car and lifted Christopher through the gap between the front seats. She sat with him on her lap. It wouldn't do to have him jammed up against the steering wheel; they both had more room like that. Cars appeared over the hill behind her, head-lamps like searchlights, making slices of light move across the back of the driver's seat. It must look strange, Val thought, an old woman sitting in the back seat of the car with nobody in the front. Oh, let them look. She was too exhausted to care. Christopher drank his milk and was happier. She studied his big eyes, his fat cheeks. He'd put on weight. He was clearly thriving with her looking after him, and she felt proud of them both. They were a fine pair together. Two's company, partners in crime. Christopher was used to her now. He would have forgotten his old life with the other mama who didn't want him.

Val put her hands under his arms and bounced him gently on her lap. 'That's better, isn't it, dearie?' she said. 'Poor lamb. Been pulled from pillar to post tonight, haven't you?' His eyes caught the light from a car coming over the hill. Those huge, trusting eyes looking up at her. 'I know I said we'd be staying in the guesthouse for a while,' she said, putting his hands against her mouth and kissing his little fingers. 'Silly Mama though, got caught dressing up in her fur coat and slip,' she said. 'Silly Mama! Say it, Christopher! Silly Mama!' She kissed and blew raspberries all up his arm, from his hands to his shoulders and up onto his cheek. Then she did the same the other side. 'Silly Mama!' Christopher beamed. 'And now that naughty man Howard is making accusations about us,' she said, putting her cheek gently against Christopher's tummy. 'Naughty Howard.' She was still for a moment. 'That naughty man,' she said quietly, hurting at the thought of what might have been.

'I'm like Montgomery Clift in *A Place in the Sun*,' she said suddenly, sitting up and looking at Christopher lying in her lap. 'It's a film, Christopher – a classic. Montgomery Clift plays George Eastman, who is engaged to Alice but falls in love with Angela, played by Elizabeth Taylor. Oh, she was gorgeous in that film. Anyway, with George wishing he could be with Angela, his fiancée Alice has become a nuisance, and George wants her out of the picture. George and Alice go out in a rowing boat and Alice falls into the lake and drowns. Poor George is arrested and convicted of killing her, even though he didn't do it. He was innocent.' Val picked up Christopher's little hands and held them in her own. 'Alright, Montgomery Clift's character had *wanted* Alice to die, but that didn't make him a murderer, did it? No, it didn't. It was an accident. The police, the priest, they all leaped to conclusions.' She kissed each of his hands, one by one. 'Just like Howard! Our story is just the same, isn't it, Bonny-Boo? I'm no different, accused of a crime I haven't committed just because Howard thought we looked a bit suspicious. Well, we're not going to hang around there for the police to arrest us, are we?' The baby looked up at her with his big, unquestioning eyes. 'No, we're not.' Val turned off the interior light.

For a while, they sat together in the back of the car. Val played Peekaboo and sang Christopher nursery rhymes: 'Old MacDonald' and 'Baa Baa Black Sheep' and 'Hey Diddle Diddle'. When they sang 'Pat-a-Cake', she moved his hands as if kneading a pudding. She reached into the bag for the music box and turned the wheel and they listened to 'Sur le Pont d'Avignon', even though it was too dark to watch the girl dance. She lay Christopher in her lap and let him kick his feet against her. Occasionally they would hear the murmur of a car's engine, see the bright beam of its lights. Christopher was happier now and was making gurgling noises. She cupped his cheek in her hand, pressed his little nose gently with her index finger.

'You're a trooper,' she said. 'My dear little Bonny-Boo.' She leaned her head against the window and closed her eyes. She was so tired.

'We should move on, I suppose,' she said, after a while. 'Wherever we're heading, it'll be a long way.'

She climbed out from the back seat and fastened him back in the front. They pulled out of the lay-by. She stopped further up the road at a T junction and looked at the signs. Think. Where now? Left to Dolgellau, right to Welshpool. She glanced at the child in the dark. She turned right, and they were heading south.

*

After a couple of hours, Shrewsbury started to appear on the road signs. Val thought about Suki. How many years since she'd seen her? Eighteen, twenty? They'd been really close right up to the time Suki moved away, but quite quickly afterwards they'd lost touch. Suki had been a wonderful neighbour. So supportive of Val during those terrible days. Allowing her time to grieve, looking after Rafe while Val went out walking. After Len's accident, it was as if Val had been ripped apart with a jagged blade. Time after time she would leave Rafe with Suki and charge along Palmer Street towards the sea, the heartbreak she'd been holding in all day bursting out of her mouth. She would march along the front, snatching at her tears with the cuffs of her gabardine raincoat. Once she reached the last of the beach huts at Uphill, she would turn around and walk all the way back to Marine Lake, climbing the steps at Anchor Head and leaning against the railings above the ruin of Birnbeck Pier, hollering her exquisite grief into the wind. The walks became longer and more frequent, but she was never able to blast off the hurt that clung to her skin like a membrane.

Suki never minded. 'Rafe's always welcome,' she'd say. 'When you've got four kids, one more makes no difference.'

Val knew it wasn't as easy as all that. Suki's kids told her about Rafe's sulks and outbursts, about the time he'd pulled all the limbs off his Action Man and caved its torso in with a hammer. 'Don't be angry with him,' Suki told Val. 'He'll be missing his dad. He's bound to be traumatised after what he witnessed. He'll be alright. Just give him time.' Suki knew the one thing that pacified him was painting. She used to find things around the house for him to copy. She took him to the library and helped him choose books about drawing. She'd sit all the kids around the kitchen table with paper and paints and scissors and glue. Rafe liked it next door. Val thought he liked it more than his own home.

Again she felt annoyed with herself for not keeping in touch with Suki. Christmas cards had dried up a decade ago. Why had she allowed a friendship like that to disintegrate? They'd been so close. She'd had some good friends over the years, but they'd all fallen by the wayside. Whatever had happened to Marion? Once Val became lost in her private world of secret evenings and dressing up, she'd let her friends drift away. She wouldn't have been able to explain to them why she did it. She just needed to. It helped relieve her pain. She could forget, just for a time. She could be Len's girl again.

She stopped the car on the approach to Shrewsbury, rummaged in her handbag for her embroidered book. There it was, Suki's address: 37 Victoria Street. When she'd bumped into Suki's daughter Becky in Weston, Val remembered her saying that Victoria Street was right next to the prison. Becky had joked in front of her toddler how it might be handy when they were visiting, if he was being a monkey. It would probably be easy to find.

Suddenly Val was excited to see Suki again. It was very late, but Suki wouldn't mind. Suki never got hooked up on things like that.

'Oh, what does it matter?' she would say, 'when it's been this long?' And she'd nudge Val with her elbow and grin, run her hand down Val's arm, like she used to. Val pictured Suki sweeping her into the kitchen, talking ten to the dozen, wanting to know all her news, putting the kettle on. She wondered if she would still have that teapot in the shape of a cupcake. It wouldn't matter how late it was. That was Suki. Val would be able to tell her how lovely it had been to bump into Becky; how well she'd been looking; how thrilled Suki must be to be a grandmother. Suki had always loved babies. She was so smitten with Val's little Duncan when he was first born. 'I'd rather keep you for a fortnight than a week!' she said when she'd first held him, and Val thought it was the oddest yet nicest compliment someone could pay a child. Oh, wait until she saw Christopher! She'd want to cuddle him and coo over him just the same way she'd cooed over Rafe and Duncan. She would tell Val all about life in Shrewsbury, and they'd reminisce about the old days. Val could tell her all about how Weston had changed, how Suki wouldn't recognise Meadow Street if she saw it now. It wouldn't even matter that Val was in her fur coat and heels. Apart from Rafe, Suki was the only person who'd seen her dressed like this. One evening Suki had come round, hammering on the back door as if the house was on fire, so that Val had no choice but to jump up and answer it in her ball gown and tiara. Anyway, turned out it was only something about a blockage in their shared drain at the back. Val had been mortified, but Suki hadn't made a big thing of it, didn't bat an eyelid when Val told her she wasn't going out. She'd just winked and told Val she looked glamorous and never mentioned it again. That's the type of person she was. She just accepted people the way they were.

Even though Val was tired, the nearer she got to Shrewsbury, the more excited she was to see her old neighbour. It would be as if the years had fallen away. As for Christopher, well. Val could tell her the baby had been left deserted and Val had come along at the right time and Suki would say she had done the right thing. Suki would make it alright.

Sure enough, on the approach to Shrewsbury, there were signs for the prison, and it was easy to find Victoria Street. It was a terrace a bit like Palmer Street, although the houses were wider and grander, with cornicing around the windows. They had small front gardens behind low walls. Hall lights shone through the stained-glass panels above some of the doors. Val pulled up outside number 37 and turned off the engine. The clock on the dash said 02:14. She looked up at the bedroom window.

She lifted Christopher out of the car, stood on the front path and pressed the doorbell. A dog barked. It sounded like one of those little dogs that get under your feet and yap too much. A dachshund or a yorkie, perhaps. Val stepped back from the doorway and looked up at the window. It was still dark. She pressed the bell again. The dog was behind the door, yapping away. Val peeped through the letterbox. 'What is it, Trix? Who is it?' she heard a man calling down to the dog. Oh, god! The internet man. It hadn't even occurred to her that someone other than Suki would open the door. She remembered Becky telling her now, about the man Suki had met online. Val hadn't expected her to be living with him. Suddenly it all felt wrong. She thought about how she must look, standing there on the doorstep in her negligée and fur, her bouffant hair. She turned back up the path towards the car, but it was too late. She'd only got as far as the pavement when the man appeared at the door.

'Can I help you?' he said, peering at her. 'And do you know it's two o'clock in the morning?'

'Oh, er . . . I'm sorry. I was looking for Suki,' Val said.

The man ran the palm of his hand down over his face. 'Who are you?'

'I'm Val.'

The man looked at Christopher, then turned round, stepped back into the hall and shouted up the stairs. 'Suki! You'd better come down here. It's her!'

'Who?' Suki's voice in the distance.

'Your old neighbour! With the bloody baby!'

Val wondered how he would have known she used to be a neighbour. She hadn't told him.

'Oh my god! What?' Val heard the disbelief in Suki's voice.

Suki appeared in the doorway in her dressing gown. 'Val!' she said. 'What are you doing here?'

She picked up the barking dog. She looked different. Her hair was short and dyed a dark red. Her figure was smaller and trim, as if she did a lot of exercise. She must be well into her sixties, but she'd barely aged. If anything, she looked younger. Val thought of her own cracked face under all the powder. Compared to Suki, she must look a hundred. The dog was still yapping and Suki passed it to the man who took it off down the hallway. She stood there on the doorstep and gawped at Val.

'You must think I'm crackers, turning up at this time of night,' Val said. 'I think I might have got myself into a pickle.'

'I'm flabbergasted,' Suki said. 'I was only telling Mike I knew you, just a few hours ago.'

'Were you? Well, there's a coincidence!' Val said, pleased that Suki must have been reminiscing.

'Well, not really . . .' Suki said. She pulled a face.

'I'm sorry it's late and I woke you,' Val went on. 'There's been a bit of a to-do. I was having a bit of a holiday with this little sergeant major and, well, I won't explain now, but it all got a bit complicated.'

'You don't need to explain, Val. I know what's happened.' Suki was staring at Christopher. 'It's true, isn't it?'

'What's true?'

'The news. That you've stolen a baby.'

So Suki had been watching the news too, and seemed to have jumped to the same conclusion as Howard. 'Stolen?' Val said. 'No! Christopher's not stolen.' She held him tighter than she had before.

Suki looked alarmed. 'Look, you'd better come in,' she said. She led Val through the hall into the kitchen. The work tops were polished marble. The deep-red cupboards and drawers had no handles so they looked like sleek, uninterrupted lines. Everything shone. Suki's man was leaning against the butler's sink, still holding the dog and stroking its head. Val clipped into the kitchen, feeling silly in her feathered high heels. She should never have come. It would have been alright if it had been just Suki, but the man was staring at her. Val saw him throw a questioning glance at Suki.

'You do know you're being looked for?' Suki said. 'You're all over the news, Val. We watched the Ten O'clock News tonight. I knew instantly. Soon as I heard it was Weston and saw that CCTV image. And then they said about the fifties clothes . . .'

Christopher was beginning to splutter. Val bounced him gently against her shoulder. She rubbed his back. 'He gets the windies, you know,' she said. 'Just like Duncan used to, d'you remember?' She looked at the floor, at her bunioned feet in those ludicrous shoes.

'I don't think that baby was yours to take, was he, Val?'

Val looked up at her. 'I'm his grandma,' she said, weakly, and held him closer to her and put her cheek against the top of his arm.

'Some people might buy that, Val, but not me.' Suki was looking at her suspiciously. 'You haven't got a grandchild. I didn't think Rafe ever *had* any children.'

Val could feel herself becoming upset. This was all so mixed up.

'No one wanted him, Suki. He's mine.' She was trying not to cry.

'You've got it wrong, Val – he's not yours.' Suki's expression was hard. She wasn't being kind the way she always used to be.

'No, you don't understand,' Val pleaded. 'He's not the baby on the news. He was on the pavement all alone. His mother left him there for me to find. There was nobody else around. She was one of those teenager mothers who can't cope and leave their babies in an obvious place so that someone kind will look after them.'

Suki was shaking her head. 'No,' she said. 'This baby is called Noah and he is very much wanted. His mother was on the TV news last night, making an appeal. She's so upset. She's desperate.'

'No, no, this one's not called Noah. He's Christopher.'

Suki was frowning and shaking her head.

'I have seen the news about a missing child,' Val said. 'But it's not this one, Suki. It can't be.' Val gripped Christopher more firmly. 'It can't be.'

Why didn't Suki understand? Val had found him. He was a foundling. Simple.

'I'm afraid you're wrong, Val.' Suki softened then, and put her arm round Val's shoulder. Val felt the familiarity of her, her gentleness. She was back in Suki's kitchen in Palmer Street, with the shock of Duncan, then Len, and all her ragged grief. Suki pulled her in closer and smoothed her hair and Val felt herself buckle. The stress of these last days finally burst out of her, and she began to cry. She wanted Suki to make it alright, like she always used to.

Suki's husband was staring at them in disbelief. 'This is ridiculous,' he said. 'What are you doing standing there discussing it, while time ticks away? You need to phone the police, Suke,' he said. He picked the landline from its cradle on the worktop and passed it to Suki.

Val's heart began to hammer. 'But I've done nothing wrong,' she said quietly to Suki.

'Listen, Val,' Suki said. 'I know all the loss you went through back then. But this isn't the right thing to do, you know.'

Val blinked back her tears.

'How's Rafe?' Suki said suddenly.

Val blinked and nodded. 'He's alright. He's really well.' How could she tell Suki she hadn't seen her son for nearly thirty years?

The man put the dog down in its bed near the back door. 'Just phone the police, Suke,' he said again.

'Give us a minute,' Suki said.

'What are you waiting for?' he said, angry now. 'Think of the baby's mother, Suke. You saw her. She was frantic.'

'Just let me talk to her, will you? You can see how upset she is. We go back a long way, you know.'

The man glared at her.

'He's right, Val,' Suki said, taking her arm away. 'We do need to get Noah back to his mother. And you know, if you turn yourself in you might not even be in that much trouble.'

'I haven't done anything wrong, though,' Val said. She jiggled the baby at her shoulder.

'His mother is so upset,' Suki said. 'She's beside herself.'

'But I'm his mama now,' Val said weakly. The idea of giving Christopher to anyone was inconceivable. 'He needs me.'

'Fuck's sake,' the husband said to Suki, striding out of the kitchen. 'I'd say the mother was more than upset. She's going through hell. She needs that child back. Phone the police.'

'Hang on,' Suki said. She followed him into the hallway.

'For god's sake, how long d'you need?' he said, as he stomped upstairs.

'This needs to be done carefully,' Val heard her say. She lowered her voice to a whisper. 'I haven't seen her for twenty years. You can see the state she's in.' She was following him up the stairs, pleading with him.

'Yeah. Mental. She's a loony tune, Suke, if you ask me. She needs sectioning, not sympathy.' Val could hear them up on the landing now. Even though they were trying to keep their voices down, she heard every word.

'Don't talk about her like that. She's had a lot of hurt in her life. She's vulnerable.'

'She's taken someone's child.'

'Shhh, she'll hear you.'

'I don't give a shit if she hears me,' he hissed. 'I don't care whether you used to be neighbours or not. It's half past two in the morning, I've got a child abductor in my kitchen, and the real mother's out there going through purgatory . . .'

Val crept along the hall. They were out of sight, around the crook in the landing. She opened the catch of the front door and pulled it gently behind her. She stepped onto the path, her heart pounding. She strapped Christopher into the car seat and turned to look behind her. The front door was still closed. She climbed into the driver's seat.

'Val!' Suki was out on the path, heading for the road. 'Val, stop! Wait!'

Val slammed the car door but it wouldn't shut properly. She looked down. A corner of her coat was caught. She opened the door, yanked in the coat and slammed the door again. Then she jabbed the key into the ignition, started the engine and pulled away.

TWENTY-SIX

By midnight, Rafe had bubble-wrapped his whole life. He had catalogued, packaged and labelled over three hundred of his paintings, posters, sculptures and books, ready for the launch of his pop-up shop the following weekend. Each item had a corresponding handwritten card, and he had organised the cards into piles, secured with elastic bands. Despite the hollow feeling in the pit of his stomach at getting rid of all this stuff and the memories it triggered, he had rather enjoyed the process of researching the artefacts and selecting the information to include on the card, then writing it in black ink with his fountain pen. He felt like an archivist, or a curator at a museum. He looked around the sitting room at all his packed stuff and tried to convince himself that the flat would benefit from a good clear-out anyway. He hadn't been able to clean for months with all the surfaces and floor space so cluttered. Maybe he'd sell the lot, give himself more room in the flat and not need to worry about money for a while.

All that remained to do was book a van. To reward himself for his hard work, he took the olives from the fridge and opened the remaining bottle of wine he'd brought with him from the cellar at Florence Road – a sixteen-year-old Margaux. He carried it into the sitting room with the olives, poured himself a glass, and sat at his computer.

The van hire was expensive, even for a day. Rafe clicked back to the email from the owner of the pop-up shop and looked at the price. The cost of the van and the shop together was extortionate. He logged into his bank account. His balance was less than he thought. He should have checked his account and found out the cost of the van hire beforehand. He'd assumed it would be just about do-able, but he hadn't checked the figures carefully enough. There was no way he could afford to do this.

He poured himself another glass. He stared at the computer, clicking between web pages, checking the costs, trying to think of a way he could still open the shop at the weekend. Perhaps a few trips in a taxi would do it. But that would cost nearly as much. And there was so much stuff – it would take hours. Perhaps he could just take the big artworks – the Mapplethorpe and the Freud. But it was too much of a gamble. The chances of him selling both in one weekend were slim. If they didn't sell, he'd be out of pocket. And who would go into a near-empty shop in the first place? He'd been imagining how it would look, with his art up on the walls, all the artefacts arranged on antique tables, his tasteful labels, and handwritten cards. He'd even had an idea for an eye-catching window display and was planning to stay up a bit longer to make lettering and bunting from pages of old *GQ* magazines. All that effort, it had all been a waste of time. He was too skint even to get the stuff to the shop. He poured another glass of wine. He tried to think of a way to make this happen, but there *was* no way. He didn't know anyone with a van. He couldn't borrow any money. He realised he didn't know anyone well enough to ask him for help. All those people from Florence Road – Louise and Susannah and Marcus. Where were they now? He never saw any of them anymore. And Simon, Jim's brother. Well, it was obvious where *his* loyalties lay. He felt bitter towards them all now, dropping him when he and Jim split up. They'd been Jim's friends, not his – he realised that now. Oh, no doubt Jim would still see them all the time. Still be hosting parties. Bigger ones, probably. They'd invite Clem's friends now. Imagine that – all those loud shirts and designer spectacles in one space. Ha! So fucking pretentious.

The alcohol had begun to make his head loll. He clicked back onto his emails and made himself write to the woman about the pop-up shop and tell her he wouldn't be able to take it after all. He tried to concentrate, too drunk to focus on the text. In the end he wrote one sentence, read and reread it, making sure it contained the word 'Sorry', and clicked Send. As he stood up from the desk he swiped at a pile of handwritten postcards, scattering them all over the floor. Then he burst into tears. He sat on the sofa and held his head in his hands. It all came out in long shuddering sobs – the way he'd pushed Jim away because of his own stupid insecurity; Clem; money. Even Simon. He caught his breath, taking loud audible gasps, then lay back and swigged the wine from the bottle. A thought came to him. Maybe Jim would help him. He had plenty of money, that was for sure. That was why he'd let Rafe have the gallery when they broke up. It was small fry compared to his other investments. He had other things going on behind the scenes that Rafe didn't even understand – funds, shares in all sorts. One of those people whose money made money. Rafe pulled out his phone from the pocket of his jeans. He'd never deleted his number. Why would he? He lay looking at Jim's name, then clicked on it. It was ringing. It was a while before he picked up.

'Hello?' He sounded drowsy. 'Rafe?'

'You knew it was me, then?'

'Of course.'

'That means you must still have my number in your phone.'

'What's this about, Rafe? I was asleep.'

'Sorry.'

'What time is it?'

'Is that all you care about when you get a call from the former love of your life – what time it is?'

'What is it, Rafe?' Jim was beginning to sound irritated.

'Um. Oh, it doesn't matter.'

'What?'

'I was going to ask you to borrow some money.'

'Money?' A pause. 'Is everything OK?'

Suddenly Rafe couldn't bear for Jim to know how broke he was. He might be drunk, but how could he admit he was having to sell all their old possessions in one of those pop-up shops Jim found so vile? What was he thinking?

'Rafe? What is it you need? If you're in trouble . . .'

'What do I need?' His words were slurring. 'Hmm, now there's a question. What do I need right now, or what do I need in the future?'

'Rafe, you're really drunk.'

'Because the answer is you, Jim. Doesn't matter what the fucking question is. The answer is always you.'

'Look, Rafe. It's late. I've got to go.'

'Oh, yeah. Back to Clem, is it? Snuggle up with Clem? Is he next to you, is he?'

'I'm not having this conversation with you, Rafe.'

'Just tell me, is he next to you?'

'He's my husband. Of course he's next to me.'

There was a pause.

'I can't deal with knowing that,' Rafe said. 'How am I supposed to deal with it?'

'I don't know. But it's been five years. You've *got* to try and move on.'

'I can't. I love you.' Rafe took another glug of wine.

'Listen, I'm gonna go now. Please don't call me again. OK? I'm sorry. I'm really sorry. Good night, Rafe.'

Jim had hung up. Rafe stared at his phone. Nice one, he snorted. Humiliating yourself yet again. Fucking nice one. He got up from the sofa to put on some Mahler and turned the volume right up, then lay back on the sofa swigging the rest of the wine from the bottle. He wanted not to care anymore. He wanted nothing to matter. He could drink himself into a coma for all he cared. It was what he deserved for being a failure. His limbs felt heavy, and the bottle fell to the floor, spilling the last of the red wine over the deerskin rug. His eyes were closed. The only sound in the room was the click of the stylus running over the grooves at the end of the record.

TWENTY-SEVEN

Val drove through the centre of Shrewsbury, following green signs to main roads. She looked across at Christopher who was wide awake and staring up at the streetlights. She had no idea where she was going. She'd think about that while she got over the shock. She should never have come to Shrewsbury. Suki had got it all wrong, just like Howard, talking nonsense about Christopher being stolen. Accusing her of all kinds. Putting two and two together and coming up with six. Val had been so looking forward to seeing her, but it hadn't felt easy like it had been at Palmer Street. She wasn't the same Suki. That internet husband lurking, throwing his opinions around. Val thought again of poor Montgomery Clift in *A Place in the Sun*, sent to the gallows for a crime he didn't commit. No one had listened to him, either. They'd come to their own convenient assumptions about his guilt, just because he fitted a certain profile.

She reached a T junction and took the A5, heading south. It

was as good a road as any. Christopher was making a trilling noise with his tongue, his little arms reaching forward and back. She loved how he was always exploring. She reached over to the dashboard for his tortoise and held it near him and scrunched its shell.

The petrol gauge was nearly empty. It would be best to stop for fuel earlier rather than later, Val supposed. Even if Howard hadn't called the police, Suki or her husband surely would have. Uselessly, she tried to pat down her hair, but it sprung up again. She rubbed at her face, but she'd left her make-up remover at the guesthouse, and it just smeared. A car came up behind her and she caught her reflection from its headlights in the rear-view mirror. For a second, she saw what she was, and she was ghastly.

At the next service station Val pulled onto the forecourt behind a white van. The driver leaned against the side as he filled up. He wore a football shirt and had so many tattoos on his arms it looked as if he was wearing a jacket. He looked across at Val and she turned her face away. A camera was fixed to the corner of the shop, another one on a post by the exit. She looked at Christopher through the car window. She hated to leave him, but she'd draw less attention if she went in alone. Anyway, time was of the essence now. She had a sense that this adventure might be coming to an end, that the night was closing in on her. Inside, the woman behind the counter watched her as she went over to the baby things and picked up some cartons of formula milk. It was a different brand to what Christopher had had before, so she hoped he'd like the taste of it as much as the other one; that it wouldn't upset his stomach. You were supposed to introduce new things gradually – she remembered the health visitor telling her that. She glanced through the window at the car. She picked up a sandwich and a bag of mints. A vending machine selling hot drinks hummed against the back wall. She would have done anything for a cup of tea, but she didn't want to linger any longer than she had to. She stood at the counter while the woman scanned the items. The woman had a smoker's face and wore a ring on every finger. Val tried not to meet her eye, but she saw the TV monitor on the wall behind her, showing her car on the forecourt. She felt the cameras cutting into her like lasers. As she drove off, the woman came out from behind the counter and stood in the window leafing through the pages of a newspaper. A few miles beyond the petrol station, on a quiet stretch of road before Telford, Val pulled over again to look at the map. Her eyes scanned down to the south coast. How long, she wondered, would it take to get to Brighton?

It was thirty years since she'd seen her son. Amazing how time had drifted. It wasn't as if she hadn't tried to stay in touch. She'd called and called – she still did, sometimes, but it was quite clear he didn't want to talk to her. No matter how many messages she'd left at the gallery, he never called her back. She knew he'd moved into a block of flats. She had his new address in her embroidered book: Preston Park Avenue. She'd at least got that out of him when he called her that time. He'd sounded quite upset – or drunk, she wasn't sure – said he'd had a falling out with someone and was now living on his own. After the phone call she wrote to him offering to go and see him on the train, but he didn't reply. She wished she knew what she'd done. Maybe nothing. In a way it was inevitable they had ended up estranged like this. It had never been easy with him. He'd been such a destructive child. She wondered if they'd ever really bonded at all. As a teenager he'd been even more difficult – thumping around the house and slamming doors. Particularly, she noticed, when she was having one of her Elizabeth evenings. Was that where all his resentment came from, or was there something else? She never found out. Once he'd moved to London, she barely saw him after that.

She pulled back onto the main road, having memorised the road numbers that would take her beyond Birmingham. The A5 was a dark dual carriageway. It was three in the morning and there was very little traffic around. The odd lorry trundled through the darkness, the occasional car. Suddenly the road signs changed to blue, and Val felt a surge of panic. There hadn't been a motorway on her old map. She wasn't expecting this. Keep calm, she said to herself. There won't be too much traffic, not in the middle of the night. If she just followed the signs to Birmingham, well, she was going the right way.

There were no lights on the motorway, and it was too dark

to see Christopher, but he was quiet for now. She assumed he'd gone to sleep. She reached across and felt his little hand, closed tightly in a ball on the blanket. His skin felt warm and soft. She put the back of her hand to his mouth to feel his breath. She wished she could hold him. As soon as they got to Brighton, she would give him the biggest cuddle for being such a good boy.

Lack of sleep was making her eyes heavy. Her head lolled while she was driving and she had to shake herself awake. It might be as well, she thought, to grab forty winks while Christopher was asleep. Who knew when she'd have the chance again? Certainly not when he was awake and upset from being in the car too long, or needing a bottle or a nappy change. There wasn't anywhere to pull off the motorway, but Val knew you could stop on the hard shoulder if you needed to. At least, she thought that was right. The motorway wasn't busy at this time of night, and any traffic would go sailing past her. She felt her eyelids closing and she forced them open. It would make sense to stop now, then get on the road again when one of them woke up. She indicated left and pulled up on the hard shoulder.

It was a relief to sit in the quiet of the car with the engine turned off. Val leaned back on the headrest, put her hands in her lap and closed her eyes. Barely aware of the dull drone of passing traffic, she felt her body melt into the seat. Then the soft buzz of sleep.

TWENTY-EIGHT

Howard couldn't sleep. All through the early hours he'd lain in bed looking into the darkness, turning it over and over. He knew he should have called the police right away. He'd intended to; he didn't know why he hadn't. But then the thought of them crawling all over the guesthouse, barraging him with questions when he was tired and confused, sullying his feelings for Val – he couldn't face it. He wasn't ready to admit she was a criminal, not even to himself. He needed to let it sit, at least for an hour or two.

It took a while last night before he realised she had gone. After he'd left her to get changed, he'd returned to his room briefly to find his phone. He couldn't think when he'd last had it. He looked down the side of the armchair, in the bedside table. Then he remembered he'd put it in the chest of drawers for safekeeping. He stood and waited while the phone turned on to make sure it was charged. He didn't use it often. Then he went downstairs and waited in the lobby for Val to come down with the baby. He wasn't sure how long it would take her to get out of those underclothes with all the straps and hooks. She'd want to take the make-up off too – he knew that from the self-conscious way she'd rubbed at her face, trying to remove the lipstick and those black eyebrows. That had upset him most of all, how she'd been trying to tone down her make-up when she thought he wasn't looking.

Next thing he knew, Pamela was coming in from putting the bins out, saying she'd seen Val drive off with the baby. 'In her underwear and a fur coat, Howard,' Pamela said. 'You should have seen her. She looked a fright.' Howard's heart was in his throat. How could she have gone? He was only in his room for a couple of minutes. How could he possibly have missed her? Now he wouldn't even have the chance to see her again, let alone accompany her to the police.

He looked at Pamela wiping her hands on her apron and clicking the door on the latch. It irked him how she'd said Val looked a 'fright'. What right had she to judge? Somehow, he didn't want to involve Pamela. He couldn't stand the thought of anyone else knowing. Not yet. He'd ring the police himself and do it calmly and quietly without any hysteria. Once people in the guesthouse started finding out it would all blow up, and he didn't want to become part of a big drama. And Val would be pilloried. Tried and convicted without the chance to defend herself. He owed her more loyalty, more dignity than that. He'd already seen how shamefaced she was being caught out

265

like that; he couldn't bear to humiliate her any further. He left Pamela in the lobby and ran up the stairs to Val's room to check for himself. Pamela was right, of course. Val had gone.

Back in his room he paced up and down, phone in his hand. More than once he pressed the first two digits into the keypad to contact the police. But he couldn't do it. He wanted to think it over, be on his own for a bit. He'd phone them first thing in the morning.

He lay with his head on the pillow and stared across the room. He couldn't get her out of his mind. Whatever she had or hadn't done, he was besotted with her. Yesterday, it felt as though two lonely people had turned towards each other and met in the space in the middle. He'd had such a connection with her; they seemed to fit together. He tried to recollect her scent, concentrate on the floral smell of her perfume. He wondered what it was. Something old fashioned, he supposed, a bit like Val herself. He liked that she was old fashioned. You never saw women like that anymore; at least he never met any. He liked her generosity, her naivety. She was damaged, he could see that now, but there was goodness in her heart. That's what was missing nowadays; everyone so uptight, or downright rude. He, Val and Christopher, they had been so gentle together, encased in their own little bubble of bliss. Howard smiled to himself. Bonny-Boo. Such a delightful young chap. Maybe that was part of the attraction too, spending time with that little lad. Be a grandad next to Val's grandma. A perfect family they would have been, something he'd never managed with Cheryl.

What was left for him now? Who was he kidding, thinking he was happy here, eating all his meals alone, trying to engage the kitchen staff in conversation at the end of their shifts when it was obvious they wanted to go home? He'd convinced himself he wasn't lonely, but Val had given him a hint of what it might be like to have a companion again. Living in one room, staring at birds in a tucked-away little seaside town – was that really living? He sighed, punched his pillow into shape, lay back down and closed his eyes.

TWENTY-NINE

The scream of sirens drilled into Val's sleep. Blue flashing lights in the rear-view mirror approaching from behind. She woke with a jolt. By the time she'd come round and realised where she was, the vehicles were already passing her. A police car chasing someone along the outside lane at astonishing speed. The blue lights got smaller and smaller until they disappeared. Val's blood pulsed. Such a distressing way to wake up. The clock on the dashboard told her she'd barely been asleep ten minutes. She looked across at Christopher, still sleeping soundly beside her. She smoothed the back of his hand with hers. 'Not a care, have you, Bonny-Boo?' she said. She lifted his hand gently and bent to kiss it. She wouldn't sleep again now, not with her heart pounding from those sirens. Might as well carry on. She pulled off the hard shoulder and back onto the carriageway.

They passed junctions for Wolverhampton, for Walsall, for West Bromwich. A turning up ahead for Birmingham. She wondered whether to come off, but then she didn't want to go into Birmingham itself. No, it was probably better to stay on the motorway. It was all so confusing. She sat hunched over the steering wheel, concentrating in spite of her tiredness. She tried to think of the towns between the Midlands and Brighton. What signs should she look for? The M54 became the M6 became the M40. She was pleased with herself for keeping calm and negotiating all the intersections. You're doing well, Val, she said. She was feeling more confident about being on the motorways.

Until she hit the M25. She didn't remember seeing that one on the map either. It was only five in the morning, but it felt like a racetrack. The panicky feeling she'd had on the M5 after leaving Weston was back. She sat up tall and stiff, gripping the steering wheel. Traffic whipped past her on all sides. A taxi came alongside, and the driver gestured to her. He was pointing to the other side of the carriageway. What did he mean? A van behind her flashed its lights. Val realised she should move over, and she pulled into the left lane. She could go more slowly there. Get her breath back and try and gather herself. There were so many more junctions than there'd been on the M5. Every few minutes there seemed to be a turning. Slough. Woking. Leatherhead. How would she know which one to take? She tried to picture the places on the map, but she wasn't even sure which county they were in. Were any of them on the way to Brighton? Traffic thundered past. Finally, she saw a turning marked Brighton. The M23, signed to Gatwick, Crawley, Brighton. Oh, thank goodness, thought Val. It was luck more than anything that she'd made it this far. She turned off the M25 and took a deep breath.

The sun was coming up. A patch of sky had lightened the horizon and was casting pale grey streaks through the clouds. After the long night travelling through the dark, the glimmer of the new day made Val feel tired. She remembered stories of people falling asleep at the wheel and opened the window. She passed the turning to Gatwick Airport and thought of all the people setting off on their holidays. She'd never been on a plane. She thought of Elizabeth Taylor endlessly criss-crossing the Atlantic in that private jet Richard had bought her as a birthday present. The photographs she used to gaze at in magazines, of Elizabeth on the tarmac in one of her turban hats and her little dog in her arms. The plane, the yacht, the luxury cars – Val's life was a world away from Elizabeth's. She licked her fingers and rubbed at the fake birthmark on her cheek. Daylight spread further across the sky and Val could see Christopher now whenever she glanced across. His little mouth was moving, his dreams fluttering behind the translucent skin of his eyelids.

The A23 went on and on. Val felt ragged. Around Crawley her eyes were so heavy she had to work hard to keep them open. She blinked repeatedly, trying to keep them focussed on the road. She scanned for signs that would tell her how many miles it was to Brighton, but there were none. Twice her head lolled, and she jerked awake. Seconds later she felt herself nodding off again. If she could just have some sleep, even a few minutes, just close her eyes. She drove on, past the turnings to Haywards Heath, to Burgess Hill, to Hassocks. She was too tired to drive. At last, she saw a lay-by and pulled in. She turned off the engine, reclined her seat and closed her eyes. Just at the same time, Christopher woke up. Please Christopher, she thought, not now. Please give me a few minutes. But his little hiccoughs were already building into wails and his hands were grasping the air.

Val unclipped his straps and lifted him against her shoulder, hoping to be able to lull him back to sleep. But his feet stepped up and down on her tummy, and his cries were loud in her ear. 'Shhh,' she whispered. 'Mama just wants a little nap. Shhhh. Your mama's exhausted.' She held his body against hers, but he wouldn't be still and lay twisting in angry frustration. 'Please, dearie,' she said. 'I just need a few minutes. *Please.*' She held him tighter, hoping strong hands would calm him, but he wasn't going to settle now. She burst into tears. The responsibility of him was overwhelming. 'Please, Bonny-Boo,' she said. 'If you'll just let me sleep now, I'll look after you for ever. I'll look after you for the rest of your life.' But he fussed and kicked, and his cries drowned her words.

There was no possibility of sleep. She put her seat back upright. It was nearly seven and the A23 was busier. Traffic

271

thundered past. She got out of the car and stood in the lay-by with Christopher squirming in her arms. 'It's alright, dearie,' she said. 'It's not far now to Brighton. Not far at all.' She felt a pang of guilt, trying to reassure him when she had no idea what arriving in Brighton would mean for either of them. She wondered why she was even heading there. She couldn't imagine Rafe was going to greet her with open arms. It was hardly going to be a welcoming committee. But where else was there? Howard or Suki must have called the police by now. She couldn't go home. Another guesthouse was out of the question; it wasn't fair on Christopher to keep dragging him from one place to the next.

Christopher was winding himself up into a proper paddy. This was what Rafe always did. She was losing heart. How much longer could she sustain this? She was seventy-two. Her body ached. It was too hard. She paced up and down the roadside, Christopher screaming so hard he was fighting to catch his breath. In the morning air she was cold with her bare legs and only a negligée under the coat. She felt utterly alone. If only Len were here. Len would have made it better. He would have taken the baby off for a walk and let her sleep. He used to do that with Rafe. 'You get your head down for a couple of hours,' he used to say when Rafe was screaming the house down and there was nothing anyone could do to soothe him. 'You have a rest, love. I'll take this little blighter out for a bit.'

The light was improving, and the breeze was making the long grass at the edge of the road bend and sway. The traffic droned. Christopher continued to cry. Val took the tortoise from the dashboard and squished its shell, but it just made him angrier. She walked him to the end of the lay-by and back, exaggerating her steps to make him bounce. She thought of the man she'd seen when she was having her hair done, with the little girl on his shoulders. If she'd known all the trouble she'd have to go to when she kicked off the brake on that pram on the way home from the hairdresser, would she have done the same thing again? She thought about it as she hobbled along the tarmac. Yes. Yes, she would. Even with him yelling and fighting in her arms, she'd still have walked away with him. Besides, if she hadn't, then who would? Anyone could have taken him. It was in his best interests, not just hers.

She squeezed into the back of the car and balanced Christopher on her knees while she punctured another milk carton. But Christopher wasn't having the bottle. He flailed and screamed, backing away when she offered it, punching the air with his little angry hands. Val leaned back against the head rest and closed her eyes while he screamed. If he wasn't hungry, then what was it? She didn't have the strength. She tried again with the bottle, but he squirmed and spluttered. It was making him angrier. She propped him up on her shoulder, but accidentally hit his head on the side of car. Christopher exploded, bawling, his face so red he could barely get his breath. Val climbed back out of the car, shielding his head as she lowered herself through the door. She walked to the end of the lay-by again, showing him the cars on the road, moving him from one shoulder to the other, turning his body around this way and that. Nothing worked. Still he writhed. He yelled and yelled. Val stood at the gravelly edge of the tarmac, her stomach a knot of stress. People were looking over from their cars, making her remember how she must look.

Perhaps she should try changing Christopher's nappy again. He was only wet, he didn't really need it, but it would be worth it if he calmed down. Once again, Val climbed into the back and lay him on the seat. She fumbled in the tartan bag for the nappies and wipes and changed him while he screamed, his legs poker straight in fury. In the end she had no choice but to squash him back in the seat and continue to Brighton. He fought her, arching his back so that she had to push him down to strap him in. His cries were deafening up against her face like that. She pulled away, her blood hammering, her body rigid.

Back on the main road, finally she saw distance signs for Brighton. Eight miles. Five miles. The dual carriageway ended, and the road turned into the main drag down into Brighton. By the time London Road had become Preston Road, Christopher had cried himself out, and the sound was reduced to the odd shuddering sob as he caught his breath. To their left, the huge expanse of Preston Park was full of dog walkers, even at this time of the morning. Val found Preston Park Avenue that ran along the northern edge of the park and crawled up the road. She saw the name of Rafe's block of flats and stopped the car.

THIRTY

The first hint of morning appeared as a curved line of light above the curtain rail in the bay window. Dawn was becoming gradually brighter by degrees, until daylight filtered through the curtains, casting the room in a grey light. From the estuary came the tremolo call of a curlew.

Howard got out of bed and drew back the curtains. He picked up his field glasses from the table in front of the window and squinted out onto the sand flats. There were indeed curlews out there, wading around on their gangly legs, pincering crabs with the long bills they used like chopsticks. Howard lowered the binoculars. He couldn't enjoy the birds. What did it matter now, his pointless record-keeping, the silly tallies in his notebook? Who cared that he hadn't seen an osprey? He raised the binoculars to his eyes again, this time turning to his right to look out at the stretch of sand he had walked with Val. He followed the line of the beach, then focused on the railings where they had stood across the water from the pier. Was that only yesterday? Already it felt like months ago.

He peered at the railings again, and smiled sadly when he thought about the excitement in her eyes when he told her the legend of Cantre'r Gwaelod. Suddenly he felt angry. Who was she? Certainly not the woman she'd purported to be. She'd pulled the wool over his eyes. Cheryl always said he was too understanding. His wife had walked all over him and now this 'Val', or whoever she really was, had taken him for a fool too. What a mug. Pathetic, Cheryl used to call him. Well, she was right. What on earth was he thinking, becoming so smitten with a woman he barely knew. She was a criminal. A baby snatcher and serial liar. Oh, well done, Howard, falling for Britain's Most Wanted. There you were, floating on air through the sand dunes, wining and dining her like a soppy old romantic, when all the time you should have been phoning Crimestoppers. Sitting in front of the TV last night, head so full of his own happy-ever-afters, he hadn't even twigged that the real Val Hinsby was the lead item on the news. And then the bungled attempt to get to the truth. He shouldn't have tried to reason with her, make plea bargains. He should have left all that to the police. He frowned. What if they took him in for questioning? It did look a bit suspicious. Aiding and abetting, isn't that what they call it?

Although he could hardly bear to be confronted with it again, he turned on the television for the breakfast news. Straightaway the presenters were talking about the baby abduction story, and showing the CCTV image of a woman pushing a pram along the seafront at Weston-super-Mare. Howard peered at the screen. It was Val alright; there was little doubt. He sat forward in his armchair and concentrated on the pictures in front of him and what the presenters were saying. The criminal language they were using did not marry up with the woman he had spent the day with yesterday. The police officer leading the investigation said they were 'concerned for the baby's welfare'. Howard thought of the kind way Val had with Christopher, her soft, sad smile when she cared for him, how she'd cradled him in the carrier and rocked the car seat with her foot while they'd had dinner. Whether or not she had lost her grip on reality, she wouldn't harm the child, Howard was certain of that. She looked after him as if he were her own. She wasn't a criminal, not really.

The programme switched to the press conference and the mother's appeal to the public. Howard listened to how the woman talked about her son. 'He's everything. He's my world,' she said, before breaking down and being led away.

Howard shook his head, castigating himself. What had he been thinking? What was he playing at? That poor mother, caught in a living nightmare, and there was he lying awake all night pondering this and that, swooning over Val. By not calling the police right away, he was as deluded as she was.

'I'm sorry, Val,' he said. He couldn't protect her any longer. He should have done this hours ago. He reached for his phone and dialled the number on the television screen.

THIRTY-ONE

The sound of the doorbell was distant at first, as if in a dream. Rafe lay on the Chesterfield fully clothed, the needle still clicking over the runout grooves in the middle of the record. The bell rang again. He stirred slightly, but his body didn't really move. His mouth was dry, and a headache gripped his scalp like an elastic band. The doorbell came again, long and shrill. Rafe opened an eye. Who the hell? One of the neighbours, perhaps. The Mahler *had* been rather loud last night. Still he lay there, not wanting to confront the day ahead let alone a stranger at his door. The rattle of the letterbox. 'Fuck's sake.' He opened his eyes. Squinted at the rectangle of grey daylight at the window. He hauled himself up from the couch, stumbled across the room and lifted the stylus off the record. Pain hit the inside of his scalp. His watch said ten to eight. He was grumpy now as well as hungover. He stomped into the hall and saw a figure behind the fluted glass in the half-light. He ran his hand over his face and opened the door. The sight of her seized his heart.

'Fuck me.'

'Hello, Rafe.'

'Hang on, am I still in my fucking dream?' His mother was a gargoyle. It was like all his nightmares turning up at once.

'Rafe.' Val hadn't rehearsed what she was going to say. She felt ridiculous now, nervous even. 'I know it's been a long time, Rafe, but I wouldn't have come unless I was desperate. I've got myself in a bit of a situation.'

'What d'you mean? What situation? Why are you here?' His heart was hammering. He rubbed the back of his head, blinked his eyes heavily. 'What the hell are you *doing* here? It's not even eight o'clock in the bloody morning. And why have you got a baby?' he said, gesturing towards Christopher.

'He's looking at you, Rafe,' Val said, smiling. She moved a bit nearer. 'Look, Bonny-Boo, this is your Uncle Rafe.' Her voice was sing-song, lost for a moment in her baby world.

Rafe looked alarmed. 'Whose kid is it? What are you doing with a baby?' he said. What horrified him most of all though was the sight of her. 'So, I haven't seen you for thirty years, and you think it's alright to turn up on my doorstep looking like that. You can't resist it, can you? It's like you're taunting my dreams.'

'Rafe, I can explain. I might be in a bit of a predicament.'

'Predicament? I'm not surprised. Look at you! You're quite something to fucking behold, aren't you?' He ran his hand over his hair, pushing it back off his face. 'Ever since I left home, I've been trying to get this . . .' He swept the space between them with his arm, gesturing at her. '. . . out of my head. And the next thing I know, you turn up on my doorstep looking like some poundshop Judy Garland. What the fuck's the matter with you?'

'Rafe—'

'Are you actually trying to mess with my head? I thought I'd left all that – *you* . . . Sorry – *her* – in Weston.'

They stood on either side of the threshold, looking at each other. Then Val said, 'I'm sorry, love. Turning up here unannounced after all these years, and with this little one.' She jiggled the baby in her arms. 'I know it's a lot to take in.' Rafe was staring at her in disbelief. 'But d'you think we could come in?' she said. 'I'm so tired. I'm really tired. I need to sit down.'

Rafe frowned at her. He looked back into the hallway behind him. He shrugged. He was too hungover to argue. 'Alright,' he said, and held the door open. She clipped into the hallway. She smelled like a pensioner.

'Sorry, the sitting room's full of stuff. Be careful. Everything's stacked up ready to go.'

'Go where?'

'I was going to do a sale . . .' He rubbed his face. 'Doesn't matter.'

He picked up the empty wine bottle from the rug, noticing

it had left a pink stain on the deerskin. His head pounded as he leaned forward.

'You wouldn't make me a cup of tea, would you? I'm ever so parched.'

Rafe stared at her for a minute. He hadn't seen the feather shoes before, but the familiarity of the coat took him right back to those dreadful years at Palmer Street. The thick black smudges along her eyebrows, her hair backcombed up so that you could see daylight on the other side. He felt nauseous.

He shuffled out to the kitchen and filled the kettle. His head throbbed. He filled a pint glass with water and downed it, gasping, and drew the back of his hand across his mouth. He rummaged in a drawer for painkillers and swallowed them with more water. He stared at the bags in the hot water, putting off the task. He didn't want to make tea and carry it in. He couldn't deal with her. Making tea for her reminded him of being in the kitchen at Palmer Street. The smell of Calor gas when he lit the cooker ring with the hob lighter. The vinyl wallpaper with its pattern of oranges and lemons. His mother's Bakelite cigarette lighter on the table and the strange silk underwear draped over the clothes horse next to the sink.

Finally he carried the two mugs of tea into the sitting room. His mother was sitting on the Chesterfield with the baby on her lap, singing 'Pat-a-Cake'. When he put her tea down on the coffee table, she stopped and looked up at him.

'What's happened with all these postcards?' she said, looking at the cards all over the floor.

'Oh, just . . .' Rafe shrugged. Trust her to turn up the day he had a raging hangover and the flat looked as though there'd been a burglary. Even though he didn't care what she thought, he was still embarrassed by the state of the place. The state of himself.

'And what about all this stuff?' she said. 'Are you moving house?'

'No, I was going to sell it.'

'Sell it? Why?'

'Don't need it. Got no room for it.'

'That seems a shame, Rafe. There's some nice stuff here by the look of it.' She turned her head away from the baby to blow on her tea. 'Not so sure about him, though,' she said, nodding at the Freud self-portrait. Rafe had taken it down from the wall, but, in the end, hadn't had the heart to sell it. 'Whyever would you want to do a painting with someone's privates out like that?'

Rafe looked at her.

'That's a lovely cup of tea,' she said. 'I really needed that; I can't tell you.'

'You haven't answered my question,' Rafe said. 'Whose kid is that?'

Val sipped her tea. 'Oh? This one? I'm looking after him for somebody,' she said.

'What d'you mean looking after him for someone? Who?'

'Just someone who needed a break from him.'

'What? Who? I don't understand. And, more importantly, why have you brought him here?'

Val stood up. 'You wouldn't just take him for a while, would you?' she said, passing Rafe the baby. 'I'm really sorry, but tiredness has just hit me like a train. I've got to go to sleep. I'll tell you the whole story later. I've been awake all night, Rafe. Can I just go and lie down? Please. Just give me a couple of hours and I'll be right as rain.'

'What?' Rafe stared at her, astonished.

'Please, Rafe. I'm so tired I could keel over. Everything he needs is in his tartan bag. There's a pram in the boot. My car's parked right outside – it's the little red one. You could even take him for a walk if you fancy it. Here's my car keys, look. He could do with a change of scene, some stimulation. He's had too much sleep, whereas I've had none. Is this your bedroom down here?' She clipped down the hall.

'What the hell?' he called after her. 'You're taking the piss!'

'I'm sorry to turn up and do this,' she said, pulling off her mules. 'If you'd known the night we've had.'

'You can't just dump a kid on me and help yourself to my bed,' he said, incredulous, still staring at the back of her. The gall of the woman.

'Please, Rafe. I've got no choice. I can't talk to you until I've had some sleep.'

284

'What's the baby's name even?' he called after her, but she had already closed the bedroom door. 'What's his name?' he shouted down the hallway.

'Christopher,' she called, through the door. He could hear the exhaustion in her voice.

'Fuck's sake,' he muttered, going back to the sitting room with the baby in his arms.

He wasn't sure he'd ever picked up a baby in his life, let alone been left in charge of one. He'd never even considered one. It was featureless, really, with its small nose and barely there eyebrows. People always talk about the smell of a baby's head, but when Rafe put his nose against its hair and breathed in, it smelled of mints and L'Air du Temps. 'Fuck's sake,' he said again. What on earth was he supposed to do with it? He pulled the giraffe out of the tartan bag and held it out to Christopher. Christopher reached for it and clutched it in his little chubby hands. Rafe lay him down on the deerskin rug while he picked up the postcards from the floor. Christopher started to splutter. Rafe looked across at him, hesitated for a moment.

'Wait there,' he said, picking up Val's car keys.

Outside on the pavement he fixed the parts of the pram together and pressed down on either end of the carrycot to make sure it was safe. Then he went back inside to fetch Christopher. He lay him in the pram. When he clipped the straps together, he pinched the skin on his finger. 'For god's sake,' he muttered. 'Stitched us right up, hasn't she?' he said to the baby as he wheeled the pram down the pavement. He turned and looked back at his block of flats. He felt on edge, having to push an unknown baby around Brighton before he knew the full story. But it would be easier to have it in a pram than crying in his flat.

A brisk breeze was coming up from the sea and it felt cool on Rafe's face. Actually, he could do with a walk and some fresh air. His head still banged, and his tongue felt like a carpet. He needed to be out of that cloying flat and far away from his mother. What was she thinking, arriving on his doorstep out of the blue, dressed up like all his worst nightmares? It was as though she was mocking him. Where had she been all night? Why hadn't she slept? Who did she know well enough to be looking after their baby? He didn't remember her being particularly close to anyone apart from Suki, and she'd moved away years ago. Whose child was this that he was pushing in the pram? Oh, who cared. Whatever her story, he hated her. He thought of her in his bed with all her powder and fur, and his stomach turned. She could have her sleep, and then she could get the fuck out of his flat.

A little way down the hill he crossed the road into the park, lifting the pram wheels carefully off the kerb. Leaves in their autumn colours of reds and russets and yellows, floated and danced on the breeze. A squirrel darted across the path and scuttled up a tree. Rafe trundled the pram along the rough track at the edge of the park. It was difficult trying to negotiate the swivel wheels over the stones and tree roots, so he crossed the grass onto the wider path. The wheels moved easier on the tarmac. Down the hill near the tennis courts, a man was pushing a buggy coming in the other direction. They smiled at each other, as if acknowledging shared experience. Both up early and taking their kids for a walk or dropping them off at the childminder on their way to work. How full some people's lives were. Rafe wondered if he looked the right age to be pushing a pram – whether the man would assume he was a grandfather rather than a father. At fifty-two, his hair so grey now, he could more likely be a grandparent, he supposed.

He crossed at the zebra crossing, then walked down the main road under the viaduct, threading through the maze of streets in the North Laine. It was quiet in these streets so early in the morning, Brighton's traders and shoppers yet to come to life. He passed tattoo parlours, vintage emporiums, wine bars and jewellers. An archway of metallic pink and purple balloons decorated the doorway of a shop selling cupcakes. A brewery lorry was stopped on a kerb and the driver clanked aluminium barrels along the pavement and passed them down through a trap door into a cellar. Rafe stepped into the road to avoid scaffolding where a shop front was being painted in wide scarlet and yellow stripes. He turned into a narrow alley where every building and wheelie bin was covered in graffiti.

A barber's shop on a corner was open early, two men chatting over the drone of hair clippers. Rafe pushed his own hair back off his face, ashamed of how far he'd let himself go. He used to walk around the North Laine all the time with Jim, but he rarely came here nowadays. Had he really fitted in here? He felt like he no longer belonged.

Each time he had to manoeuvre the pram, he did so tentatively, pushing down on the handle to lift the wheels over the kerbs, turning corners at a shallow angle, making the movements smooth, so as not to jerk and upset the baby. He didn't know what he'd do if it started to cry. Instinctively he found safer places to cross than he otherwise would, waiting at crossings rather than jaywalking diagonally over streets, making sure cars had stopped before stepping into the road. His hands felt strange wrapped round the handle of the pram, but there was something calming about pushing it. There was no rush, just the slow trundle of the wheels along the streets. The baby was awake and watching everything. Rafe liked how he seemed alert, keen to learn about his surroundings. How lucky he is, thought Rafe, with his life ahead of him. A clean page. What Rafe would give for that.

They reached the seafront and went down the slope to the walkway alongside the beach. Cafes were setting out tables for the day, and the shops under the arches opening their shutters. A solitary skateboarder clunked over ramps near the shingle. He was trying to perfect a trick mounting a low wall. Time after time his board clattered to the ground, and he picked it up by stamping on its tail and catching it mid-air. Rafe detoured around the ramps so the noise wouldn't startle Christopher. He stopped on the boardwalk and leaned over the handle of the pram.

'Lots to see along here, little fella. Perhaps you'd like to get out in a minute, have a proper look around. Eh? Is that what I'm supposed to do? You'll have to help me. I'm new to all this.'

He watched the baby's eyes staring at his. He held the baby's fingers between his own and the baby grasped his middle finger. With its tiny hands and huge eyes, it made Rafe think of a bushbaby.

'What did she say your name was?' he said. 'Christopher, wasn't it?' The baby continued to stare at him.

'Christopher,' Rafe said quietly. 'Hello, Christopher. Who are you then, eh?'

He wheeled the pram to the shingle at the edge of the beach and parked it next to a bench, angling it towards the burnt ruin of the West Pier. He unclipped Christopher's straps and lifted him out of the pram. It felt rather a lot, having to support his head and hold all his limbs at the same time with only two hands. Rafe sat on the bench with Christopher on his lap, propping his head in the crook of his arm. He pulled the blanket from the pram and wrapped it around the baby and tucked it around his body and legs.

'There you are,' he said. 'That's the West Pier, Christopher. What's left of it, anyway.'

The baby gazed towards the sea and Rafe studied the tiny movements of its mouth, the network of veins under the thin skin of its ears, the patch of scalp at the back of its head where the hair looked worn away or perhaps had yet to grow. Peculiar how a baby is so brand new, yet has the features of an old person too. He liked how the baby's face was open and curious; how he seemed to be always listening. It was interesting watching him. It was almost as if Rafe could see his brain developing before his eyes.

Behind them, the observation tower had already opened, and the viewing pod, shaped like a great glass doughnut, rose steadily above Brighton. The morning sun was reflected in its huge windows. A handful of tourists were up early, and stood against the glass looking out, taking in the views across the English Channel, the city and the South Downs. It made Rafe think of the story of *Charlie and the Great Glass Elevator*. He remembered Val reading it to him, sitting on the edge of his bed in the back room, smoothing his hair. She was a good mother much of the time. Despite her bizarre rituals, she'd tried her best. It hadn't been easy for her. He'd never felt very close to her, but he'd felt loved. He couldn't deny her that. He took a deep breath. His head was clearing.

Above the skeletal ruins of the West Pier, a mass of starlings performed their regular aerial display, rolling and swirling in an ever-changing formation. Rafe had never seen them do this in the morning before; it was normally an evening thing. 'Wow, look at that, Christopher!' he said. 'The wonders of nature, that.'

Christopher was making tiny noises as he watched and Rafe could feel the faint vibration of him in his arms.

'Done us both good, having a walk,' Rafe said. 'Bit of sea air always perks you up.' He gave Christopher a little squeeze, feeling the connection between him and this human being. He was a sweet little chap. Rather than feeling saddled with him, Rafe found he was enjoying his company. Very odd, his mother turning up like that. She hadn't told him whose baby it was, or why she'd been up all night. She could explain all that later, and once she'd explained she could be on her way. He didn't want her there. It might have been different if she'd come to Brighton looking normal, suggesting they patch things up. He could have warmed to that. But there was hardly going to be a reconciliation between them while she was still wearing that bloody coat.

He and the baby sat quietly together watching the waves swell around the ruined stumps of the old pier. A seagull bobbed on the surface of the sea, and starlings roosting on the pier chattered and chirped. A middle-aged couple in matching anoraks crunched along the shingle with a spaniel, the woman repeatedly slinging a tennis ball into the sea for the dog to retrieve. Rafe wished he could stay there sitting on the bench in the fresh breeze, listening to the sound of the waves pulling back across the shingle. Even with the baby it was good to be down on the front so early, watching Brighton waking up and breathing in the fresh air. If he could stay in this moment for ever, he'd never have to deal with the Jobcentre, his lack of money, his bubble-wrapped possessions that had been a waste of his time. Or his mother.

After a while he felt the movements of Christopher's body – the tiny jerks of his hands, his little fidgets. They should probably move on before he began to get fractious. Rafe clipped him back in the pram and tucked him up in the blanket. His long hair fell forward, and he stood up and brushed it back. Perhaps next week he'd get around to going to the barber. He pushed the pram along the seafront towards the marina. The clock at the entrance to the Palace Pier said it was only half past nine, but already the air smelled of burnt sugar from the candy floss kiosks, and the electronic bleep of computer games hummed through the open doors of the arcade.

He wheeled the pram alongside the tracks of the Volks railway, the wind blowing his hair around his face. Shafts of sunlight shone weakly through the clouds, making a patch on the surface of the sea glint and shimmer. A runner sped past wearing fluorescent shorts and a T-shirt that said: *If I collapse, can someone pause my Strava?* All that energy, all that ironic knowingness of certain Brighton types. It made Rafe feel old and tired. If I collapse, he thought, can someone just leave me where I fall?

When he reached Duke's Mound, he turned away from the seafront towards Kemp Town. It felt wrong to be near this seedy place with a baby. He felt disgusted with himself, thinking of all the times he'd been with men in those grubby bushes. What good had it ever done? It was no wonder he was depressed if that was his only entertainment, his only company. He pushed the pram up the hill and considered again how he had let his life slip by since breaking up with Jim. Why couldn't he put things right? It wasn't too late. He just needed to stop degrading himself at Duke's Mound, use dating apps like any sensible person. He could still sell his stuff, and start looking properly for work. It wasn't beyond him. There must be something out there he could do. Alright, he was probably never going to run an art gallery again, or curate any major exhibitions, but goddamn if he couldn't get a little job. It only needed to be part time. Small steps, that's all it took. How could he get his confidence back if he didn't even try? He pushed the pram with renewed determination. Why let Jim define him? Was he really nothing without Jim? He'd been his own man long before they met. Achieved good things, worked up from nothing to being well known and well respected in the London art scene. He had a wealth of skills. He just needed to find himself again. Look at the state of his mother, back at the flat. She hadn't changed a jot in all these years. Still an unholy mess. Compared to her, he seemed capable. If he could just muster up some inner strength, get a lucky break, maybe he could begin to get back on his feet. As for all the stuff he'd priced and parcelled, well, if he couldn't afford a van, he'd just have to sell it on eBay. It was a pain to have to post everything, but it wasn't the end of the world. Stop whinging and get on with it, he told himself. He could still make some decent money so long as he put a minimum reserve price on everything. Anyway, he'd done most of the hard work last night. He even had half a mind to take it up to the new owners of Florence Road. This stuff belongs on your walls, he would say. It was all chosen for this house. Have it. Have the bloody lot.

Starving, he stopped at the deli on the corner. Emilio sprang out from behind the counter when he saw the pram.

'Ah, I love the bambinos!' he said, leaning over the baby. '*Ciao, piccolino,*' he said. '*Ehi, segnor carino!*' He stroked Christopher's cheek.

'Is not your baby, no?' he said, turning to Rafe and laughing.

Rafe shook his head and smiled. 'Nah,' he said. 'My mother's looking after it for someone.' He shrugged. 'I don't know whose it is.'

'Not the missing baby on the news, is it?' Emilio joked.

'What baby on the news?'

'Oh, have you not seen that poor mama at the press conference? Is terrible. From uh . . . Oh I don't remember the name of the place. Funny name. What's it called? By the sea.'

'Oh. I don't know,' Rafe said. 'I don't watch the news.' He looked at Emilio with his head in the pram, cooing over the baby. 'Anyway, how are you, Emilio?'

'I'm good,' Emilio said, straightening up. 'Too busy though. The girl who was working here – you remember her? Lily. Well, she's gone off to uni and I need to find someone else.'

'Oh,' said Rafe. He was quiet for a moment, imagining himself behind the counter. He knew about food and wine. He knew Italy. It might just be what he needed to lift him out of himself. He had to do it sometime if he was going to stop himself sliding deeper into the pit he was in. He could see himself weighing olives on the big scales at the back, cutting the Italian cheeses, wrapping hams in brown greaseproof paper, creating wonderful window displays. If he could redis-cover his confidence and talk to the customers, well, it might even be a bit like the old times in the gallery. He forced himself to say it before he lost his nerve. 'I could be interested,' he said. 'I'm looking for something.'

'Really?' Emilio considered him for a moment and Rafe thought he saw a flicker of doubt cross his face. But then he said: 'Well, I know that you know about food and wine.'

Rafe nodded. 'And Italy,' he said.

Emilio smiled. 'OK,' he said. 'Yes. Why not? Listen, I'm waiting for a delivery now, but can you pop in tomorrow morning? We could have a chat?'

'Uh, yeah. Sure. Great.' Rafe forced himself to make eye contact and smiled.

He bought four slices of pizza and ate two of them as he walked back through the park, blowing raspberries at Christopher, and zigzagging the pram along the path.

THIRTY-TWO

The flat felt dark and gloomy after the sunshine and fresh air. It was always so alive down on the seafront. By contrast, Rafe's flat was a mausoleum. There was a whiff of his mother's L'Air du Temps hanging in the stale air. Once he'd got rid of her, he would give the flat a proper clean. The bathroom tiles needed scrubbing with bleach and the kitchen could do with a proper sort out. Piles of unopened post, magazines and dirty dishes had accumulated on the worktop. A new job at the deli would be an incentive for him to clear the clutter. And this afternoon he would go and get himself a haircut.

Rafe reached into the tartan bag for some toys and squashed the tortoise's shell and rattled Peter Rabbit.

'Hang on,' he said. 'I know what you'll like,' and he held Christopher in one arm and pulled the disco ball out of its box by its ribbon with the other. He moved over to the window and held it, spinning, so that Christopher could watch the light reflected in its tiny, mirrored squares. It was absorbing watching Christopher's fascination. For someone who had never taken an interest in babies, he was surprised by the fondness he felt towards him. He had a beautiful, intelligent face, and Rafe was enjoying imagining the world through his eyes. He turned the disco ball with his finger, making it spin faster, and watched Christopher's glee.

Val appeared in the doorway. Rafe stiffened.

'Oh, he likes that,' she said.

Rafe glanced behind him. 'Feeling better, are we?' It was as if something had caught in his throat. He didn't mean to sound quite so frosty, but it was hard to mask the agitation he felt by her being in his flat. She came over and held Christopher's hand and watched the disco ball with him. Her hair was frizzier after being asleep. He didn't remember it being this dark. Why ever did she want it as black as that? She looked like the bride of Frankenstein. Close up, the hair was thin, with patches where he could see her scalp. Underneath all that teased-up hair and theatrical slap, she was an old woman. It startled him.

'Yes,' she said. 'I'm sorry to do that to you. I was so tired I couldn't think straight.'

Rafe handed her the paper bag. 'There's some pizza in there if you're hungry,' he said.

'That's kind. Thank you.'

Rafe shrugged. 'I'd only have to make something,' he said.

'Did you go for a walk?'

'Yeah.' He was still being curt. He didn't want her to start thinking she was welcome. The sooner she was gone, the better. Now she'd had a sleep, she could be on her way. 'Went all the way down to the front.'

'Lovely,' she said. 'Perhaps we could have a walk together later. I've never been to Brighton.'

'I didn't think you'd be staying that long,' Rafe said. 'Was assuming you'd be off in a minute. Once you've told me what you thought you were doing, of course. Why you've turned up out of the blue like this, and with a bloody baby. Whose child is it?'

Val looked at him but didn't say anything. She put out her hands for Christopher.

'Here, I'll take him now. He's probably due a feed, and then I expect he'll have a nap as well. He'll be tired if you've been down to the sea.'

Rafe tried not to touch her as he handed her the baby. She made his skin crawl.

'Have you got a microwave or something? If I put this milk in a bottle, can we warm it up for him?' she said.

'Yeah, I guess,' he said.

He watched his mother root through the tartan bag, pulling out packets of baby wipes and nappies and clothes, spreading them along the length of the Chesterfield.

'Here,' she said, passing Rafe a bottle and a carton of formula milk and following him into the kitchen with the baby

299

on her hip. They stood together in the small kitchen watching the bottle turn in the microwave and when the bell pinged, Rafe passed it to Val, and she screwed the teat on and shook a few drops onto the back of her hand to check the temperature.

'I'll change him and feed him, and I'll put him down in your room, if you don't mind,' she said, and shuffled off down the hall with the baby in one hand and the bottle in the other.

'Be my guest.' He tried his best to sound sarcastic. 'Help yourself.'

Rafe went into the living room and put the disco ball back in its box. He needed her gone, but it was difficult with the baby and all this to-ing and fro-ing to the bedroom, all the changes and feeds. She hadn't told him why she was here yet, and she certainly didn't appear to be in a hurry to leave.

'He's better at feeding than you ever were,' she said as she came back from the bedroom, pulling a linen square from the shoulder of her fur coat. 'You used to bring half of it back up again, cover me in baby sick.'

Rafe felt his back stiffen. 'Oh, here we go. You're doing it already,' he said.

'Doing what?'

'Criticising what I was like when I was a baby.'

'I'm just telling you what you used to do. Proper little rogue you were. Always sick. Always cranky.'

Rafe felt his anger beginning to rise. 'Oh, don't think I

don't know it. I know I was a nightmare. You told me enough times. And just for the record, I couldn't help it – I was a baby, remember?'

'I'm not saying you could help it. There's no blame, Rafe.' She shrugged. 'You were just hard work, that's all.' She tidied the baby things off the Chesterfield, put them back in the tartan bag, and sat down.

'Why do you always tell me though? I'm sorry I wasn't an easy baby. I'm sorry I wasn't Duncan.'

'Don't bring him into this,' Val said. 'He's got nothing to do with it.'

'Yes he has. He was the perfect child, while I was never good enough. You made it plain enough. I know you think the wrong one of us died.'

Val looked aghast. 'Don't be ridiculous.'

'It's true. After Duncan, I was always a disappointment. Talk about black sheep! It's no wonder I left home – escaped from you – the first chance I had.'

'Well, you certainly couldn't wait to run away, that was clear. Swanning off to London, not giving a by or leave. Changing your name.'

'What's that got to do with it?'

'It's the name your dad and I christened you with.'

'Can you blame me? Who wants to be saddled with a name like Ralph?'

'What's wrong with Ralph?'

301

Rafe scoffed. 'Even in the 1970s it was a terrible name for a child.'

'It was your dad's middle name.'

'I know. That's why I didn't change it completely. It was only a small tweak. I modified it. Ralph to Rafe. It isn't that different.'

'Well, it sounds different to me. It's a completely different name. Anyway,' she said, 'it's not important. I don't know why you're getting so het up.'

'I'm not getting het up. I'm just telling you I needed to start afresh when I moved away.'

Val raised her eyes. 'Typical of you, that,' she said.

'What d'you mean?'

'Well, moving away. You had to be different.'

'I wasn't trying to be different. I just needed to get away from Weston.'

'You always did think you were better.'

'I wasn't better.'

'Why did you go, then? What was so wrong with Weston?'

'It was stifling. Small-minded tinpot little town. Anyway, it wasn't just Weston. It was you.'

Val looked as if she had been punched.

'What d'you mean it was me? Why?'

'You were supposed to be my mother,' Rafe said. 'And look at yourself.'

Val bowed her head. 'I know I look a bit of a mess,' she said. 'I've barely had any sleep, and—'

'All this . . . shit,' Rafe said, sweeping his arm up and down in front of her. 'Don't you see, it freaked me out. You drove me away with your pantomime clothes and your clown make-up. Look at yourself. You look like Ken fucking Dodd.'

Val stared at the floor and swallowed.

Rafe carried on, his anger at her stupid, fake persona finally vented. 'I never understood what you were doing. I didn't want to understand it. All I knew was that I hated it. None of my friend's mothers did that in the evenings. But my mother was like some freak.'

Val put her hand onto his arm, but he shrugged it away.

'I could have put you in the circus. Roll up, roll up, look at my monstrosity of a mother! One minute she's plain Val Hinsby, living in a two-up, two-down in a quiet little seaside town, and the next she's Elizabeth Taylor, movie starlet, swanning around in fur coats and jewels, thinking she lives in the Hollywood Hills with Richard fucking Burton. Mad as a bastard hatter, she is! Roll up, roll up!'

'Rafe, please . . .'

'Come to think of it, I'm glad you've turned up, actually, because there's quite a lot I want to say to you. We might as well have it out. Like how damaged I am. You never talked to me about anything. About my dad. You never explained. It felt that there was this great big thing that was wrong, but all you could do was sit there being weird in your stupid make-up and that *fucking* coat.'

He saw her face fold then.

'I didn't know it upset you so much.'

'Well, it did. The worst thing is that you didn't even seem to notice how much it was driving me away.'

'I didn't dress up very often.'

'Really? Don't make me laugh. You did it all the time. By the time I left it was virtually every night.'

'I wasn't aware I did it that much.' She pulled a hankie from her pocket and dabbed her eyes.

'And that stupid thing you used to say all the time – "Tell Mama all" – in that phoney Hollywood accent. It sounded so . . . insincere. It frightened me when I was a child. What was all that about? Why did you say it?'

Val was quiet for a moment, running her finger along the hairs on the hem of her coat.

'It's a line from *A Place in the Sun*,' she said. 'Elizabeth Taylor whispers it to Montgomery Clift while they are dancing.'

'Oh, why am I not surprised?' Rafe said, rolling his eyes.

'She says to him: "You seem so strange, so deep and far away, as though you are holding something back." And that was you, Rafe. That was how you seemed to be. And then Elizabeth tries to coax it out of him. "Tell Mama," she says, with the camera right up close to her face. "Tell Mama all."'

'But . . . don't you think it's weird?'

'It's a wonderful film.'

'Not the bloody film. You! Saying all that shit. Dressing up. Can't you see how deluded you are? It's like you're possessed or something.'

Neither of them spoke for a time. Val stroked the fur on the front of the coat forwards and back, changing the direction of the pile.

'I'm sorry,' Val said quietly. 'I never understand why I do it. I can't explain it. It just makes me feel better. It makes me feel close to your dad.'

Rafe considered this. She'd always talked about his dad but had still never managed to tell him anything.

'I just wanted my mum,' Rafe said. 'But all I had was this . . . parody. Some lampoon of a Hollywood actress.'

'I'm sorry,' Val said. 'I was grieving. I'm still grieving. I don't seem to have ever got over losing your brother and your dad.'

Rafe turned round. She looked small and fragile sitting there on his Chesterfield in all that make-up, like a doll.

'You always seemed so far away,' he said.

'I felt like I'd been hollowed out,' Val said. 'I still do.'

There was a silence. Rafe wondered whether he should put his hand on her shoulder or something, but he couldn't, quite. He didn't want any intimacy with her. It had always felt too cloying at home. Even her perfume suffocated him.

'Will you do something for me?' he said.

Val looked at him and nodded.

'Will you get changed? I find it hard to talk to you with you dressed like that.'

Val bit her lip. 'I haven't got anything else with me,' she said.

Rafe looked puzzled. 'Why not? Where are your normal clothes? You still haven't told me what you're doing here. Why were you up all night? And who does this baby belong to?'

'Shall I go and wash the make-up off my face?' Val said, getting up. 'Would that be better? I can see it upsets you.'

'It does more than that,' he said. 'It haunts me. So, yeah, if you could at the very least take the war paint off . . .'

Val disappeared into the bathroom.

'I'll go and make us some coffee,' Rafe said.

When she came back, she stood in the doorway rubbing her face with a towel. Her violet eyes seemed to have dimmed over the years; they looked more of a watery grey. Rafe put the mugs on the coffee table.

'That's better than nothing,' Rafe said. 'Thank you. You don't need all that garb, you know.'

Val sat on the Chesterfield. She looked fragile. She picked up a cushion and held it against her stomach.

'I pushed you away, didn't I?' she said.

'Yes, you did.'

'I didn't realise. I'm sorry.'

'It's done. It's what it is.'

Rafe balanced on the arm of the sofa and sipped his coffee.

Val noticed how his feet were dry and scaly like a bird's, his yellow toenails thick as cheese rinds. He seemed like a sad man. How long had he been like this? He'd lived his whole life since she'd last seen him in Weston-super-Mare. Then, he was on the cusp of manhood; now his face was lined and his hair was grey. How could it be he'd lived his twenties, thirties, forties, without her having seen him? How could they have let that happen? One thing she was certain of though, was that she loved him. He was her family and she loved him.

'I couldn't help it, but perhaps if I'd known how much it upset you . . . I could have tried harder not to do it. I know it's silly.'

Rafe drew his hand over his face.

'Everything comes from that, doesn't it? What happened to Daddy. It's like this fulcrum in the middle of the two separate versions of our lives. Yet no one ever talked about it.'

'What d'you mean?'

'You never explained what happened to him that day. You didn't talk to me about it. No one did.'

'I couldn't talk about it,' Val said. 'Because there was nothing to say.'

'That's ridiculous. There must have been plenty to say. I was four. All I've got are these distorted images in my brain. It's like I witnessed this huge tragic incident, but no one explained what it meant.'

'Because no one knew what it meant.'

'Really? You must have an idea. Surely you know . . . whether he meant to do it.'

'I do know. But I never wanted to admit it, not to myself. Certainly not to you.' She looked down at her hands. 'But I think I do know.'

'You never told me anything,' Rafe said. 'You never explained. All these years and it was this big undiscussed secret.'

'What do you want to know?'

'What do you think? What do you bloody think?' He didn't speak for a moment, then said, quietly: 'Did he jump on purpose? Do you think he intended to kill himself?'

Val swallowed. She picked at a bit of loose skin along the side of her nail.

'I never knew for sure,' she said. 'But yes, I do think he meant to do it.'

Rafe's throat tightened. In his heart he'd always known it, but no one had ever said it out loud. So, it was true. All his worst fears had been confirmed. He remembered the bald man bent over his dad, trying to breathe life into him. The sudden and shocking force of him pumping up and down on his chest, his fingers laced. The circle of people gathering round, their unnerving hush. What a waste of energy. His dad hadn't wanted to be revived. He'd been trying to die.

'But you always called it an accident,' Rafe said, looking at Val.

'Because to call it anything else would have been . . . unimaginable.'

'But that's like denying it. You can't live your life in denial.'

'I know. I've always denied it. It was easier that way.'

'But you owed it to me to tell me. Why did you keep it from me?'

'You were a child, Rafe. I didn't want to burden you.'

Rafe stood up then, walked across to the window.

'I wasn't a child when I left home. I was eighteen, and still you kept silent.'

'I thought it would hurt you too much.'

'Irony is, it made it worse for me though, didn't it? I've been burdened with it all my life.'

'What d'you mean?'

'Losing my dad. Nothing ever explained. It's resulted in . . . all these questions. Doubt. My whole life I've been scared I'll lose what I love. And then when I did find the one person who meant the world to me . . . I drove them away.'

'Oh?'

'There was someone I loved. Very much, as it goes. His name's Jim.'

Val looked at him with surprise.

He laughed. 'You don't know the first thing about me, do you?'

Val ran her fingers over her neck.

Rafe laughed to himself. 'Well, if we're spilling secrets we should have shared years ago, I might as well come out. I thought you would have figured it out by now.' He watched his mother stroke her chin. 'Oh please tell me you don't have a problem with it.'

Val hesitated for a second. 'No,' she said. 'No, it's not that. Goodness me, no. I've always known, or at least suspected. But it was your story to tell, not my place to pry.'

'Oh.' Rafe looked at her, surprised. 'And does it bother you?'

Val shook her head. 'Not in the slightest,' she said. 'All I cared about was for you to be happy, love.'

'Oh.' Rafe said again. All those teenage years tearing himself apart, feeling like a disappointment, wondering whether to come out, and all the time she didn't give a hoot about his sexuality. Maybe if they'd talked more, been more honest with each other.

'Well,' he said, 'it was only ever a big deal to me while I was living in Weston, anyway. Once I moved to London it didn't matter. And I didn't see much of you after that.'

'You hardly saw me at all after that.' She sniffed back tears, ran her finger under her eyes. 'I never saw you,' she said, her voice cracking.

'I know.'

'You didn't phone me for months when you left. I didn't know if you were dead or alive.'

'Can you blame me? I wanted to forget you. I wanted to forget all of . . . this.' He gestured to her coat.

310

Val blew her nose. 'So, what happened? With this Jim?'

'I couldn't bear the thought that he'd leave me, and in the end I suffocated him.' He swallowed. 'We ran some shops and a gallery. We had this amazing house. I had a brilliant life. Then I blew it. And since then, I've just . . . crumbled.'

'I'm really sorry to hear that,' Val said. She looked at her son sitting there on the edge of the sofa, his shoulders mantled, his movements small and nervous. Those raptor feet. She wanted to cuddle him and make it alright. She wished he would lie down so she could stroke his hair like she used to when she read him stories in his room at Palmer Street. Why had she allowed her grief to consume her to the extent that she had ostracised her own son? He was the very person she should have clung to, and should have let cling to her.

There was a silence. Val turned her wedding ring round her finger.

'Why d'you suppose he did it?' Rafe asked. 'Was it because of Duncan?'

Val nodded. 'His mind was so disturbed,' she said. 'It completely broke him.'

Rafe nodded. 'I suspected as much. I just wish you'd talked to me properly. When I was older, I mean. All these years I've carried round these questions. How could he have done that when he had us? He had another son. Didn't he love me?'

'Of course he loved you.'

Rafe was tracing a line in the carpet with his toes. 'I often think about when he took me swimming,' he said. 'It *felt* like he loved me.'

'He loved the bones of you, Rafe. It's just that after Duncan . . . I don't know. He just couldn't find peace.'

'We should have had this conversation years ago,' Rafe said. 'I've been in the dark, my head all messed up with wondering.'

Val looked stunned. 'I didn't realise,' she said. 'I just always assumed you knew. I see now. It would have been better if I'd been clearer with you.'

'Too right,' Rafe said. 'And not been living in a Hollywood fantasy,' he added.

'I can see that,' Val said. She knew now why he'd gone. She understood how her behaviour had affected him. They sat in silence for a time. 'What did you say you're doing with all this stuff?' she said, nodding to all the bubble-wrapped paintings. 'Is it all yours?'

'It all came out of the old house, the one I shared with Jim. When we split up, we divided it between us. I need to get rid of it.'

'Why?'

Rafe shrugged. 'Could do with the space. It reminds me too much of better times. And, well, if you want the truth . . . I'm completely skint.'

She peered at the desk. 'Is that the watch I sent you for your birthday?'

'Yeah. Sorry.'

'Oh, Rafe. If I'd known you were struggling with money, I might have been able to help.'

Rafe bowed his head.

'Why didn't you tell me?'

'I was hardly going to call you to ask for money out of the blue when I hadn't seen you for thirty years. And I haven't wanted to see you. I'm sorry, but that's how it is.'

There was a silence. 'If only I'd known . . .' Val said. 'That when I dressed up . . . I've always been a bit ashamed of it, but if I'd known it upset you as much as that . . .'

'It wasn't just the dressing up. It was all of it. Dad. Duncan. Realising I never measured up to him. I was a pain and he was perfect.'

At that Val tutted. 'That's not true.'

'It was stifling in that house,' Rafe said. 'And it always felt so . . . sad.'

Val sniffed back her tears, held her fingertips under her eyes. 'I've missed seeing you,' she said. 'I've missed knowing who you are.'

'If you'd been like this a bit more,' Rafe said.

'What d'you mean? Like this?'

'Well . . . normal.'

He slid off the arm of the sofa and sat next to her, the space between them full of everything that might have been.

'You could have at least returned my calls once or twice,'

Val said. 'I lost count of how many times I rang, and you never phoned me back.'

'I know.' Rafe looked at his mother and felt a pang of sympathy for her. 'I'm sorry,' he said. 'But there was just too much resentment there.'

'Can I make it up to you? What do I have to do?'

'You could stop trying to be some trashy film star. Just be my mother.' He nodded to her coat. 'And you could start by ditching the clobber.'

Val brought the two edges of the collar together to cover her slip. 'I only ever did it sometimes, in the evenings,' she said quietly. 'I wasn't harming anyone.'

'Weren't you?' said Rafe, rattled again. 'Oh weren't you?' He gestured around his flat. 'Look at me . . . look at my fucking life, and tell yourself again you weren't harming anyone.'

Val felt like she was going to cry. What had she done to him? She was quiet for a while.

'I know I haven't been right for a long time,' she said. 'But it's not too late, is it?' She thought about how being Elizabeth had driven her son away, had wrecked the possibility of finding happiness with Howard, and she knew she would have to go. She didn't hate Elizabeth Taylor. She could never do that. She hated her version of her, and how she had allowed it to ruin her life. She had always thought of it as an escape from her life, but it was far from that. It had trapped her. It was time for Elizabeth to go.

'No, it's not too late.'

They sat side by side for a time, almost touching.

Val took a sharp intake of breath.

'What is it?' Rafe said.

'There's something else I need to admit to myself,' she said.

'What's that?'

From the bedroom came the first stuttering cries of Christopher waking up.

Val wiped her eyes and sniffed. 'I'd better go and get him,' she said. 'Doesn't matter.'

She came back with the baby, who looked bleary with sleep. 'Oh he's had a lovely nap, haven't you, Bonny-Boo?'

Rafe watched the way she held the baby against her, swaying and kissing its head. He noticed the way she leaned into him, hovering her nose near his mouth, trying to catch the smell of his breath. She stood over near the window and put her cheek against the top of his head and moved gently from side to side, her eyes closed. She was lost in him. Rafe imagined her as a young mother with him and his baby brother.

Val tugged the changing mat out of the tartan bag and lay Christopher down and changed his nappy. She found some clean clothes and dressed him. Rafe watched as she held his little feet and marched his legs up and down. She wiggled each of his toes and chanted 'This Little Piggy', and when she said 'Wee, wee, wee, all the way home,' she made a spider with her hand and ran it up his leg and his body and all the way under his chin. She leaned over him and kissed his tummy and blew raspberries on his cheeks. She sat back on her heels and rummaged in the bag and pulled out Peter Rabbit and shook him so that he rattled. Then she bounced him along her arm and made him leap high in the air and land on Christopher's tummy, then up on his chest and cheeks and up to his ears. She lifted out the music box and wound it up and it played 'Sur le Pont d'Avignon'. Val opened her eyes and mouth wide and looked down at Christopher and then turned to watch the girl dance.

Something felt odd.

'Whose baby is that?' Rafe said.

Val ignored him. She was leaning over the baby, her hands either side of him now. She bent her elbows to lower herself over him to kiss him on one cheek, then rise back up, lower herself again and kiss the other. Her coat was undone, and her bosoms looked like two isosceles triangles in that 1950s-style corset.

He'd watched her once, through a crack in the door. He must have been thirteen or fourteen. In that bra and some strange elasticated thing, painting her lips scarlet. 'I'll be down in two minutes, Richard!' she'd called in her fake American drawl. 'Has the car arrived? I told the driver seven-thirty.' She'd looked over to the door then and saw Rafe standing there. She covered her chest with one hand and swiped at her make-up with the other, trying to rub off the spot on her cheek.

Val was moving her head to one side, then the other in time with the tune from the music box, smiling at the baby. She bent down to blow a raspberry on Christopher's cheek.

'It's so nice,' she said, turning round to Rafe, 'having my boys together again. Being with both my babies.'

Something jolted inside Rafe. 'You didn't answer me,' he said, his voice rising. 'Whose baby is that?'

Val went quiet then. The music box had stopped. She picked Christopher up and hugged him to her. 'He's just such a good boy,' she said. 'He's a really good baby.' She walked up and down the room, lifting Christopher gently up and down in front of her. 'Yes you are, aren't you, Bonny-Boo?' she said, bringing him towards her to kiss his cheek, then lifting him up, away from her again. 'Yes you are. You've been such a good little boy.' She sat on the Chesterfield with the baby on her lap facing her. 'Good as gold.' She opened her eyes wide like a surprise. 'Good. As. Gold.' She put her hands around his tummy and moved her knees up and down and clicked her tongue to sound like a horse trotting. 'Oh, you'll like this one, Christopher. We haven't done this one yet,' she said, and she started chanting a nursery rhyme. 'This is the way the lady rides: nim, nim, nim,' she said, making him bob up and down. She moved her legs slightly faster. 'This is the way the gentleman rides: trot, trot, trot.' Then she bounced her legs up and down as fast as she could. 'And this is the way the farmer rides: gallopy, gallopy, gallopy!'

Christopher's little body was flown faster and faster into the air, his face startled with glee, his little body rocked this way and that. Val stopped and her knees were still again. She changed her grip, holding him under the arms. 'Again?' she said, moving her ankles up and down, making her knees rise and fall. 'This is the way the lady rides: nim, nim, nim,' she chanted. Rafe was becoming more and more unsettled. Why wouldn't she answer him? It was as if she was ignoring him on purpose.

'You're not listening,' he said. 'I asked you a question.' He had raised his voice a little, but she was oblivious, wrapped up in her nursery rhyme and the baby on her lap. Before the baby woke up it had felt as if they were turning a corner and that she was a normal person. But now Rafe had lost her again, and she was back to being the woman he remembered from Palmer Street. Mad as a bloody hatter. A freak. Still she carried on. 'This is the way the gentleman rides: trot, trot, trot,' she sang, smiling at Christopher, her delighted face as wide as his. She was lost in it, her knees speeding up, bouncing the baby up and down on her lap as if she really believed that he was in the saddle, and she was the horse.

She was hiding something. Rafe grew more and more alarmed. He pulled his phone from the pocket of his jeans and tapped on the news. Something Emilio had said earlier was beginning to chime.

'And this is the way the farmer rides . . .' sang Val, her

knees going up and down like the clappers. 'Gallopy, gallopy, gallopy, gallopy, gallopy, gallopy, gallopy, gallopy!'

The CCTV image of a woman pushing a pram along Weston seafront appeared on Rafe's phone. He peered closer. It was very grainy. Could it be? He clicked onto the news story. His heart lurched.

'Oh my *fucking* god,' he said.

'You'll have to mind your language now, with the baby around,' Val said, looking over. 'They pick up all sorts you know, even at this age it's all going in—'

'I don't fucking believe it,' Rafe said, still looking at the screen. He went quiet then, peering at the phone, moving his finger to scroll down the page.

He clapped his hand to his forehead. 'Oh my god, what have you done?' He looked across at his mother and moved his head slowly from side to side in disbelief.

Val had stopped bouncing the baby and looked worried.

'Were you going to tell me, or just wait for me to find out?'

'Tell you what?' Val looked at the floor, unable to meet his eye now. She knew very well.

'D'you want to tell me where you got that baby?'

'There's a story going about on the news, Rafe—'

'A story going about? You're a national headline!'

'No. You see . . . there was a misunderstanding. I thought he'd been left on his own. He was on the pavement, and I took him. He needed someone to look after him.'

'Oh, what bullshit. Do you really expect me to believe that? It's obvious what's going on here. You kidnapped him, didn't you? You've stolen him.'

He held out his phone to her. 'Look! Look at that! What the fuck have you done?'

'He wasn't wanted, Rafe. He was left all alone.'

Rafe jumped up. 'Bullshit! He wasn't. He belongs to someone. You can't just take someone else's kid. What on earth were you thinking? You mad bitch!'

Val started to cry. 'I don't know,' she said. 'I don't know what I was thinking.'

'I can't believe you've taken someone else's child.'

'He needed looking after . . .' Val said, but her voice trailed off. It was no use. She didn't even believe the words herself anymore. For the first time since she walked away from the observation wheel with the pram, she gave in to her guilt.

While Rafe stared at her she thought again about the plot of *A Place in the Sun*. She remembered it more clearly now. Although Montgomery Clift hadn't actually pushed the girl into the water, he'd wanted to. He didn't think he'd committed a crime, but in his heart he was guilty. 'Perhaps you've hidden the full truth of this even from yourself,' the priest says to him at the end of the film when he's in jail awaiting execution. Val could remember it all now: walking along the seafront after having her hair done, the big wheel turning, the metal pods clanking in the wind. A woman's voice up above her, singing 'Wheee' to a child. Deep down, she'd known all along.

'I thought he'd been left, Rafe. Oh, I don't know what I thought anymore. I just saw the pram and it was like the last fifty years hadn't happened. It was my baby boy. His little hands were up around his ears, his little face to the side . . . He looked just like Duncan. And he was all tucked around in this yellow waffle blanket, d'you remember the one we used to have? And . . . Oh, Rafe, you don't know what it was like losing Duncan. It was as if he'd been snatched out of my arms.'

Rafe looked at her aghast. 'But you can't just take a baby!' He raised his hands in exasperation. 'It's about the worst thing you can do! Have you any idea how serious a crime it is?'

'I know. But I've been so confused.'

'Confused? You're fucking deranged. I've always known it. I thought we'd made a bit of headway just now. I thought for a minute that my mother might actually be a reasonable human being. But not a chance. Serves me right for being so stupid. How dare you involve me in this! You let me take him for a walk around Brighton, none the wiser. For god's sake, you made me an accomplice! How dare you just turn up when you're in trouble. I'm just trying to get back on my feet.' Rafe was shouting now. 'What on earth has been going through your head the last three days?'

Tears ran down Val's face and she wiped them with the back of her hands. 'I don't know, Rafe. I don't know what I was thinking.' A dark guilt twisted inside her. The last three days had been such a mess. She didn't know what was what.

'I've been trying to deny it,' she said. 'Living in a bit of a fantasy, I suppose.'

'No change there, then,' Rafe said.

'When I think back,' Val said. She screwed up her face a little, trying to concentrate. 'I might have heard his mother up in the wheel. "Wheee!" she was saying. "Wheee!" But I think I must have shut it out, Rafe, because I didn't want to hear it.'

'What?' Rafe said. 'How could you?'

'I don't know. The trouble is, I never seem to know what's real and what's not. Everything is always so . . . blurred.'

Rafe looked at his mother sitting there in that absurd outfit, clutching the baby on her lap and crying. He saw how damaged she was. He softened a little. What she'd done was monstrous, but he could see she hadn't done it through malice. He considered what it would have been like for her, losing her child and then her husband. It was the first time he'd seen her through adult eyes, and it was only now that he understood her. She needed to be helped, not shouted at. Suddenly he felt very sorry for her. He sat down next to her, put his hand on hers.

'Why did you come here?' Rafe said.

'I don't know. I suppose having this little boy . . . it made me think of my own babies. It made me think of you. You and Duncan, and how I lost you both.'

Rafe studied her, then said quietly: 'When you took the baby, what was going through your mind?'

'I don't know. It was blank really. He was just lying there under that yellow blanket, reminding me of the baby I lost. I just felt compelled to take him away, to keep him safe. It just felt right somehow, pushing him home.'

'So then, what were you intending? What was your plan?'

'I never had a plan,' Val said. 'I left Weston and drove to Wales. I had a lovely time there, Rafe. I met a man, actually. He was old fashioned, like your dad. He was wise and kind and he was nice to me. It was like there was this wonderful understanding between us. Oh, I can't explain. And then I ruined it.'

'How?'

Val sighed.

'He was lovely, Rafe, he really was. We walked on the beach at Aberdovey, and he told me a story about a lost land in Cardigan Bay. There was a whole kingdom out there, he said, but it flooded, and everyone drowned. And there's a bell under the pier that rings every time the tide comes in, to remember all the lost souls. It's sad and beautiful at the same time.'

'So what happened?' Rafe said. 'With this man in Wales?'

'I . . . He saw me dressed up in all this,' she said, holding out the lapel of her coat.

'Oh god.'

'He said the police were looking for me, but I didn't believe him. I didn't want to believe him. I was just upset because he'd seen me like this.' She looked down at her coat, touched her hair. 'So I fled. I ended up at Suki's, actually.'

'Suki's? What on earth for? When?'

'Last night. Early this morning.'

'Why?'

'I saw the signs to Shrewsbury. I thought she'd be pleased to see me. I suppose it was seeing Suki that made me come here. It reminded me of those times. Of you.'

'So what did Suki say, you turning up out of the blue like that?'

'She and her husband, they'd seen me on the news. They had an argument about whether to call the police. Then I fled.'

'Well, the police are going to find you soon enough, whether they called them or not. I'm surprised they aren't knocking on the door already. They could be here any minute.'

'Oh. Do you think so?'

'Too right,' he said. 'Listen. Whatever your reasons, whatever you thought you were doing, you're in serious trouble. We need to get the baby back to his mother.'

Val looked alarmed. 'But I can't give him up,' she said, holding onto the baby. 'He's used to me now. He needs me.'

Rafe shook his head. 'No,' he said. 'No, he doesn't. He needs his mother.'

Val was close to tears again. 'I can't lose another baby,' she said.

'But he's not yours to keep.'

Val was rocking gently back and forwards. She lifted her knees a few times weakly. 'This is the way the lady rides: nim, nim, nim,' she said, and smiled sadly. She held Christopher to her and rested her head on his little shoulder.

Rafe considered her. He'd listened and sympathised, but now he wanted her out of his flat. He didn't want the police knocking on the door. All his life the past had dragged him down, and he wasn't going to let it anymore. Besides, there was a woman out there who wanted her baby back.

'You know what you've got to do,' he said quietly.

'I know. I know that now.' She ran her hand over Christopher's head. 'Have you got the police interview with the mother there?' she said. 'On your phone? Can I watch it?'

The woman wasn't the teenage mother Val had imagined, desperate to get rid of her child. She was older, in her thirties perhaps. Val stared at her face as she spoke. She looked like any mother would, living through her worst nightmare. She hadn't abandoned her baby at all. She'd asked the man in the kiosk to keep an eye on the pram. It was a quiet day, she said. The baby was asleep and she didn't want to wake him. She'd promised her little girl a ride on the wheel on the way back from pre-school. There was a cold wind and she thought they'd be better off going another day, but her daughter had persisted, and she didn't want to break her promise. She'd parked the pram next to the kiosk, but when they got off the wheel it was gone. The man must have taken his eye off it for a moment. Noah was everything to her, she went on. He was loved. He needed her. Val heard her voice crack. She watched her break down and sob; watched the woman police officer put her arm around her and lead her through the door at the corner of the room. Val felt the full weight of what she'd done. How could she? Of all people, she knew what it felt like to lose a baby. To inflict that on another woman, well it was unforgiveable. She deserved everything she had coming to her. They should throw away the key.

'I want to go to the police station, Rafe,' she said. 'I want to walk in there and tell them what I've done and give Christopher back to his mother.'

Rafe nodded. 'Well, thank god you've seen sense,' he said. 'I'll come with you. Make sure you get there.'

'There's no doubt I'll get there,' she said. 'I've done a terrible thing. I can see that now. But if you come with me . . . I'd like that.'

'If you turn yourself in, they might be more lenient with you further down the line,' Rafe said. 'It's better that way.'

Val nodded. 'I know,' she said.

Outside, the wind had got up, making Rafe's letterbox rattle.

'Shall we go?' Rafe said.

Val nodded. She remembered how bereft she'd been when she lost her boy. They stood up together and Rafe reached out to take the baby. Val hesitated, holding him to her. She buried her face against the sleeve of his cardigan and breathed him in. She loved this little boy. 'I don't know if I can do this,' she said. 'I don't know if I can be parted from him. He's my Bonny-Boo. He's part of me, now.'

'Come on,' Rafe said. 'Let's put him in his pram, eh?'

Val passed Christopher to Rafe, running her hand over the baby's head. 'Sorry, Bonny-Boo,' she said. 'I've got to hand you back. It's going to break my heart, but I've got to give you back. You weren't mine to take.' They stepped out of the front door and fastened him into his pram.

Rafe looked at his mother standing there in her slip and bare legs. 'Could you at least do your coat up?' he said.

Val had been so preoccupied with Christopher that she'd forgotten for a moment how she looked. She pulled her coat around her and fastened the furry buttons.

'How far is the police station?' she asked.

'Half an hour walk, I suppose,' Rafe said. 'It's right down in the town.'

'On the way,' Val said. 'Can we walk along the front? I want to be with my boys down by the sea. Just for a few minutes.'

Rafe looked at her. He was about to say something sarcastic but he stopped himself. 'Course we can,' he said.

THIRTY-THREE

Val pushed the pram, Rafe walked alongside her holding onto the side of the handle, just like he'd done when he was a little boy. They crossed the road into the park and walked down the rough track under the trees before moving onto the wide tarmac paths that flowed down towards the city. White clouds scudded across the sun, and shadows passed over the lawns like stop-motion. The wind tugged at the branches of the trees. The park was busier than when Rafe had been out earlier. An elderly gentleman in whites and a Panama hat stood on the edge of the bowling green, inspecting the grass, bending down to peer across the surface, like a snooker player weighing up a shot. People were sitting on the terrace around the circular walls of the Rotunda Cafe, making the most of the October sun. In the rose gardens, a young man in a Brighton and Hove Council polo shirt was standing on the mulch, cutting back plants and throwing the dead heads into a wheelbarrow. Val remembered reading about Elizabeth Taylor having a rose named after her. A hot-pink bloom it was, with double petals and magenta edges. Suitably showy.

They left the park and crossed the road near the viaduct. They walked through the back streets as far as the railway station, then down the hill past the clock tower to the seafront. Rafe glanced up at people as they passed, worried they would identify Val as the woman they'd seen on the news. He imagined possible scenarios of being accosted, accused, held in an armlock in a citizen's arrest. But everyone was going about their business, not looking, not noticing. A bin lorry crawled along Queens Road, stopping to empty the wheelie bins that the shops had left out along the street. They felt the smelly air blast their faces, the stench of rot. They turned onto the front and walked along the main road, lined with the grand decay of Brighton's regency facades. A bassline thumped from a car stereo. They crossed the road and walked down the slope to the walkway along the beach. The pram bumped quietly over the boardwalk. Val had to be careful not to step in the cracks with her heels. The plastic straps of her mules were cutting into her feet. She considered taking them off altogether, but she could hardly walk along in bare feet. That wouldn't be right. Children were climbing on a rusty anchor outside the fishing museum. A group of women were doing yoga on rubber mats on the beach, reaching up to the sky with long fingers. Rollerbladers shot past on the boardwalk, rumbling over the planks.

Just before the pier, Val and Rafe stood at the carousel with its twisted golden poles and grimacing horses and listened to the pneumatic melodies of the barrel organ. Val thought of Gordon MacRae in the film *Carousel*, standing on the platform of his fairground ride trying to drum up business, then spotting Shirley Jones in the crowd and lifting her up onto the revolving platform. She imagined Mary Poppins on her jolly holiday, the horses jumping off the merry-go-round to charge along the racecourse. She thought of the runaway carousel in that final scene of *Strangers on a Train*, speeding up like a thing of nightmares, getting faster and faster, until finally it spins out of control and is flung off its axis, killing the dastardly Bruno. She remembered the time she had taken Rafe on the carousel at Clevedon, and he'd spent the whole time whining and crying, complaining he was falling off; how she'd had to cling onto him from the rear seat on the horse, one arm around his waist and the other clutching the pole, willing the ride to end. The following day she couldn't feel the muscles in her arms, she'd held him so tight.

She looked at Rafe and put her hand on his arm. She felt so sad that she had just rediscovered her son, and now was about to lose him again. 'I'm so sorry,' she said. Rafe edged away from the pram a little and put his hands in his pockets so that she couldn't touch his arm anymore.

Next to the wall along the edge of the beach, Val stopped again. 'Will you take a photo?' she said. 'I'd like a picture of us.'

Rafe looked around, worried it would draw more attention to them. As if his mother tottering along in her fur coat and bare legs wasn't enough. How long would it take before they were recognised? Someone was bound to see the pram and the coat and put the clues together. He needed to get her to the police station without them being caught first. He couldn't face a public hullabaloo. He wouldn't be able to cope with that. She was looking at him, though, with a pleading expression. 'OK,' he said. He would give her what she wanted. Once she got to the police station, her life was going to be over. He wasn't heartless enough not to allow her this.

'Stand on the sea wall,' Val said to him. 'Hold your hands out to the sides. As if you were holding a bucket and spade. I'll stand here, just in front of you.'

Rafe felt foolish standing there with his arms out wide. He knew what she was doing. He remembered that photo of her with the pram and him on the sea wall, the one that sat on her dressing table in her bedroom at Palmer Street, beside the brushes and powders. The atomiser with its crocheted puffer and tassel. The sickly-sweet scents and the strange underwear with straps that hung down and all those purple dresses in the wardrobe. He shook his head, threw out the memory.

'I'll need long arms,' he said. 'But I'll do my best.' He held the phone out as far as he could and tried to take a selfie of them.

'Make sure you include the pram,' Val said.

'It's not going to fit us all in,' Rafe said. 'I can't get the camera far enough away.'

A man in a camel coat overheard them.

'D'you want me to take it?' he said, holding out his hand for the phone.

Rafe felt a stab of alarm. But the man simply took the photograph and handed Rafe back his phone.

'I think I've got you all in,' he said.

'Thanks,' smiled Rafe, glancing at him nervously. The man walked off along the pavement towards Hove.

Val peered at the screen.

'Whatever happens now,' she said, 'will you send me the picture?'

Rafe imagined printing it off and sliding it into an envelope addressed to HMP.

'Sure. OK. Sure.'

They pushed the pram up the slope, Rafe still holding the side of the handle. Around the entrance to the pier, the briny tang of hotdogs hung in the air. Onions sweated on hot metal plates. Gritty clouds of pink candy floss hung in polythene bags on the sides of kiosks, blowing around in the wind. Multi-coloured windmills spun in buckets of sand. Sticks of rock. Hoop-la. Hook-a-Duck. Win a prize every time. Rafe saw the excitement in his mother's face. It was as if the charm of seaside kiosks and being on the prom with her son and a baby in a pram had brought back her joy.

Zoltar, the mechanical fortune teller, sat in his glass box in a gold turban and with his pointy black beard, as he'd done for a hundred years. In exchange for a few coins, he rocked backward and forward, hovering his hand over his crystal ball and spilling words of wisdom to tourists.

Val idled near him, enchanted. 'Oh, have you got a pound?' she said to Rafe.

He shook his head. 'Nah,' he said. 'Come on, we need to get on.' He already knew what her future held. Yet she was still living in a fantasy world. Half an hour ago she'd been rocked when she saw Noah's mother on television. Next thing she wants her fortune told. Rafe took her arm and walked her on, away from the pier. He was uneasy. He hadn't minded bringing her on this route, indulging her with the photo. These would be her last moments of freedom after all. But that was enough now. They'd spent long enough down here. The thought that they could be stopped any moment was making his heart hammer. He kept expecting a tap on the shoulder. He wasn't prepared to be part of any media circus. The promise of this new job meant he could begin a new life, one that was purposeful but anonymous. He pitied his mother, clicking along the pavement in her silly shoes. It upset him that she was as lonely as he was. He wondered whether he should try and help her, tell the police she was not in her right mind. She needed psychiatric help, not putting behind bars. But then he looked at her again, clip-clopping along, and he felt impatient and annoyed. She'd infected enough of his life already. He didn't want her trashing his new start as well.

They crossed over Old Stein and walked north, away from the sea.

'Oh, look at that!' Val said as they walked past Brighton Pavilion. 'It looks like a great big wedding cake!'

When Rafe had first moved to Brighton he'd been enchanted by the incongruity of this preposterous Indian palace plonked in the heart of a very British seaside town, but now its vulgarity annoyed him. For a moment he remembered the cartoon drawing of it on the side of Jim's cake.

'Yeah, I guess,' he said.

'And those minarets stuck on the top there, they look like melting ice creams,' Val said. She was childlike. She smiled and pushed back the hood of the pram. 'Look, Christopher,' she said. 'Look at this funny building.' She stopped again and stood at the side of the pram and she watched the baby. Her face crumpled. 'Oh, Rafe,' she said. 'I don't know if I can do this. I don't think I can be parted from him.'

'You've no choice,' Rafe said.

For a moment it crossed Val's mind to protest that this was all a mistake, that she was the baby's mother, but she knew it was futile. That argument had worn thin, even in her own mind. She had everything coming to her.

They walked up Edward Street, Val's fluffies clacking up the pavement. The plastic straps had made nasty gashes across her bunions, and she was hobbling now, trying to put the weight on the outside of her feet. Her lolloping gait reminded her of Charles Laughton in *The Hunchback of Notre Dame*. 'Why was I not made of stone, like thee?' Quasimodo says at the end of the film, leaning against a gargoyle on a ledge at the front of Notre Dame, having lost Esmeralda. Val knew what he meant. It would be easier not to be human, not to feel.

'D'you think I'll go to prison?' she said.

Rafe pressed the button on the crossing.

'I don't know,' he said. 'Yes, probably.'

They stood side by side and waited for the green man.

'Will you come and see me?' Val asked, scared of the reply, needing to know. Every fibre of her urged him to say yes.

The lights changed and they crossed to the sound of the beeps. Rafe didn't speak for a while. Would he?

'I don't know,' he said. 'I don't know.' Maybe. In time.

They turned into John Street and walked up the side of the Jobcentre towards the police station. Rafe thought of the people in there, sitting on the red chairs waiting for Chelsea. If the job at Emilio's took off, he'd never have to go into that building again.

As they approached the police station, their steps slowed. Val had the same feeling as when she'd pushed the pram along Palmer Street three days before. Weightless, floating above herself, pulled from the gravity of normal life. Was that only three days ago?

She could hear the mother's voice loud and clear now. 'Wheee!' she'd said in the observation pod above Val's head. 'Wheee!' she'd sung to her child, clearly audible above the click and grinds of the wheel. Val went back over it all. The policeman on his motorbike; the hotel in Abergavenny where Christopher had screamed all night; the long drive to Aberdovey; the wonderful day with Howard; calling on Suki in the middle of the night. For all that time, the mother had been waiting. Val could explain she'd made a mistake. She'd thought he'd been abandoned at first, but as time went on, she had become confused.

There was something important she wanted the mother to know though: that she'd looked after Noah like he was her own. He hadn't wanted for anything, and he'd been content. That he was an adorable angel.

Outside the station, Val stopped and put the brake on the pram. She turned to Rafe. 'I'm scared,' she said. 'I know I deserve this, but I'm scared.'

Rafe made himself put his arm around her shoulder. 'You'll be alright,' he said. He couldn't bring himself to say 'Mum'. They stayed there for a moment while the automatic doors opened and shut. Val looked in her handbag and pulled out the wad of cash she'd been carrying around since she left Weston. She pressed it into Rafe's hand.

'Here,' she said. 'You have it.'

'There must be hundreds of pounds here,' Rafe said.

'Take it,' Val said. 'It's the least I can do. Anyway, I won't need it, will I?' She kicked the brake off the pram.

Rafe watched her swivel the wheels to face the police station. Should he offer to go in with her? Did he owe her that? After willing her to get here, this now felt sudden, final. He hesitated, then nodded towards the entrance. 'Do you want me to . . . ?'

Val shook her head. 'I'll do this bit on my own,' she said. 'You go now.' She reached up and kissed his cheek. 'You're a good boy,' she said.

Rafe stood on the pavement and watched his mother totter in through the sliding doors.

Acknowledgements

I am profoundly grateful to the following people who have supported me and my writing, and who have helped bring this book to life:

Thank you to my brilliant agent Annette Green, for taking me on, and for always having my back.

Heartfelt thanks to Kate Ballard, the loveliest editor in the business. Your talent and expertise meant that this novel became the best version of itself. I feel as if I hit the jackpot with you.

Thanks to Nicky Lovick, for your sharp eyes and forensic copy-editing.

Thank you to the whole team at Allen & Unwin, for believing in my story and in me, and for all your excellent work.

I owe a huge debt of gratitude to Dexter Petley, Writer, Editor, Alchemist. Thank you for seeing something in my writing way back when, and for showing me I still had a lot to learn. I'm not sure this novel would exist if it weren't for your wisdom and generosity.

I am very grateful to my tutors and peers at Bath Spa University: Celia Brayfield, Nathan Filer, Philip Hensher, Samantha Harvey, Richard Kerridge, Anna-Marie Crowhurst, Jennie Beck, Vicky Argyle, Sarah Fox, Lydia Owen Edmunds, Emma Nuttall, David Pearson, Ian Schutzman, Jack David, Debs Cooper, Abbie Taylor, Paul Horsley, Re'al Bakhit, Nick Millo. Your insightful feedback and shrewd suggestions helped enormously as I developed my story; you have all contributed to this novel.

To Jo Thulborn. Oh, where to start? Your belief and support have meant everything. Thank you for indulging me by always wanting to talk about my writing, for being my sounding board, and for cheering me on. Thank you, my darling friend, for all our years of priceless times; you have brought such richness and joy into my life that I can't imagine having lived it without you.

To Cath Hine. Thank you for your constant support and encouragement, for always being interested and always asking questions. I cherish our wonderful friendship, the way our minds meet, our walks and laughter, and everything we have shared.

Huge thanks to Paul Vickery, whose artistry and talent leave me speechless. Thank you for sharing your knowledge of the creative industry, for the practical advice, and for calling me a writer. Thanks for London larks (and New York capers), sixties movies and hairy spiders, and for all of our history and all of our laughs.

To Jo Backhouse, whose creativity I find so inspiring. Thank you for being my friend and writing companion, and for the joy of our ever-criss-crossing lives.

Enormous thanks to Cat Lane, for your unstinting belief in this novel, your cheerleading, for all the troubleshooting and the 'what-if's. Your advice and technical help have been invaluable, but not as invaluable as your extraordinary kindness.

Thank you to Andrea Jacobson, for your warmth and intelligence, and your offers of help.

Massive thanks to Clare Donoghue, for understanding Val right from the beginning, and for telling me to stick to my guns.

Thank you to Dave Battcock, Andrew Wille, Tracey Eveleigh-Jones, Luana Codo, Chris Ewan, Jeremy Backhouse, Matthew Laight, Sebastian Abbo.

Thank you to Marion Willey, for our closeness, and for everything, really. I am so grateful for the way you encouraged me while I risked everything to pursue this dream of mine. Love you, Momma.

To Caroline Mussons, my wonderful sister. Thank you for your love and loyalty, for all our precious times together, and for always asking about my novel in the hot tub. (We'll always have the Imperial! Some of the best hours of my life.) I adore you.

To Asia, Gabriel and Louis. You brilliant, gorgeous three. I love you so much I could burst. And yes, there will be 'Buns for tea!'

And to Rob, for your endless emotional support. I know at times it (I) can't have been easy. Thank you for your patience and understanding, for taking my ambition seriously, and for never minding that I am always in the library. It means the world. You mean the world. All my love and thanks for ever.

I once overheard a snippet of a conversation, about a woman who was rumoured to walk around a seaside town dressed as Elizabeth Taylor. I would like to extend my gratitude to this woman, who was the inspiration behind this novel, but whom I never knew.